The World in Half

ALSO BY CRISTINA HENRÍQUEZ

Come Together, Fall Apart

The World in Half

Cristina Henríquez

Riverhead Books

a member of Penguin Group (USA) Inc.

New York 2009

RIVERHEAD BOOKS
Published by the Penguin Group
Penguin Group (USA) Inc., 375 Hudson Street, New York, New York 10014, USA • Penguin Group (Canada), 90 Eglinton Avenue East, Suite 700, Toronto, Ontario M4P 2Y3, Canada (a division of Pearson Canada Inc.) • Penguin Books Ltd, 80 Strand, London WC2R 0RL, England • Penguin Ireland, 25 St Stephen's Green, Dublin 2, Ireland (a division of Penguin Books Ltd) • Penguin Group (Australia), 250 Camberwell Road, Camberwell, Victoria 3124, Australia (a division of Pearson Australia Group Pty Ltd) • Penguin Books India Pvt Ltd, 11 Community Centre, Panchsheel Park, New Delhi–110 017, India • Penguin Group (NZ), 67 Apollo Drive, Rosedale, North Shore 0632, New Zealand (a division of Pearson New Zealand Ltd) • Penguin Books (South Africa) (Pty) Ltd, 24 Sturdee Avenue, Rosebank, Johannesburg 2196, South Africa

Penguin Books Ltd, Registered Offices:
80 Strand, London WC2R 0RL, England

Published simultaneously in Canada

Library of Congress Cataloging-in-Publication Data

Henríquez, Cristina, date.
The world in half / Cristina Henríquez.
p. cm.
ISBN 978-1-59448-855-9
1. Panama—Fiction. I. Title.
PS3608.E565W67 2009 2008040372
813'.6—dc22

Printed in the United States of America
1 3 5 7 9 10 8 6 4 2

Book design by Meighan Cavanaugh

For Ryan

The World in Half

One

Origination

More than three thousand miles below the surface of the earth is its core. It's taken scientists a long time to learn anything about it. Most of them would readily admit that they know more about every other planet in the solar system than they do about the pit that's at the center of ours. But seismic waves have taught us a few things. There's a liquid outer core and a solid inner core. The convection currents in the outer core dictate our magnetic fields. The inner core is made of pure iron. Its temperature hovers around 5,000 to 6,000 degrees Celsius. At one time it was molten, so the fact that now it's not means that little by little the planet has been hardening itself from the inside out. I think about that a lot. And then again, I think maybe the scientists don't know anything. None of them, after all, have ever traveled to the core of the earth. It would be impossible for any human to get so close to such a fiery heart.

. . .

My mother is humming in the bathroom when Lucy arrives. It's the last Thursday in December, and gusts of bitter wind rattle the house periodically. The sky outside is as gray as a stone. She's been in the bathroom for more than an hour now, and so far she has completed the entire score of *West Side Story* and at least a dozen repetitions of "O Christmas Tree." She won't admit it, but she's nervous. "If this woman's coming here to see me," she said yesterday, "I might as well make sure she sees something good." I tried explaining that Lucy wasn't coming to judge her.

"Yes she is."

"Trust me, she's not."

"Don't be naïve," she said. "Everyone is always judging everyone else."

Lucy shows up, exactly like she said she would, at eight a.m. sharp. Through the window I can see her—a heavyset woman in a camel-colored mohair coat and a man's fedora—shifting her weight from foot to foot and rubbing her hands together to keep them warm. She has a giant canvas tote bag slung over one shoulder.

"Ding dong," she says, when I open the door. "Avon calling."

"Excuse me?" The frigid air from outside rushes in.

"I'm sorry. That was a joke."

"Are you Lucy?"

"I like to start things off with a joke. Folks usually get a kick out of it. You might be too young to understand that particular one, though. It started in the sixties. Or was it the fifties?" She waves her hand. "It's not important. Yes, I'm Lucy. Lucy Carter from Sunrise."

We have to wait another thirty minutes before my mother comes out of the bathroom. In the intervening time, I make Lucy a cup of hot tea, which she sips on the couch while we talk idly about whether each of us is from the area (Lucy is originally from Minnesota, though she's lived here since she was six years old), and the dreary winter they're predicting we'll have this year, what I'm studying in school, and how expensive gas is these days. Because it would seem awkward not to point it out, I explain why there are towers of magazines stacked up against one of the living room walls. The magazines are my old copies of *Science* that my mother dug up from the basement a few days ago. She woke up that morning and said, while she peeled the shell off a hard-boiled egg, "Do you know what we need, Mira? We need order." The next thing I knew, she was dredging up every back issue of every magazine we'd ever owned and sorting them by issue date. The *Science* magazines are next to my *National Geographic*s, the yellow spines layered on top of one another straight as railroad tracks. Lucy eyes the towers approvingly and says, "Well, that makes as much sense as anything, I guess."

When we've exhausted all that and still my mother has yet to make her entrance, I take Lucy on a quick tour of the house. I show her where we keep the flashlights and the batteries in case the power goes out, and where we keep a fire extinguisher under the kitchen sink. I tell her which days the trash is collected, and what time the lamps in the living room are set to turn off every night, and how to jiggle the toilet so that it flushes on the first try. I tell her that I've already written out a rent check for the month and that she needs to drop it at the owner, Mrs. Sakac's, house on Colfax before the fifteenth. I show her that I've stuck a Post-it note on the check with Mrs. Sakac's address. Lucy takes it all in without asking questions or for clarification. Just as we're about to head down to the basement so that I can show her how to use the washing machine, the knob to the bathroom door rattles.

"Hold on," my mother calls from inside. "I'm coming."

The knob rattles again. We wait.

"It's locked," my mother says.

"Unlock it," I say.

There's nothing but silence. The knob is still. I step forward and try to turn it. "Mom, unlock the door."

"Hold on."

I don't dare look back at Lucy. It's embarrassing. I just keep my hand on the knob and listen through the door while my mother fiddles and curses and, finally, turns the lock. When she walks out, she's wearing a plaid wool pencil skirt, a purple turtleneck sweater, sheer brown hose, and her best heels. She pauses outside the bathroom door, as if she's just stepped onto a stage. Then she says, as though nothing happened, "Were we going down to the basement?"

Later, after my mother has given Lucy her own tour and after the two of them have had time to ease into some semblance of comfort with each other, we all sit together at the kitchen table and go over the routine: Lucy will move into our house for the next three weeks. She will sleep on the couch. "I'm hoping you can provide sheets and blankets, but I'll bring my own pillow," she says. "Nothing against your pillows. I'm sure they're fine. But my neck needs a buckwheat pillow, and I've found that most people don't keep those around." Lucy will be with my mother all day, every day. At this, my mother makes a face. "Well, I'm not going to Velcro the two of us together. I just mean I'll be in the house whenever you are. And if I need to leave the house, I'll bring you with me. And if you need to leave the house, I'll take you anywhere you want to go." My mother opens her mouth and Lucy quickly corrects herself. "Not anywhere. But you know what I mean." Lucy will do all the driving. She will use her own car. "It's a reliable Volkswagen Rabbit," she assures us. "Never had a single repair." She will implement safety precautions around the house: cover the outlets with plugs; lock up our household cleaners; install night-lights. She will help my mother in all the ways that she can and all the ways that are necessary, but she is not, she takes care to stress, a babysitter. For anything for which my mother doesn't require assistance—"I would guess that's still most things at this point," Lucy says—my mother will be on her own. Nor is she here as hired entertainment. "I can be very entertaining," she says, "but that's hardly the point." Lucy knows, because I marked it on the paperwork, that my mother had to leave her job a month earlier. One of the lawyers in the office where she worked as the receptionist approached her one day after a batch of billing statements my mother was supposed to have sent got returned to the office for lack of postage. He told her that they were all fond of her and had always known her to be capable, but that the work had gotten away from her lately, and that they didn't want to fire her, but they hoped she would see it was time for her to leave. My mother, who almost never goes with the flow of anything, said she did see. During her lunch that day, she scribbled a letter of resignation. Since then, though, my mother hasn't quite known what to do with herself. After spending her entire adult life working—never calling in sick, dismissing the idea of vacation—she has no clue how to pass the time. For her, being unemployed is like wandering through a dark and beguiling forest. I assume, though, that's what Lucy is referring to when she says she's not entertainment. She's not here to fill my mother's time for her, only to keep her safe.

"When are you starting?" I ask.

"I believe I just did."

. . .

The next night, because it's New Year's Eve and because Lucy insists, I go out with my friends. Before I leave the house Lucy asks if she can take a picture of me. "I've never seen you look so nice," she says, taking no pains to hide the amazement on her face. I'm dressed in a shimmering silver V-neck blouse, black trousers, and black boots. My hair is long and straight down my back, my bangs long and straight across my forehead.

"You've only seen me yesterday and today," I point out, smiling. But then my mother comes out and corroborates Lucy's opinion.

"Mira! No jeans!" she says. "Is this always how you dress around your friends?"

"Yes. I wear disco balls to my geophysics classes."

"I know you thought that was funny, but you should consider it. It would be an improvement over jeans all the time."

Lucy backs me against a wall and takes a picture. "One more with the flash," she says.

"Lucy," I point to my shirt. "I'm pretty sure I've got the flash covered."

"For once," my mother says, and I roll my eyes, hoping that it comes off as good-natured, before pulling on my coat and walking out the door.

It's dark by the time I get to campus. Asha buzzes me up to her room and hugs me when I walk in. She has jazz—her favorite since she took a class on Thelonious Monk last quarter—playing softly.

"You look so good!" she says. "Were we supposed to get dressed up? Do you even know where we're going? Juliette's still talking about going to the Med, but I don't know if I feel like it."

Asha is wearing dark jeans, a slim black turtleneck, and green sneakers. She is, as one of the guys in her dorm told her once, a classic Indian beauty, with thick, wavy hair and flawless golden skin.

I sit on her bed, covered with a Jamawar shawl. "You know she only wants to go there because of Ben, right?" I say.

"That waiter? What's his last name? Linwood? I think he was in my biology lab."

"Did you tell Juliette? She's practically killing herself to find out anything she can about him."

"Exactly why I didn't tell her. If she knew where he was every Tuesday and Thursday at three-thirty, she would probably stalk him."

Asha is leaning over her dresser, lining her almond-shaped eyes with heavy black eyeliner. She licks her pinky and dabs at one of the corners. Then she turns to me and, shaking her finger, says, "So you don't tell her, either."

Juliette and Beth arrive together about ten minutes later. They walk into Asha's dorm room wearing dresses—Juliette a corduroy shirtdress with a wide brown belt around her waist, and Beth a very plain sleeveless black dress that hits at her knees. She has tights on underneath.

The four of us met the first week of freshman year at a barbecue in the courtyard that two of the neighboring dorms threw to welcome new students. Juliette and Beth lived in the same suite, so they came over together, clinging to each other the way everyone did in the beginning just for the comfort of having someone to do things with. Asha was monitoring her veggie burger on the grill and I was talking to my RA. Later, I got in line for a hot dog behind Juliette and Beth. Juliette brokered the introductions, and then Beth and I learned we were in the same major (geophysical sciences), which Asha overheard and which, because she was in the sciences, too (chemistry), prompted her to introduce herself to us a few minutes later as we sat cross-legged on the grass, eating and licking salt from potato chips off our fingers. With the scent of charcoal wafting through the air, we sat outside talking to one another long after all the others at the barbecue had thrown away their plastic plates and wadded napkins and returned to the safe cover of their dorm rooms, until dusk fell and the mosquitoes came out and Asha jumped up because she kept getting bitten. Someone—it must have been Juliette—suggested we all have breakfast together in the dining hall the next morning. We've been friends ever since.

"What the hell?" Asha says when she sees them. "Why didn't anyone tell me we were supposed to be dressing up?"

"What do you mean, why didn't we tell you?" Juliette asks. "It's New Year's Eve."

"This is just the dress I use for interviews," Beth says, before sitting beside me on the bed and putting her arm around my shoulder, squeezing me in a sideways hug. "How are you?" she asks.

"I'm okay," I say. She gives me the most pitying smile, lips together, turned down at the corners.

"What interviews?" Asha asks.

"What are we listening to?" Juliette wants to know.

"Sonny Rollins. ''Round Midnight.' It's a standard," Asha says. "What interviews?"

"It's nice. Can I download it from you?"

"Sure. What interviews, Beth?"

"The interviews I'm trying to set up for summer internships. Didn't I tell you I'm trying to get a job at Fermi Lab?"

"Okay, before the three of you get all caught up in your ultra-fascinating science talk, where are we going?" Juliette asks, after coming over and giving me her own hug.

"I heard you wanted to go to Medici," I say, winking suggestively.

"First of all, I can't believe you just winked at me like that," Juliette says. "What are you? Some kind of Playboy Bunny CIA operative?"

I laugh.

"Second, I wouldn't *mind* going to Medici, unless someone has a better idea." Juliette adjusts her purple plastic glasses before dropping a glance on each of us in turn. "Medici it is, then."

The restaurant is just filling up by the time we get there. We slide into a booth near the back and order sandwiches and onion rings and root beer floats. It feels good to be there with them, eating the food we've always eaten and having the conversations we've always had. We watch for Ben and try to keep Juliette from making a fool of herself when she sees him, since every time he passes through the room she threatens to wave him down and tell him that she thinks he's amazing. "You don't even know him," Beth says. And Juliette replies, "Look at him. What more do I need to know?"

The restaurant is warm and dim, the dark wood furniture worn and etched with people's names and initials. Wilco is playing on the sound system. We finish our onion rings and order mocha pie as the students continue to amass and get louder. When Juliette stands up and announces she's going to the bathroom, Asha says she'll accompany her to make sure she only goes to the bathroom and doesn't somehow veer off course into the path of a certain Ben Linwood. Juliette sticks her tongue out at Asha, and Asha says, "You better keep that thing where it belongs." Beth and I laugh.

As soon as they're gone, Beth says, "Did I tell you before that you look really nice tonight?"

"Why does everyone keep saying that?"

"We usually only see you in your sneakers and jeans."

"Excuse me, but I wear tops, too."

Beth smiles. "I'm just saying, it's nice to see you dressed up." She presses the back of her fork against some leftover piecrust still on her plate and watches it crumble through the tines. Then she looks up. "I can't believe you're not going to be here next quarter. Who's going to meet me for coffee at the C-Shop?" She sighs and lays her fork down. "Did I tell you I saw Dr. Herschel on the last day of finals? He asked me how you were. I didn't even know he knew we were friends. I mean, he has a lot of students to keep track of. Although maybe I shouldn't be surprised since all your professors love you." Dr. Herschel is the chair of the Geophysical Sciences Department.

"What did you tell him?"

"I said you were fine." She looks at me and blinks. "Just tell me one more time that you're fine."

"I'm fine."

At midnight, as anyone might have predicted, Juliette jumps up from our booth, streaks across the room to where Ben is standing with an empty round tray tucked under one arm, takes his face in her hands, and kisses him. He drops the tray, but boy if he doesn't kiss her back with gusto. Asha walks over to the group of guys at the booth behind us and asks, with exceeding politeness, if any of them would consider spending his New Year's kiss on her even though she is not dressed as prettily—the word she uses—as her friends. All four guys raise their hands.

When she rejoins Beth and me at our table, I say, in a lightly mocking tone, "Would any of you consider—"

"Stop," Asha says, blushing.

"I thought you weren't allowed to date American guys," Beth says.

Asha writes on a napkin: "Date." And under that: "Kiss." "Do those look like the same thing?"

"I don't know," I say. "What's the Hindi translation?"

"Hilarious," says Asha.

When we leave, it's gotten so cold outside that we run the whole way back to Asha's dorm, our lungs stinging by the time we arrive. Juliette and Beth are both staying overnight, sleeping on the floor, but because I didn't clear it with Lucy first, I tell them I'm going back. We hug good-bye and I promise to call them the minute I get back from Panama. They want pictures, they say, and if anything, anything at all happens while I'm there, they want to know about that, too. They'll be keeping their cell phones on.

Outside, on the sidewalk, I walk past my car, across the street, down a narrow path that leads to the heart of campus. In the distance the sounds of horns and the unnerving snap-pop of amateur fireworks punctuate the air, but from where I stand I can't see another soul. There is nothing around me but the towering Gothic buildings, the stark trees, the snow-dappled grounds, and the deep black sky, opaque as velvet, domed overhead. I fist my hands into the pockets of my coat and take a long breath, the cold air tingling in my chest. Pieces of my hair sweep lightly against my cheeks, caught in the icy breeze. Not even a month earlier I walked by this same spot, one of hundreds of students streaming silently past, on my way to class or to my dorm. Now, though, I have other places to go.

. . .

Two weeks ago, I was in my mother's bedroom, looking for a medical bill that she wanted me to find. Her doctor's office kept sending us a bill that she swore we had already paid, and though she called and tried to straighten it out with them, they insisted that they had no record of the payment. The person on the other end of the line apparently told my mother that if she could produce the record in question and send it in, they would be able to sort everything out and cancel the charge.

When I walked into my mother's room that day, the bed was unmade. The pillows, flattened where her head had lain, were propped against the wall. The flimsy wooden dresser with its trifold mirror was piled with every trinket or piece of jewelry she had ever owned: chipped seashells she proudly told me once were from the Atlantic; barrettes I hadn't seen her wear in years; chopsticks; plain rings; beaded necklaces; tarnished brooches; nail polish bottles; sample tubes of perfume, the liquid inside browned like whiskey. And next to the dresser, a metal filing cabinet, four drawers tall.

I started with the second drawer from the top, the tabs of the file folders ruffling against the underside of the drawer above as I slid it out. The folders weren't labeled, so I flipped several past my fingertips and peered inside. Receipts, credit card statements, instruction manuals—the usual. When my fingers pried open a folder near the back, I stopped. It looked like it was full of letters. Some of them were typed on onionskin paper, some handwritten in blue ink. All of them were in Spanish—I could see that easily—and addressed to my mother. *Querida Catarina,* they said, one after the other. I pulled the folder back enough to see the name signed at the end of each: Gatún Gallardo. I caught my breath. My father.

The topic of my father has always been off-limits in our house. For a long time, the sum of my information about him consisted of knowing that he was a man my mother had an affair with while she was stationed with her husband in Panama. I always thought of him as a man who, upon learning she was pregnant, decided he didn't have much interest in raising a child, so he let her, and me, go. It isn't a story my mother ever verified. It isn't even a story that I tested out loud. It's simply what I pieced together from what little I knew about him, about their situation, about the past. And it seemed easy enough to believe. My father, after all, had never contacted me, and on the few occasions I brought him up, my mother usually told me not to worry about him or else just gazed at me with the kind of excruciating sorrow that would shut anyone down.

Of course, other details leaked out over the years. At some point I learned his name and that he had lived in Panama City, Panama, his entire life. I knew that he was fifteen years older than my mother and that he smoked cigarettes. I knew that he worked at the Panama Canal, that he had a wide jaw and a huge smile, that he was skinny as a toothpick, that he kept a comb in his back pocket. And I thought I knew that he was a man who had broken my mother's heart. Until I read the letters.

Dear Catarina,

You've gone home. You've gone back to the United States. The butcher you knew on the base was the one who told me. He said, "Oh, the North American girl? She went back home. She was never really happy here." Don't worry. I'm not angry. But I don't believe that you were never happy here. I think you were happy with me, no? Or maybe all along I was mistaken. Did I do something to make you leave? I don't know what's happened. For days, I kept expecting you in the evenings only to find that you didn't show. I sat at the kitchen table where I had a view of the street and looked for hours for the shape of you lit against the streetlights, walking on your toes as you always did toward my front door. Every day, I grew more confused about where you could be and why I hadn't heard from you. I was going crazy. And I was worried that something had happened to you. You can't imagine the thoughts that ran through my head! So on Friday I went to the base even though I know I wasn't supposed to, even though a hundred times you told me not to, and discreetly I asked around about you. Then the butcher told me you had gone (he really is a foul-smelling man, as you had said). You can't imagine how much I miss you. I hardly know the point of getting up anymore in the morning if I'm not going to see you at night. Are you coming back? Are you okay? Please write to me.

Yours,

Gatún Gallardo

Dear Catarina,

I was so happy to receive your letter. Thank you for explaining everything. I can't believe it! A baby! We made a baby! I told my mother, who is very excited, too. I can't believe it. We have good medical care here in Panamá, but of course I understand that you want to be near your own family. When may I come to visit? I want to put my hands on your belly. I want to see you with a baby in you. Of course I'll also come when the baby is born. I could move to the United States permanently. I could apply for a visa now. Or maybe you want to move back to Panamá so we can raise the child here? I'll wait to hear what you prefer. I'm so excited, *mi pajarita,* I could burst! I'll wait for your next letter so we can make our plans.

Yours,

Gatún Gallardo

Dear Catarina,

I've been checking my box every day, but so far, no letters from you. I hope you haven't sent one that got lost. I can imagine it drifting off the plane and twirling down into the ocean, being eaten by a fish. Or maybe you haven't had time to write. I hope everything is fine. I think about you and the baby constantly. I was almost fired from my job the other day because I fell asleep on my lunch break dreaming of the two of you.

Yours,

Gatún Gallardo

Dear Catarina,

I received your latest letter three days ago. It left me confused. I don't believe you would have written the things you did if you understood how I felt about you, how I still feel about you! I understand that you don't want to come back to Panamá. I understand that you want to raise our child in the United States. There are more opportunities in your country than here. I know how important it is to you that she has a good education. But I don't understand why you're telling me not to come there. I can apply for a visa. I have a good record. We can get married. We can spend every day for the rest of our lives together. We can fall asleep with each other every night. We can raise our child together. I don't know what you mean when you say, "It's not a good time here." Tell me when will be a good time. I will wait for the good time. I miss you and I want to see our baby, who, if my calculations are correct, will be here in the world soon. Please write.

Yours,

Gatún Gallardo

Dear Catarina,

A baby girl? I'm sure she's beautiful. I hope you are fine, too.

Yours,

Gatún Gallardo

Dear Catarina,

It's been a long time. I didn't think, not in a hundred years, that I would feel this way about you. All of my original feelings are still here, under the surface. They will always be here if you want to find them. But now

I don't know what to say. I can hardly believe it was you who wrote the letter. Why did you tell me not to come there? And why will it be better for everyone if I stay away? And how can I forget about you? I know, because of other things you wrote and because of things you told me when we were together, that it's not you saying this! It's your parents, forcing it upon you. They don't believe I'm a suitable father because I'm Panamanian, because I don't have enough money, because they don't like my brown skin. I know you told me about what the United States used to be like, how the people with color in their skin had to use different bathrooms and different drinking fountains and different seats in the movie theaters and on the buses. But that was a long time ago, no? Everyone knows now that that was wrong, no? I don't believe that people there haven't changed. I don't see how it would be a problem for me there. She's our baby, after all. She's partly made of me. I just want to see her. Please, Catarina. I don't know what else to say but please. Show me that you're still the courageous, impudent girl I knew. Don't listen to your parents or anyone else but yourself. You don't need to do anything but open the door. I ask nothing else of you. I only want to see her.

Still yours,

Gatún Gallardo

Dear Catarina,

I know you're sorry. Did you think I didn't know that? And yet, to see my name, and only those two words, and your signature afterward. I cried like a child. I cried like a man who has lost everything.

But I'll honor your wishes. I've only ever wanted to give you what you desire. I'll stay here. I won't try to come there. I won't try to contact her. You can tell her whatever you want about me, I suppose.

I'm returning to this letter after a few days. I don't know what else to say. I will be thinking of you always. I have photographs of you. The one of you in the hammock, after you fell out the first time, is my favorite. I look at it every day. Even after all of this, I can't help but love you. I love her, too, of course. Maybe she'll sense that even though I won't be there to tell her. This will be my last letter.

Yours with a heavy heart,

Gatún Gallardo

I stared at that last one for a long time, my heart thrumming in my chest. The handwriting was all capital letters. In the earlier ones he had drawn little cartoonish sketches after the signature, which was always his full name and the only thing in cursive.

It took me nearly an hour to read them all, translating in my head as I went. A few times, I had to stop and look something up in my Spanish–English dictionary, the filmy plastic cover rolled back at the edges, soft as petals.

When I gently laid down the last letter, I could see translucent circles near the edges where the oil from my skin had seeped into the paper. I pinched the paper again between my fingertips in exactly the same spots and slid it with shaky hands, along with all the others, back into the folder.

Both Lucy and my mother are there to bid me good-bye the day I leave. It's a Sunday, three days after Lucy arrived. I would have liked more time at home with them both, to make sure this arrangement was going to work out, that Lucy would be able to handle my mother and that my mother would at least tolerate Lucy, but everything about this trip was so last-minute that there wasn't much I could do about the accelerated timing. I found the letters and I made a reservation. I was afraid that if I thought about it all for too long, I wouldn't go through with it at all.

Lucy and my mother are sitting together at the kitchen table, my mother doing the crossword and trying to persuade

Lucy to help with the clues she can't unravel, and Lucy eating a bowl of cereal. Next to my mother's elbow is a paper towel with a heap of eggshell and the white of a hard-boiled egg on top. She always digs out the yolk and eats it first.

"Good morning," Lucy bellows as I walk in.

"Good morning!" I bellow back, smiling. I feel good, alive with the frisson of anticipation. I feel like anything is possible.

"What's all this yelling?" My mother frowns.

I pour myself a bowl of dry cereal and sit at the table with them, and the three of us pass the time talking about my mother's puzzle and then, for a while, about what Evanston used to look like before a movie theater and glass condominiums and an Urban Outfitters moved right into the middle of it. "They closed Sherman Restaurant!" my mother exclaims at one point, and Lucy gasps and throws a hand to her mouth at the indignity.

When the doorbell rings, my mother gets up to answer it.

"Hello, Catherine. Happy New Year."

George Grabowski is standing on our front step wearing a Chicago Bears parka. In his hands he's holding a potted plant, the base wrapped in metallic cellophane.

"I brought you this," he says, proffering the plant. "New life. New year. I thought it would be appropriate."

"George Grabowski. Our neighbor," I whisper to Lucy. "He's in love with my mother."

Lucy raises her eyebrows.

He isn't bad-looking, George Grabowski. He has ruddy cheeks, and flecks of gray in his eyebrows and sideburns, and he keeps himself clean-shaven. But he has never, in all the years I've known him, made any sort of progress in his quest to woo my mother. I was there when he told her once that she was beautiful. My mother replied, "Well, perhaps I should make you an appointment with an eye doctor, then?" George managed to look only amused, not crestfallen.

"Hello, Mira," George says, waving at me past my mother.

"Happy New Year," I say. I grin at Lucy.

She smiles and whispers, "She doesn't like him?"

I shake my head.

George tries his best to keep up the conversation at the door several minutes longer while Lucy and I try our best to listen without appearing as though we're listening. When my mother walks back to the table a few minutes later, the plant in hand, she says, "What am I supposed to do with this thing?"

"Take care of it," I mumble with a half-eaten spoonful of cereal in my mouth.

She stares at me blankly. "How?"

"You took care of me. I think you can figure out how to take care of a plant."

Lucy takes the pot out of my mother's hands and examines it as if she's appraising it. "Don't worry. I'll help you."

The taxi arrives not more than an hour later. The driver carries my suitcase to the curb and drops it in the trunk with a thud, letting it fall awkwardly against the spare tire, then waits in the car while I say my good-byes. Lucy looks on from inside the house while my mother and I stand in the front yard by the flagpole we never use. The ground is damp from melted snow and my feet sink a little into the soil.

"So you're leaving," my mother says. "For how long again?"

"Three weeks." I'm shivering with nerves.

"Well, I wish you had told me about it earlier."

"Come on. It's not that long," I say. There's a certain pleading laced through my voice that she not make this more difficult than it already is. My determination is fragile. If she makes enough of a fuss, I might cave. I might stay. "It will be over before you know it."

She pinches her lips together and stares at my shoulder. "I meant to ask you, have you seen my black beaded necklace?"

She's asked me the same question three times in the last week. "It's on your dresser."

She nods, her nose blooming pink from the cold. "Three weeks is a long time," she says.

I wince.

"Who knows what could happen in three weeks," she says.

"Nothing will happen."

Everything around us is quiet except for the clink of the rope beating against the flagpole in the breeze.

She sighs, then smiles. "Have fun."

"Your black beaded necklace is on your dresser," I say.

Two

Orientation

All the times I imagined it, I thought that what I would see from an airplane window would be this: rivers as thin as dried earthworms, treetops as lush as clumps of moss, patches of farmland laid out like pressed handkerchiefs, mountain valleys rounded like soft dimples, the earth in miniature. But the only thing outside the window is white air with, occasionally, bands of sunlight radiating through. It's beautiful and breathtaking, being that close to the marbled sky, but it isn't what I hoped to see.

The man in the seat next to me smells of a garlicky sweat, a stench that lifts off him each time he stirs, and he often does, stretching his arms over his head and cracking his fingers. I try to ignore him and read the copy of *Principles of Geology* that I brought with me. I got it in high school as a graduation gift from my earth sciences teacher. The pages are worn and highlighted and notated and dog-eared from all the times I've read it. The man touches me once when I doze off, to announce excitedly, "Drink cart," and point to a flight attendant standing in the aisle with a plastic cup raised in her hand like a trophy. I order water. He orders a tomato juice with lime and a tiny bottle of vodka.

The two of us, along with at least a hundred others, are en route from Chicago to Houston. From there I'll continue to Panama City, Panama. I have no idea what to expect. I know everything I've read about it in my guidebook—how much to pay for a taxi from the airport, what the temperature will be like, what areas of the city to avoid, what kinds of payments merchants will accept. But that's all superficial. I don't know what really to expect, underneath all of that.

After he finishes his drink, the man next to me says, "So, do you speak English?"

"Me?"

"You know English?"

"Yes." I don't feel like telling him that I know Spanish, too. Not absolutely, totally fluently, but well enough. When I was younger, my mother tried to teach me a little—the words for colors and numbers and animals and foods—anything she had learned when she lived in Panama. When we exhausted her vocabulary, she sent me every Wednesday night for a year to a Spanish class at the YMCA. She was always like that, pushing me to spend my time learning and studying and learning and studying because, she said, that was the way to become more than you knew you were. By the time I got to high school and started taking Spanish as an elective, I was the best student in my class. My teachers couldn't believe how naturally it came to me. And they couldn't believe, when they heard about it, that I hadn't minded, all those years, taking Spanish classes outside of school. It wasn't exactly that I hadn't minded, though, as much as that I hadn't known better. I didn't know until I was older that not everyone my age was spending weeknights learning a second language. I didn't consider the reason for it, either, but I think it boiled down to this: Spanish was just something my mother had fallen in love with, the way other parents are in love with music or baseball or books. She wanted to share it with me the way people want to share the things that mean something to them with those they care about. And she wanted to give me a connection to some part of my background. She wanted to hold open a doorway to myself.

"Just checking," he says. "I fly this route all the time, and a lot of times the people sitting next to me only know Spanish. Texas is full of Mexicans."

"Texas is a big state," I say. "I think it's probably full of a lot of people."

He shrugs. "So that's where you're going? Texas? You have family there?"

"I'm just connecting there. I'm going to Panama City."

"In Florida?"

"In Panama."

"Panama. Isn't that a Van Halen song?"

"I don't know." I do know. The first time I heard it on the radio, I almost couldn't believe my ears. But I don't feel like indulging him.

"That's where they have the canal, right? And the hats, too. Panama hats, Panama Jack." He nods approvingly.

"The hats are from Ecuador," I say.

"Come again?"

"The hats are actually from Ecuador."

"Ecuador hats? No"—he frowns—"that doesn't sound right. I'm pretty sure you've got that mixed up. They're *Panama* hats."

"I know that's what they're called, but they're made in Ecuador. They got popular when Theodore Roosevelt toured the canal, when it was being built, and he wore one. People started calling them Panama hats and the name stuck." I don't know why I'm telling him. As if he cares. I just want to prove that I know what I'm talking about. I always feel I have something to prove when it comes to the topic of Panama.

"If you say so." He raises his plastic cup and lets an ice cube slide into his mouth. "So why are you going? You visiting someone?"

"I'm not sure."

"What do you mean you're not sure? Either you're visiting someone or you're not."

"I don't exactly know my plans yet."

"How long are you staying?"

"Three weeks."

"Have you ever been there before?"

I shake my head. Maybe if I stop talking, he'll return the favor. I peek around him, to a perfectly normal-looking passenger across the aisle, and wish I'd been assigned a different seat.

"Three weeks without plans in a place you've never been before?" He widens his eyes. "Good luck."

Ordinarily, I am not a brave person. Not that I walk around all the time afraid of things, just that I almost never do anything that requires considerable courage or abandon. I do what's asked and what's expected and what I'm supposed to do.

I don't jaywalk. I wait in line at a register to ask questions that other people simply walk to the front with and shout at the cashier as she handles another transaction: Where's the escalator? Can I make a return in this line? Which way to the shoe department? I pack up my things in the library and take them with me when I need to use the bathroom. I put money in the meter even if I'm running in for something I know will take only a minute. I sample lotions only from the labeled tester. I give back the extra change if someone gives me too much. I turn in my school assignments on time.

The first geologic exploration of the South Pole was in 1911, in the midst of the Heroic Age of Antarctic Exploration. Roald Amundsen, the man who completed it, was an adventurer to the marrow of his bones. As a young boy, he used to sleep with his bedroom windows open in the winter to get his body accustomed to the cold he would one day endure as the explorer he knew he wanted to be. The second person to reach the South Pole was Robert Falcon Scott. He died trying to get back to his base, and I have often imagined that he did not particularly want to go on the trip in the first place. All he had to look forward to, after all, was ice and bitter cold and the great occupying space of the unknown. He may have acted with bravado and been brimming with confidence, but what if he was simply a man caught up in a race, a man leaving his family behind, a man who felt he had something he needed to prove?

Some people are true adventurers. But many more are adventurers by circumstance, adventurous only because their goal requires them to be. They pull on the mask of daring because doing so is the only way to get where they're going. And sometimes the mask becomes them, and by the end of their journey, the true adventurer who has lain dormant in their soul ignites and takes hold. And sometimes the mask is still just that, an outer shell, and the inner person remains unchanged. It's hard to know all the time which is which and who you are. It's hard to know until the end.

I don't know what will happen to me by the time this trip is over, but right now, at the start of it, I am Robert Falcon Scott, and Panama as well as everything that might happen there is my fantastic unknown.

. . .

I lied to my mother about this trip. More than two weeks ago, I booked the ticket online and then walked into her room to tell her I'd been invited on a Geophysical Sciences Department trip to the Cascades Volcano Observatory in Vancouver, Washington. There was no way she could have known that I was really going to Panama.

"I'll be gone for three weeks," I said. "The trip is for the first three weeks of the quarter."

She said, "There was a human head on the kitchen counter this morning."

I was sitting on her bed while she stood in front of her dresser and applied makeup. I was watching her face in the mirror. In the lower corner of it, I could see my own—my wide, dark brown eyes; my long, straight nose; my pale lips, shiny with ChapStick; my black hair pulled into a low, haphazard ponytail loop; my bangs cut in a blunt line, dusting the tips of my thick eyelashes.

"A human head?" I asked.

She nodded.

When I walked into the kitchen, there was a cantaloupe on the counter.

Back in her room, I said, "I think it's gone now."

"What is?"

"Mom, did you hear me before?" I didn't know why I was pressing it. She had already taken the news better than I thought she would.

"You mean about the trip?"

"Yes."

"I heard."

I wasn't going to tell her the rest: that I had arranged to take the entire next quarter off. Later, I would. But not yet. I wanted to avoid the inevitable fight the news would trigger. My mother would argue that taking a quarter off was the first step down a slippery slope that ended with me, in a heap at the bottom, quitting school altogether. There was no way to explain to her that taking a quarter off was no big deal, that people did it all the time. Even when I talked to the dean about it, he'd said I was the third person that day to come to him with the same request. He'd told me that my scholarship would remain intact as long as I took off for no longer than one year. Everything would be fine. But none of that would matter to my mother. To her, it would signify the beginning of the end. She had always made it clear that there was no messing around when it came to school. She wanted more for me than she had for herself. That sort of thing. By the time my mother was my age, she had been herded to a small, local Catholic college along the banks of the Hudson River at the insistence of her parents, who wanted to keep her close by. The point of going to college, as my mother tells it, was not so much to gain an education as it was to find a husband—a singular obsession with her parents, who believed, even in the late seventies, that the best any woman could do was to find a good man. In the shadowed wings of my mother's life, her parents were conspiring to help her winnow her marriage prospects until they finally settled on one man, a U.S. Marine named Brant Strickland, whom she wedded before transferring with him to his station in the Panama Canal Zone. He and my mother were divorced less than a year later. "It wasn't right from the start," she told me once when I asked her about it. "It wasn't right from the start or from the middle or from the end. It was never right." And why hadn't she gone to college after that? "Because, Mira, after that you were making your grand entrance."

She held out a tube of lipstick the shade of apricot and said, "What do you think of this color?"

"I promise I'll be back soon," I said, unwilling to let it go. "And someone will be around, you know, to help you."

"All fine," she said, and gazed again at the mirror. She pressed her lips together and released them with a faint popping sound.

As soon as I step off the plane and into the airport, I get swept up in the masses of people hurrying all together in the same direction, like a school of fish darting through the terminal. I walk with them, gripping the strap of my orange bag, half reading the backlit advertisements for hotels and travel excursions and banks that hang on the walls. It looks like any airport. Not that I've been to one before today. But it's not so different from O'Hare or Hobby. Maybe the lighting is dimmer. The furniture is older.

At the passport vestibules, everyone sorts instinctively into two lines: one for Panamanian citizens and one for everyone else. I get in the line with everyone else. I know it's where I'm supposed to be. Of course it is. But I can't help looking at the Panamanians who snake their way through the stanchions—women carrying woven-plastic bags, women wearing gold jewelry, men with leather shoes and mustaches, men in linen shirts, everyone's skin darker than mine—and feeling a twinge of displacement, as if almost, maybe, I could be in that line with them. I'm not sure why, but I want them to know that. I want them to know that I'm not just any tourist visiting their country, that I have a claim to this place and a reason for being here, that I belong to them, at least a little bit. I wonder whether, or how, they would treat me differently if they knew.

When I get to the scratched Plexiglas window, the man on the other side peers at me under heavy eyelids. He opens my passport and stamps—thud, thud, flips a page, thud, the rhythm of my pounding heart—then slides the passport and my tourist card back under the window.

In a way it's amazing that I even have a passport. Until now I've never once had the fortune to use it. The year I turned sixteen, I begged my mother for a passport as a birthday present. She drove me to Circus Joe's Burger Palace and sat me in the old-fashioned photo booth they had by the register and told me to smile. The bulb flashed four times. "This was cheaper than going to Walgreens," she said, when I came out.

"What do you mean?" I asked. Somehow, I didn't realize that she had brought me there to get my official passport photo. I had been pestering her for a passport, sure, but she hadn't given any indication that she was actually going to get me one. I thought that we were merely going to Circus Joe's for a birthday lunch, and that when she sent me into the photo booth it was for a commemorative birthday snapshot.

"The post office is even worse. They should be ashamed of what they charge for a passport photo."

"This can't be my photo," I said.

"We haven't seen them yet. I'm sure they're fine."

"No, I mean it has to be official. Circus Joe's isn't official."

My mother stared at me. A giant plastic elephant, lion, and bear stood frozen in parade through the middle of the restaurant. Then, a strip of photographs came sliding forth, as if the booth was sticking its tongue out at us. My mother bent down slowly and plucked the strip out of the tray. "I know that," she said evenly. "I just thought you might need a warm-up." Without another word, she stuffed the narrow band of black-and-white photos into her purse, and strode out to the car. She drove us straight to Walgreens.

Several weeks later, after we also went to the post office to fill out the required papers, I received in the mail a beautiful gold-stamped navy booklet. By then, my mother was long past the embarrassment of her mistake, and she came into my room smiling, holding the passport aloft, and told me, "Happy Birthday, Mira." I spent that entire afternoon cutting out silhouettes of the countries I longed to visit—Iceland, Mongolia, France, Egypt—and sticking the pieces, like paper fish, between the pages of the booklet. The first one I cut out, of course, was Panama. I've been holding on to my passport, waiting for the day I would use it, ever since.

Hotel Centro is the cheapest lodging listed in the guidebook that also advertises air-conditioning. I'm paying for this trip with money I've saved from my scholarship stipends and from the little bit that I have in the bank from odd jobs I had throughout high school, so there isn't a lot of wiggle room as far as my budget is concerned.

I made a reservation before I left home. Over the phone, the man I spoke to told me at first that the hotel was booked. We were speaking to one another in Spanish so I wasn't sure whether I misunderstood. Then he said, "I'm joking, of course! We have plenty of rooms. You want to go to Costa Rica? No rooms. But in Panamá we have plenty of rooms. How many nights?" I started with one. I had given myself three weeks for this trip, but who knew what would happen? I didn't want to commit to anything for too long. Besides, he assured me, extending my reservation, even by increments of one night at a time, would be easy.

It's almost ten o'clock by the time the taxi pulls up in front of the building. A doorman with a gold name-badge that says "Hernán" opens the car door and, through the night air, carries my suitcase up the stairs from the street.

The lobby is small and sparsely decorated with two club chairs and a potted palm tree. A room off to the side houses a small bar, the bottles lined up against a mirrored wall like at an apothecary. Hernán places my suitcase on the floor by the front desk before stepping back a polite distance. I check in with the attendant on duty, who hands me a key for room 308. "It is the top floor," he says. "I hope you will enjoy it."

Hernán follows me up the flights of stairs, thumping my suitcase behind him. I could have managed it on my own, but I don't want to offend him by saying so. At the door, I tell him thank you and try, as gracefully as possible, to hand him a folded dollar bill for his trouble. Hernán takes it, then starts back toward the stairs.

The room is plain but clean. It smells faintly of disinfectant. There's a twin bed with a beige bedspread hanging low enough that it brushes the tile floor, a small television set on top of a white wicker dresser, a private bathroom with a standing shower, an air-conditioning unit perched in the window. The few times my mother and I have traveled, we've gone by car, and we've stayed in motels, and we've done that only if there was no way we could have pushed through the dark and our exhaustion to our destination. My mother never wants to stop and pay money to sleep. My room now isn't much different from those—if anything it's nicer—except for the fact that I'm in it by myself.

I lay my suitcase flat on the floor and turn on the air-conditioning, waiting as it gurgles to life. On the ground below, there's a lighted alley lined with a row of trash cans, and across from it, apartment buildings with ironwork balconies, almost all of which are strung with laundry.

I'm about to step away from the window when I see something move. A guy holding a bucket filled with flowers scans the length of the alley, then settles himself against one of the trash cans, lowering his face into the petals. After a few minutes, he gets up and walks away, cradling the bucket against his hip.

I don't know what to do with myself. I don't want to unpack, since I'm not sure yet how long I'll be here. I don't want to call any of my friends, since nothing has happened yet to tell them about. I'm not hungry. I'm not tired. I take a deep breath. I need to relax. I need to remember my plan. I told myself that as soon as I got here, the first thing I would do was find a phone book. That should be simple enough. I open the dresser drawers and in the bottom one, next to a pad of paper with the words "Hotel Centro" along the bottom edge, bingo. Okay. Out of my orange bag, I pull my father's letters and lay them on the bed. His return address is in the upper right corner of each. I lay the phone book on the bed next to the letters and open it to the G's. I feel my heartbeat speed up. I already looked him up on the Internet, of course, before I came, but I didn't find anything. Not so much as a trace of him in the first thirty pages of Google search results. After that, I told myself just to wait. To exhibit some patience. As soon as I got here, I could get my hands on a phone book. I could see if he was listed and go from there.

I tuck my hair behind my ears as I scan the names. I almost can't bear to look, but I can't stand not to. I back away and jiggle my arms a little, like a runner getting ready to crouch down into the starting blocks. Come on, Mira, I tell myself. I approach the book again. Then I read: Gallardo, Ana. Gallardo, Benjamin. Gallardo, F. O. Gallardo, Ignacio. Gallardo, M. Gallardo, Tula. Gallardo, Tulia. Gallardo, Ynez. Eight Gallardos in all. None of them Gatún, and none matching the address I have.

It's hard to imagine my mother in this place, more than twenty years earlier. What did Panama look like when she lived here? Through the window, in the distance, there's a sliver of what appears to be the ocean. In the space between two buildings, the tiniest patch of blue, glinting in the moonlight.

I can't say why, but the sight of the water makes me think of the time, one summer, when my mother and I drove to the dunes along Lake Michigan, in Indiana. It was supposed to reach ninety-nine degrees that day, the latest in a string of four days that the temperature in Chicago had skyrocketed to near or over a hundred. Everyone in the city was going crazy, and my mother and I were no exception. We had taken to sleeping in the basement, where it was cooler, my mother stripping down to her bra and underwear and splaying herself on top of an old comforter she'd laid out on the floor. We spent an entire afternoon in the frozen-food aisle at Jewel, walking up and down, up and down, opening the freezer doors every so often to stick our faces in and pretend that we were looking for the perfect bag of peas or that we were actually considering buying French bread pizza. After a few hours of this nonsense, a manager strode toward us and handed us both paper applications, saying pointedly, "If you're going to spend this much time in my store, you might as well be on the payroll." My mother, I remember very clearly, said, "Thank you. That's the easiest interview I've ever had," and took the application, stuffing it in her pocketbook.

The next day, my mother had a new plan.

"We need to get out of here. We're driving to the dunes," she said when I came upstairs for breakfast. It must have been a weekend, if she was home from work.

"The where?"

"You know the dunes."

"In Indiana? Yeah. I didn't hear you. I thought you said we were going to the doom."

"If we stay here any longer, that's exactly where we'll be going."

She told me to wear my bathing suit under my clothes, and after that, we were off. In the car and on the road. I don't remember anything in particular about the car ride, but I do remember pulling into a parking lot and walking into a huge, shimmering sea of golden sand. Mounds and mounds of it unrolling as far as I could see, rounded and windswept, the valleys lost in shadows.

"This is so cool," I said. When I had said I knew what the dunes were, I meant by reputation only. I had heard of them, but I had never seen them in person.

"It better be cool. Or at least cooler than where we were. That was the whole point."

My mother beckoned me to the beach, where hundreds of other people with the same idea were stretched out on oversized towels or splashing near the shoreline or kayaking farther out. We owned none of the usual beach accoutrements, so we just took off our clothes and got in the water, dunking ourselves under, heads and all, until we started to cool off enough that we felt sane again. My mother floated on her back for a time, her hands sculling silently under the water, her eyes closed against the beating sun, while I stuck my feet in the sand holes where it was shallow and then reached down and pulled up whatever I could grab hold of, sorting the silt and quartz crystals and rocks in my palm and saving some to take home.

Later in the day, when the sun was dimming, we sat up to our waists in the water and watched the swallows fly from their nests in the dunes and the dragonflies bat their wings overhead. A light breeze sent the sand at the top of the mounds swirling in the air.

"This was nice," I told my mother, and I meant it. We didn't often spend time together like that. The majority of our days were about more pedestrian concerns—getting dinner on the table, finishing homework, fixing the thermostat, that sort of thing.

"You liked it?"

"I liked it."

She smiled and rubbed her eyes and looked out at the water. "You know, there are a million places in the world.

But you only need to find one that makes you happy. As long as you have one, that's enough."

At the time, I thought she was talking about being there, but now I wonder whether she was thinking about Panama instead.

Three

Absorption

Early the next morning I go looking for breakfast in the hotel bar. I spent nearly the entire night awake, curled up on the bed, alternately thinking of what I would do when the sun came up and reading the guidebook and *Principles of Geology.* By the time I finally fell asleep on top of the sheets, the air-conditioning grumbling like a bad stomachache, it was almost four a.m.

Before bed, I called my mother. I figured out when I should have landed in Washington—three hours after I had actually landed in Panama—and dialed her at home. She sounded relieved to hear from me and glad to know that I had made it to my destination in one piece, no problems. She asked how the flight had been, and when I told her I just read and that they played a movie the whole way, she said that wasn't fair, that they didn't show movies on airplanes the last time she flew. She was making soup when I called. Lucy was watching television. "She watches crap," my mother said. "Right now she's watching an infomercial for gloves that are textured so they can peel potatoes." I told her I would call her again tomorrow. "You're not going to call me every day, are you?"

"Why not?"

"It's a lot of money."

"I'm just using my cell phone. Until I run out of minutes, it's not costing us anything extra."

"Well, you don't usually call me every day from school."

"Maybe not every single day, but I get pretty close."

"Mira, you already left me with a babysitter."

"She's not a—"

"She is. And that's fine. But you don't need to call me and check up on me every day, too. I can still take care of myself, you know."

"I'm still going to call you tomorrow."

"If you must."

In the bar, the tables are empty, with menus propped up between the salt and pepper shakers. Along the counter an assortment of juices and coffee are lined up as though the employees are expecting a crowd. I take a seat at one of the tables, and a burly man with a thick mustache and fingers stout as sausages comes to take my order: a hard-boiled egg and two fried corn cakes—they're called tortillas on the menu—with a Panamanian white cheese. He wipes his hands on a white towel threaded through one of his belt loops and tells me he'll be back with my food in a minute.

When he leaves, I pour myself a cup of coffee from the silver urn on the bartop. It's so strong, even after milk and three sugar packets, that I manage to take only small sips, and even then, I struggle to get it down. Halfway through the cup, a commotion erupts in the lobby behind me.

"Lady didn't pay me!" I hear a voice yell in Spanish.

"I know. But that is the risk of this job. You know that. You have to calm down," says another voice.

"*Oye,* this is a business!" yet another man chimes in.

"What we're talking about is a business, too, *payaso.*" The first voice.

"Your business office is out on the street, not here in my lobby."

I crane my neck but I can't see anything.

"*Your* lobby? What? Now you own this building?"

Then I see him, the same guy from the alley the night before. He crosses the doorway—my little rectangular field of vision—in the direction of the front desk, his baggy pants dragging lightly against the tile floor. Hernán, the doorman, strides briskly after him as he says, "I am telling you again that you have to calm down!" and then the front bell rings repeatedly. There are some scuffling noises, but no more talking, before the lobby goes quiet again. I sneak to the doorway of the bar and peer out. The guy—he's about my age, his hair bleached the color of butterscotch—is sitting, scowling, on one of the two chairs in the lobby with his arms crossed while Hernán kneels in front of him and appears to be whispering to him sternly. The front-desk clerk stands red-faced, staring at the two of them as if on guard for an attack he believes might still happen.

From behind me, I hear, "Your food," and turn as the bartender places my plate on the table with a clatter. I linger for a moment before returning to the table.

I'm cutting off a second piece of the hot, crispy corn cake when the guy from the lobby strides into the bar and plops himself onto a stool at the counter. His light brown hair is curled against his neck, and he scratches it absently before he starts drumming his fingers on the lacquered bartop. He pushes himself forward across the counter, searching, I guess, for the bartender. A few seconds later, he spins around on the stool. Even with my eyes trained on my plate, I can feel him staring at me. I take another bite of my corn cake. He keeps staring. Finally, I look up. "The bartender is around here somewhere," I say, in Spanish.

He grins, hops off the stool, and shuffles toward me.

"How's your food?" he asks.

"Good."

He pulls out a chair and sits across from me.

I rest my fork on the lip of the plate. I don't feel scared of him, exactly, but I don't know what to expect.

He slides the toothpick dispenser across the tabletop toward himself and turns it over, catching one of the slender sticks in his palm. "Do you mind?" he asks.

When I shake my head, he pops the toothpick into the corner of his mouth, the greater part of it dangling from between his lips like a slide.

We sit for a full minute at least, neither of us saying anything, although I can feel him watching me curiously. He never turns away. Neither do I. It's like we're in some kind of silently agreed-upon contest. The rest of the bar is almost impossibly quiet, not a single particle of sound floating in from the lobby or from the kitchen.

Finally, he says, "Are you staying in this hotel?"

I cock my head. "Maybe. Why?"

"Just wondering. I haven't seen you around here before. The people who pop up out of nowhere are the ones staying here. The people who hang around all the time are employees."

"That's usually how a hotel works."

"So I'm going to guess you're staying here."

"Okay."

His skin is honey-brown, and he has wide-set, light brown eyes traced with a hint of green. One of his front teeth is chipped at the inside corner, giving his grin an air of mischief and boyishness, and his hair is cut short. He's wearing baggy cargo pants and a red T-shirt with a faded checkered-flag decal on the front.

I finger the handle of my fork and move it from one position to another on the thick, rounded edge of my plate.

"I'm bothering you?" he asks. "I just wanted to welcome you to the hotel. Make sure you have everything you need." He smiles as though that wasn't his intention at all. Not in a malicious way. More as though it was simply something to say, a token bit of exchange.

When I tell him that everything has been fine so far, I expect him to leave, but he stays put. "Just in case I see you again before your stay is over, what's your name?"

"Miraflores." I don't know why I say the full thing, since at home everyone calls me Mira.

He squints at me. "Like the canal?"

"I was named after the locks at the canal. Yes."

"But you're not Panamanian, are you? Are you a Zonian?"

"A what?"

"I guess not, then. They know who they are. They're really fucking proud of it."

"I'm half Panamanian," I say, even though I'm nervous to let the words out of my mouth. Because is he going to want me to prove it? Can I prove it? Is he going to ask me questions I don't know the answers to?

"Really? So you're half from here." He turns the toothpick around in his mouth. "And where is the other half of you from?"

"Chicago."

"In the United States?"

"Right in the middle of it."

"That's where you live?"

"Yes."

"So you live in the middle of the United States, but you speak Spanish?"

"I've been speaking Spanish to you this whole time, haven't I?"

"Yeah, but usually the Americans come here and expect us to speak English, not the other way around."

I don't say anything.

"Now I'm really bothering you, huh? You want to finish your breakfast?"

He's been propping up the toothpick with his fingers while he talks, but now he draws it out of his mouth and scoots away from the table as though he's going to leave.

"You're not bothering me," I say.

"No?" He relaxes in his chair and chews on the soggy end of the toothpick again. "So how long are you staying here in Panamá?"

I don't feel like answering his questions all of a sudden. He's kind of nosy, isn't he? And why is he asking, anyway? I don't want to give away something that would let him take advantage of me if that's his intent. Although maybe I already have.

"Hey, what was all that I heard earlier?" I ask instead. "With your flowers?"

"Ah, fucking lady didn't pay for the flower I gave her. Sorry. My language. Hernán's always reminding me there's a proper way to speak to the tourists." He looks at me searchingly. "How did you know about the flowers?"

"I could hear you from in here."

He snorts. "No shit? Sorry about that, too, I guess."

"It's okay."

"Hey, you want one?"

"What?"

"A flower. I have orchids today. Every other dude on the street is dealing in roses, but roses are so fucking ordinary. I guarantee I'm the only guy out there with a bucket of orchids. The tourists love them."

"Aren't orchids rare, though?"

"I don't sell the endangered ones, if that's what you mean. I already got in trouble for that shit once. The fucking, like, flower police or something came up and told me I was breaking all these laws. Whatever. I stick to the legal ones now. So do you want one?"

"I'm okay."

He twists the toothpick between his fingers.

"How do you know Hernán?" I ask.

"Who said I know Hernán?"

"You mentioned him a minute ago."

"You know him?"

I'm about to say that he's the doorman when I realize I don't know the word for "doorman" in Spanish. "He's the man who stands outside the door."

"It's nice that you paid attention, you know. People usually don't notice. I'll have to tell him you noticed."

"So you *do* know him."

"Hernán's my uncle. My father's brother. I've been living with him since I was about five."

"So you *really* know him."

He shrugs.

I don't know whether to press him. Maybe it's my own frame of mind and reason for being there, but I ask, "And your father?"

"My parents took off for Brazil and left me with him. They got transferred there for work, but then they never came back. Hernán's okay, though."

"Your parents left you?"

"Not at first. They sent money back, called me on the phone. But somewhere along the way they decided they liked their new life in Brazil. They wanted to stay. They didn't see a reason for me to come join them. So I don't know if they left me. They just never came back for me." Nothing in his face shows that he feels anything about the fact that his parents abandoned him, but his voice betrays a forced nonchalance.

On the floor, a parade of ants navigates the crevice between two tiles.

"I'm in Panamá because I'm trying to find my father," I say.

He takes the toothpick out again, discarding it on the floor. The ants march over it. "What do you mean?"

"My father lives here. He's Panamanian."

"Ah, the half of you from here."

"Right."

"What do you mean you're trying to find him? He's lost?"

"I've never met him. He doesn't know I'm here looking for him."

"Serious? He doesn't know you're here?" He looks at me

for several seconds while he curls his lips around his teeth. "Do you want help?" he asks finally.

"That's okay."

"Really?"

"I don't know what I'm doing."

"So I could help you. Fuck," he says, throwing his hand in the air. "You've never even talked to him or anything?"

I shake my head.

"I mean, my parents are all the way in Brazil but I could call them if I wanted. I just never want to. But Christ. You have a little bit of information on him at least?"

"I have his name."

"Anything else?"

"I have an address. He might still live there but he might not. I don't know. And I know he used to work at the canal. Maybe he still does." I turn down one corner of my mouth. I know it's not a lot to go on.

"You don't know much, huh? I guess we have somewhere to start, though. I mean, if you want my help. I know the city pretty well."

This isn't the sort of offer I normally would accept. When I was growing up, my mother taught me to be wary of strangers, especially those who seemed willing in any way to be helpful, to be nice, to be of use. But then again, coming here in the first place wasn't the sort of thing I normally would do. And what if he really can help me? I don't have that much else to go on at this point.

"Okay," I say.

He smiles wide, evidently pleased. His chipped tooth is uneven against the others. "We should know each other's names," he says. "I know yours."

I nod.

"Mine is Danilo."

Every inch of the bus is elaborately spray-painted and airbrushed. The driver's name is scripted in blue near the grill and there's an image of Fidel Castro in fatigues on the side. Before I even get on, I can hear music with a backbone of thumping bongo drums coming from the radio inside.

Danilo and I share a double-wide seat, and he taps his knees to the beat of the music while we ride. He brought his flower bucket with him because, as he explained to me as we walked through the hotel lobby, he never knew when he might make a sale. He keeps it in the aisle beside his feet.

The bus is crowded and hot and, between the voices and the music, loud. The driver keeps shouting for everyone to move back, move back. He hollers over and over, "*Péguense que tienen ropa.*" A young boy crouched on the floor beside the driver stands periodically and echoes the same remarks. Danilo shouts back once, "*¡Gracias, pavo!*" and then turns to me and says, "Those guys are the worst."

"Who is he?" I ask.

"Probably the driver's nephew or something. They're on all the buses now. Like helpers."

Danilo acts aggravated, but for me it's invigorating to be

on the bus and to feel like I'm really, truly, in Panama at last. Not just in the hotel or in a taxi or in a restaurant, but here among the people who call it home. I clutch my bag on my lap and look at everyone while a sort of giddiness fizzes inside me like a firecracker, a series of warm pricks bursting against my chest. Outside, palm trees hover overhead as we, along with hundreds of other vehicles, lurch and crawl and bump over the city streets. The driver doesn't stop at intersections. Instead, he honks twice—two little bleats to announce that we are coming through—then barrels ahead. Traffic lights are rare. On side streets, there are stop signs, and elsewhere traffic is regulated naturally by the halting ebb and flow of vehicles pressing slowly ahead, edging around each other, making their own lanes, turning where they want, stopping in the gravel along the side of the street.

"I'm glad I don't have to drive here," I whisper to Danilo.

"Eh. It looks like a fucking mess, but it's so slow that people never get in accidents," he says.

We pass stout white buildings with wavy red-clay roofs, restaurants with their names painted in block letters onto the façade, strip centers, uniformed guards with machine guns slung over their shoulders pacing the street corners, a man selling Coca-Cola and Orange Crush in bottles from a cart, apartment buildings with laundry hanging over the balconies, huge cathedrals, people holding umbrellas on street corners, kids selling fruit stuffed into long plastic sleeves, covered bus stops, wild tangles of plants in every open space.

This is it. I've been staring at the photographs in my guidebook for weeks. But now, this is it.

Danilo asked me the address before we got on. I told him: Ave A. Casa 822. He clucked his tongue and grimaced.

"What?" I asked. "Do you know it?"

"I don't know the house, but that address is in a bad area."

"How bad?"

"It's just . . . Look, it's not terrible. But it's a good thing you're going there with me. Let's just say that."

I didn't press him about what that meant exactly. I don't know, maybe I should have. But what would have been the point? The address was the address, after all, and no matter where it was, it was where I needed to go.

Another fifteen minutes into our ride, the bus stops. I don't think anything of it at first. Outside, a dog sniffs at a styrofoam container of food open on the sidewalk. But by the time the dog wanders away, we're still stopped. Two cars in the intersection in front of us start honking at each other. I glance at Danilo. He's gazing out the window across the aisle, totally unconcerned. Behind us, two men start talking about how a month earlier one of the city buses caught fire and how the passengers rushed to the back exit to get out but the door was sealed shut, so they changed course and surged toward the front of the bus instead, but with everyone scrambling and pushing and screaming and climbing over one another, most of them got trapped inside the bus and died when it went up in flames. The woman across the aisle from us is holding an ivory-colored rosary in her lap, working her fingers from one smooth bead to the next.

"Danilo," I say. "Are we close?" If we are, maybe we can just get out and walk.

"Not really."

"How long have we been sitting here?"

He surveys the deadlock in front of us. "Who knows?"

A bubble of panic rises inside me. What am I doing here, on this bus, with someone I hardly know? He could be taking me anywhere. He could be anyone. I've heard the stories about tourists who are kidnapped or murdered when visiting a foreign country, and yet here I am, trusting him. Why did I talk to him in the first place?

I look at Danilo again, at his soft earlobe and the fine hairs that gather in a little curl just below it, the buttons of his spine peeking out over the stretched, droopy neck of his T-shirt. He grips the back of the seat in front of him with one hand outstretched and, as I'm staring at him, drops his head to wipe his forehead against his arm. Then he turns to me again.

"You okay?" he asks. "You look, I don't know, strange."

I laugh in spite of myself. "What a compliment."

"I didn't mean it like that."

"Maybe this wasn't a good idea," I say.

"What wasn't?"

"I don't know."

"You mean going to find your father?"

I think I mean all of it: taking a leave of absence from

school, lying to my mother, coming to Panama, talking to Danilo, getting on the bus, and yes, going to find my father. But what I say again is, "I don't know."

Danilo straightens and focuses his brown eyes on mine. "Miraflores," he says. "What do you want to do?"

"I don't know."

"You keep saying that."

"Well, I keep meaning it. I just don't think I'm ready yet."

Danilo doesn't say anything at first. "Where do you want to go?" he finally asks.

I brush my knuckles over my lips. "Back to the hotel?"

He shakes his head. "You can't spend your whole time in Panamá in the hotel."

"I'm not. I'm on the bus right now."

"But we haven't *gotten* anywhere yet. No. We have to go somewhere."

I know where we are before he tells me. Panamá La Vieja. Old Panama. The vestiges of what the city used to be. Danilo acts surprised when I say it. I tell him I read about it in my guidebook.

"We call it Panamá Viejo," he says. Then with considerable amusement he asks, "What else do they tell you in that guidebook?"

I shrug, feeling embarrassed, offended, something.

We walk across the soft, patchy grass to a small collection of ruins: crumbling stone half-walls no more than two feet high, weathered and blackened; windows without roofs; rooms without floors; buildings that are skeletons without flesh. Weeds sprout in between the rocks. Stones are hidden beneath matted grass. At the edge of the bones of the ancient city is a three-story-tall stone bell tower, still fairly intact.

Danilo says, "It was part of the cathedral."

I follow him inside the hollow tower and stand on the grass floor. Faint sunlight runs through the tall rectangular window openings and scatters down on us as we gaze up, our hands cupped like visors over our eyes. The smell is musty and warm.

"What do you think?" Danilo asks. His voice echoes a bit.

"It's nice," I say. I'm trying to come up with a reason why he brought me here, of all places.

Danilo takes a few steps and runs his palm along one of the walls, covered with gnarled moss. "I think it's fucked up."

"What?" I drop my hand and look at him.

"This place. It's fucked up. There were pirates who came here and torched it." He turns to me. "Did your guidebook tell you that?"

"Who? They did what?"

Danilo cups a hand over one eye and pumps his other arm as if he's doing a jig. "They set it on fire."

I can't help laughing at his pantomime. "Pirates?" I say in English.

"Isn't that what I said? *¿Piratas?*"

"Henry Morgan, right?"

"That's the dude who fucked everything up."

"But I thought I read . . . I thought when he was attacked, this was a Spanish city."

"So? It was here, wasn't it?"

"But it belonged to Spain."

"It doesn't matter," he says. "It was still here. It belonged to us, even if the name of here wasn't Panamá at the time."

"The boundaries of a place are always changing," I say. He stares at me, puzzled. I'm not sure I used the right word in Spanish for "boundaries." "I mean that you can't say a place belongs to a country just because of the land it's on. A long time ago this land was Spain's, so the city would have belonged to Spain. Now the land is Panamá's, so the city belongs to Panamá. In a thousand years it could be China's, so it would belong to China."

He looks unconvinced.

"I'm saying it's all political. They're just different names for the same place. The land doesn't belong to anyone. It only belongs to itself."

Maybe my Spanish is shaky, because he still looks perplexed. But then he says, "Geography is an illusion? Is that what you mean?"

Exactly. I tried to explain the same concept to my mother once, but she didn't understand. Even Beth accused me of sounding "philosophically nonsensical" the time I tried to get into a discussion with her about it while we were waiting for the TA to post the grades for our physical oceanography class.

Danilo runs his thumb along the uneven groove at the

meeting between two stones. "I've thought that before," he says. He keeps tracing, brooding a little while I stand still in the center of the square tower. Then he says, "I still think this place is ours, though."

When we step out into the full wash of daylight again, we walk past more rubble and crumbling walls, the foundations perfectly undisturbed, as if the buildings were once little more than tiered cakes, the tops of each simply lifted off. Not far in the distance, white gulls circle over the muddy brown-blue water in the bay.

We walk until we reach a small arched stone bridge. When Danilo strides out to the middle of it and sits, placing his flower bucket behind him, I sit down, too. The sky above us is absolutely clear, although across the bay, a thick swab of pale gray clouds hangs placidly. Our feet dangle nearly thirty feet above the narrow green stream that runs under the bridge, foamy as it curls around the rocks. A plastic grocery bag wound around a tree branch flows silently below us and, after it, the small body of a dead frog, splayed like an open flower. An old mini-refrigerator is lodged in the silt on the bank. Bits of mica schist glint in the sun.

I feel light sitting there, buoyant, the panic that surfaced earlier entirely gone. I have a strong sense of being close to something, even if I don't know what. Of being on a precipice. As if sitting on the side of that bridge is the same thing as being perched on the edge of my life.

Then, out of nowhere, Danilo says, "You know, you probably shouldn't take the bus alone while you're here. The bus system in Panamá is hell. No real routes, no schedules, buses going all over the place. They're called *diablos rojos* for a reason."

"I take buses at home."

He makes a face. "I don't know. You should probably just take taxis from now on."

"How do you know the buses in Chicago aren't just as bad?"

"People just say it's crazy here. They say that no one who doesn't live here would take the bus in their right mind. Do people say that in Chicago?"

"I guess not."

"Okay," he says, satisfied. Then, "In Chicago, you have the bears, right?"

It takes me a second to realize he doesn't mean animals in a forest. "For football, yes, the Chicago Bears."

"And for baseball?"

"The Cubs." I say it in English because I don't know the word for it in Spanish.

Danilo wrinkles his nose. "What is that?"

"A cub is a baby bear."

He shakes his head. "Lots of bears."

I laugh.

After another minute, he says, "You know, there are supposed to be treasures in the water. When the pirates came, everybody panicked and dumped all their gold and shit in the river. You know, to hide it. But then most of the residents got killed, so all their stuff is still supposed to be buried down there somewhere."

I don't catch everything he says. "*Tesoros* means 'gold'?"

"Could be gold. You know, just valuables. Treasures."

"It's all under the water?"

"That's the story. No one's ever found anything, though."

There seems something final about the way he says it, as though he merely brought up the subject for the sake of idle conversation and now is annoyed that the discussion has gone on. I wouldn't mind asking him more about it—the idea of treasures somewhere beneath our dangling feet is intriguing—but I get the sense that he's far less academic about exploring topics than I am. He's more impetuous perhaps, flitting to whatever captures his attention next. I push my bangs off my forehead, but they fall right back down again, rebellious in the humidity.

"Thanks for bringing me here," I finally say.

He gazes out at the water and shrugs. "Now you can say you've seen something."

I call Beth as soon as I get back to my hotel room. The reception is terrible.

"I can barely hear you," she says.

"I know. Is this better?" I'm standing by the window.

"Not really."

"Okay, tell me if it gets better. I'm just going to keep talking and talking and I'm walking around my room and I'm walking by my bed and I'm talking and I guess I could go out into the hall but I don't really feel like doing that and I'm still walking and I don't know what to say but I'm still—"

"There! That's good. It got clearer all of a sudden."

"Beth, I'm standing in the shower."

She starts cracking up and I just roll my eyes, smiling at myself in the mirror.

"How are you?" I ask.

"Forget about that. How are *you*? You made it there okay, obviously."

"Yeah, no problems. I got in last night."

"And what's it like?"

"It's . . . I don't know. It feels like I went really far away, but it also sort of doesn't. I mean, there are all these familiar places, like Wendy's and McDonald's and Costco, overlaid on this completely unfamiliar landscape. There are plants running wild everywhere."

"There's a Costco?"

"I know! It seemed so out of place when I saw it."

"But it's not totally Americanized, is it?"

"No. It still feels like its own place. And it's bigger than I thought it would be. I mean, the city itself is huge."

"Bigger than Chicago?"

"It feels like it. It's definitely more crowded at least."

"And your hotel's okay?"

Beth is from the sort of family that books the Four Seasons everywhere they stay. Not that she's pretentious about it. She has never once given me the impression that anything I do—going to a dumpy bar, taking the el, looking for bargains at Village Thrift—is below her standards. Even so, I have the notion that "okay" means different things to the two of us.

"It's nice," I say.

"That's good."

"Yeah."

"Mira?"

"What?"

"Nothing. It sounded like you were going to say something else."

"Well, I met this guy."

"*What!* Mira, you've been there for one day! You met a guy? I've known you for two years, and you've never *met* a guy."

"It's not like that. He's going to help me find my father."

"Oh, so is he older?"

"I think he's about our age."

"What's his name?"

"Danilo."

"I can't believe this. Do you mind if I tell Juliette and Asha? All those times Juliette tried to set you up with guys in her classes. She practically had the wedding planned for you and that guy—what was his name? Jamison or something ridiculous—in her pottery class. And I know you went out with some of them, but since it never went anywhere, we knew you were just sort of scared of the whole concept of getting into a relationship, but now this!"

"What do you mean, you knew I was scared? I wasn't scared."

"You just don't have a lot of experience."

"Neither do you."

"I know. But Juliette never finds guys who are right for me. If she did, I would take her up on it."

"You could find your own guys, you know."

"I'm just saying, I'm open to at least having the experience if I could find some experience to have."

"I'm open." As soon as the words are out of my mouth, I think of my mother. "I'm open," I say again.

"Apparently."

"Come on. I just met him, Beth. I mean, I've known him for less than twenty-four hours. And all he's doing is helping me find my father."

"I'm glad someone's helping you," Beth says. She sneezes. "Sorry. I think I'm getting a cold."

"It's eighty-eight degrees here," I tell her, and I see myself in the mirror giving an impish grin.

"That's the cruelest thing you've ever said to me," Beth says.

"No, wait," I say. "This is worse: it's also sunny."

"Sunny!" Beth wails. "I'm in the middle of a Chicago winter here, Mira! I don't even know what that word means anymore."

"It means everything over here is going fine."

. . .

I call my mother after that, as I told her I would, but Lucy informs me that she's already in bed.

"She's okay?"

"She's great. And you? How are the volcanoes?"

"The what?"

"Isn't that where you are? At a volcano observatory? Am I getting the name of it wrong?"

"No, that's right. It's— They're very . . . volcanic."

"I should think so."

Then, I don't know what makes me ask but I say, "Lucy, do you think it was okay for me to come here?"

"You have to live your life," she says.

"I know. But I think maybe it was bad timing."

"There's no good timing now. It's only going to get worse. But that doesn't mean you shouldn't do what you need to do."

I press my tongue into the back of my teeth. "Yeah."

"Mira, it's okay. She'll still be here when you get back."

"Yeah." I feel like crying now.

"She'll still be here for a long time, even if you have to look harder to find her."

No one said the word "Alzheimer's" until the third doctor. The first dismissed the symptoms as depression, assuring us that my mother, at forty-five, was far too young to worry about "other possibilities," as he put it. The second, we stopped going to after my mother deemed him unacceptable because of the poor quality of his teeth.

"Am I going to die?" she asked me on the way out of the parking garage after our visit with him.

"What?" I asked. I was driving.

"I have no idea what he said to me. He could have said I was going to die tomorrow, for all I know."

"You weren't listening to him?"

"Did you see his teeth? They looked like corn on the cob. How could I concentrate with corn on the cob yapping in my face?" She shook her head and rolled down her window as we snaked through the aisle toward the exit.

"I don't think they were that bad."

"Mira, I will shoot myself in the head if I have to go on looking at his corn teeth."

"So you want to switch doctors?"

"Very astute."

Doctor number three, Dr. Wu, was the one to give her the diagnosis. I didn't go with her to the appointment. She showed up at my dorm afterward, buzzing my room from the lobby, without any prior warning that she was coming. When I went down and saw her, she had a lavender scarf looped into a small flounce around her neck and a manila envelope tucked under her arm. She was folding and refolding one corner of the envelope.

"I didn't know you were coming today," I said.

"I need to talk to you. Do you want to take a walk?"

Instantly, my stomach started kneading. By then, of course, I already had my suspicions. "What's going on?"

"I'll tell you, but go get your jacket first. Hurry up."

It was a brilliant Chicago day, the sun high in the sky, a bracingly cool wind echoing off the lake. We walked without talking. The tree leaves swished, like muffled static, as they were tousled in the breeze. I had on jeans cuffed up past my bare ankles, my black low-top Converse sneakers, and a green-and-white-striped long-sleeved tee. I hadn't washed my hair in days, so it was greasy, held back with bobby pins. We walked down the sidewalks that fed out to the east, then under one of the stone archways that held above it train tracks, then across the grassy lawn surrounding the Museum of Science and Industry. When we got past the fence to the footpath that ran along the lake, my mother took a left. She pursed her lips and pulled them back again as she cast her gaze across the water, the sunlight shimmering wildly off the surface. Small black birds circled overhead, and every now and then one of them cawed. I fidgeted with the hems of my sleeves, stretching them over the heels of my palms, as I waited for what she had to say.

After about half a mile, I stopped. "Mom, come on. You have to tell me what you wanted to talk about. I can't stand it anymore."

She turned to look at me. We were face to face on the sidewalk, my mother with her back to the lake, the sounds of the birds still coursing through the air, the sounds of cars whizzing by on the street not far from where we stood. My mother crossed her arms and pinched her lips together. In the breeze, her hair-sprayed hair lifted all together at the sides like wings.

"I failed all the tests," she said. "I have Alzheimer's."

Just like that.

I knew that she had gone for testing earlier, and that the doctor had wanted her to come back in six months, which was the appointment she just had. The tests weren't about absolute numbers. They were about establishing a pattern of decline. They were things like puzzles and answering questions about a paragraph you'd just read and counting backward by sevens. We had practiced these things together over the phone. Her performance over the past few months had been sporadic. And there had been signs that things were off—the time she got frustrated to the point of tears because she couldn't remember how to use the letter opener, the time she was late meeting me for lunch because she got lost driving to a restaurant we always ate at, the time she left the back door to the kitchen wide open overnight, the time I found her eating a peppermint candy with the wrapper still on. But I got good at convincing myself that these things happened because my mother was under a particular amount of stress right then or that what she was experiencing were isolated, and entirely normal, moments of forgetfulness.

"Dr. Wu said there was also a possibility it could be something called Pick's. But he's pretty sure it's the other thing. I have to go to a neurologist. They want to do some scans of my brain."

I felt as though my head had suddenly inflated. I felt fuzzy and hot.

"Anyway, I told Dr. Wu he was wrong. I told him I was too young to have it. Do you remember that first doctor? That's what he said. But Dr. Wu said I have the kind called early-onset." She twisted her body to look out at the lake and, when she turned back to me, said quietly, as if conferring a secret, "I think my mother had it. That must have been what it was. We just thought she was going crazy."

My mother never brought up her parents. They had both died years earlier, but even when they were alive, we had no sort of relationship with them. I had never even met them.

She had a little spasm of a shiver.

"That isn't what's going to happen to you," I said.

"It is. That's exactly what's going to happen to me." She kicked at something invisible on the ground. "Damn it."

My stomach was killing me.

"It runs in the family," she said.

I didn't think about it this way at the time, but I guess she was warning me. If it wasn't exactly a warning, I believe that she was at least contemplating a future for me that caused her more despair than her own diagnosis had brought. She was casting it out in her mind, imagining the bright and capable daughter she'd raised felled by a disease that dissolved a person's mind wholly and persistently. She must have been, because what she did next was so uncharacteristic it could have been prompted only by the most piercing anguish: She put her arm around me. She drew me to her. She circled her arms around my middle, her hands below my shoulder blades. And she held me there. I cupped her shoulders from behind and squeezed her soft arms with mine. I could feel her breathing. I could smell her hair spray in the breeze.

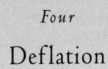

Four
Deflation

In the morning, a slice of sunlight cuts through the gap between the drawn curtains. Lying on my side in the bed, my hands palm to palm between my knees, I stare at it and wonder what's going to happen today. I have absolutely no idea, but I hope it will be something significant. I already feel as though I've fallen behind, wasting all day yesterday like I did. It was my fault, too. Danilo was willing to go to the address until I made us detour. I cover my face with my hands and rub them briskly up and down a few times, trying to wake myself up.

Thirty minutes later, I head downstairs dressed in the best clothes I brought with me: a white blouse with scalloped trim around the armholes and a denim skirt with a column of oversized brown buttons down the front. The outfit is paired with my Converse, of course, which isn't going to win me any fashion awards, but at least they're black and white, so they sort of go.

I'm hoping to find Danilo milling around, but when I check the bar, there's only a middle-aged couple sipping coffee at one of the tables. The man turns the pages of a newspaper while he drinks, letting the paper leaves collapse softly, like a failed soufflé. Outside, I crane my neck to scan up and down the street. Nothing. Then I see Hernán standing with his back against the building, his arms crossed, his cap drawn over his eyes. It looks a little like he's dozing off. I walk down to street level and tap him on the arm. He startles, then brightens when he sees me.

"Good morning," I say.

"*¡Señorita!* You look so nice. What can I do for you today?"

"Have you seen Danilo?" I ask.

"Danilo?" Hernán furrows his brow.

"Have you seen him this morning?"

"My Danilo?"

I smile. "Is there another one?"

"Why are you looking for him?"

I'm thrown off by his accusatory tone. "I was just wondering if you had seen him."

"How do you know him?"

"I don't really *know* him. I met him yesterday. He offered to help me."

Now Hernán's thick, dark brows fold toward each other, a long crease forming between them. "Help you how?"

"Just . . . nothing. If you see him, could you tell him I'm in the bar, having breakfast?"

Hernán hesitates. "Whatever you are trying to accomplish, you can do it without him."

When he sees I'm at a loss for words, his face softens.

"Who should I say is at the bar?"

"Me."

He smiles. "But what is your name?"

"Sorry. Miraflores."

He looks surprised, but doesn't comment on it other than to say, "Very pretty."

"Thank you," I say.

When I emerge again, after taking an hour and a half to eat two eggs and drink one cup of coffee until its bitter and very cold end, Hernán shouts cheerfully, "Time to go already? And unfortunately"—he shakes his head with mock ruefulness—"no sign of Danilo yet."

"It's okay," I tell him. I do feel disappointed not to have run into Danilo again, but I spent all of breakfast reminding myself that I can do this without him, just as I've been planning all along. It doesn't matter who helps me or how it happens, but I want to find my father. I spent so long believing that he was someone who didn't want to know me. But everything changed when I read those letters. My father cared about me. He cared about my mother. At least he did when he wrote them. But I believe that he still does. If I can find him, if he saw me . . . I'll shock the hell out of him, I'm sure.

But I really, honestly, think he'll be happy to see me. After all this time, to know that I came for him and that I want to know him. And I could tell him that I think my mother never stopped loving him. He may not want to hear that. If he's moved on already, it might be too much. Or he may be living every day of his life longing to hear that. And I could be the one to tell him. I could have him call her. She might tell him things she's been holding on to for decades, things she might not even remember soon that she wants to say, thanks to the insidious disease that's stalking its way through her brain. I could give her back that bit of her past, even though I'm not sure she deserves it since she's the one who exiled that bit of her past to begin with. And of mine. It was such an inexplicably fucked-up thing to do. But with everything that she's going through, hearing from him again might make her feel better. After all these years, I think she would finally talk to him again if the opportunity to talk existed. With or without Danilo's help, I need to find him.

I start in the direction Danilo and I walked yesterday to catch the bus, my orange bag slung diagonally over my shoulder. I'm not far when I hear Hernán shouting after me, "Wait, please! Please wait!"

I turn around. A car stops in front of the hotel and honks, but Hernán ignores it and strides toward me. "Where are you going?" he asks before he even reaches me, his voice raised.

I tell him the address.

He makes a face. "Why?"

Like Danilo, he asks a lot of questions. But there's a tenderness about Hernán, a protectiveness in how he treats me that I find endearing, unaffectedly sweet.

"I'm meeting someone there," I say.

Hernán takes off his cap and slicks his sweaty charcoal hair back against his scalp, then replaces the cap. "It is not a good area," he says matter-of-factly. The car that pulled up in front of the hotel honks again. Hernán whips his head around and throws up his hands. "Wait a moment!" he yells.

"How are you getting there?" Hernán asks.

"I was going to take the bus. I know which one is the right one."

Hernán raises his eyebrows. "You know which one is the right one?"

"The one with Fidel Castro."

"Ha! That is what you think? But they are all painted differently. There could be ten buses that go where Fidel goes! And then again, Fidel could be taking the day off. Those bus drivers work according to their own schedule, and you never know what kind of night the driver had last night"—he imitates someone throwing back a shot of alcohol—"that might make him skip a day of work today. I have seen it before. Ambitious guests try to take the bus to somewhere ten minutes away, and the next thing they know, they're on a three-hour trip to a whole other province! And they don't make it back to the hotel for days! No, I will call you a taxi. Do you have money?"

"Hernán, come on, that's never really happened, has it?"

"It has happened. It hasn't happened. What's the difference? It could happen. Do you have money?"

"Yes."

"Then you will take a taxi. Today, for me, please take a taxi."

Before I can argue, Hernán whistles until he attracts the attention of what looks like nothing more than a regular car, an old brown Hyundai, idling across the street, which now makes a U-turn and pulls up to the curb. Gallantly, Hernán opens the back door and motions by sweeping his arm back and forth like a pendulum for me to get in. Then he pounds the passenger-side window until the driver leans across the seat and cranks it down.

"She's going to Santa Ana. Across from the San José Church."

"Five dollars," the taxi driver replies.

Hernán balks. "The fare from here to there is two dollars."

"She's American, no?"

"No. Two dollars."

The driver grunts assent and rolls up the window. Hernán waves at me as we pull away.

I know that Hernán said I wasn't American because he wanted to get me a better fare. But it was still so odd to hear him deny it like that. No. She's not American. And yet, to the taxi driver, I clearly didn't pass as Panamanian. What does he think I am now? French? Portuguese? Dutch? When I was growing up, my mother never made any kind of point about my cultural connections, or disconnections. File it under A Topic That Came Too Close to My Father, and therefore A Topic That Would Not Be Discussed. But I do remember when, in fifth grade, a girl from Puerto Rico enrolled at my school toward the end of the year. Her mother and our principal had walked her out to the playground during recess so she could see who her classmates would be. I was kneeling in a patch of clover, looking for a sprig with four leaves, just like I'd been doing every recess since the snow had melted, while the other kids shrieked on the swings or played hopscotch on the asphalt. I looked up and saw the girl, skinny, wearing a white dress that was much too fancy for school. She was standing in front of her mother, not far from me. They surveyed the yard, and then her mother pointed at me and said, "Why don't you introduce yourself to her? She looks nice, *mi hija,* and I bet you she speaks Spanish." I didn't know what to do. I didn't want her to approach me. I didn't know why her mother would have said that about me. But I knew that I wasn't who she thought I was. I wanted to be. I wished I could have said, in Spanish, "Hey, come over here and we'll look for a four-leaf clover together," but even though I knew a few words by then, I didn't know enough. I felt embarrassed by my failings. I felt, even then as I still do now, like I've let everybody down, like there is supposed to be more to me than what I know, like there's a hollow space carved out along my side that somehow never got filled in. So I stood up quickly and brushed off my knees and ran over to the kids watching hopscotch, trying my best to blend in and fade away. I remember standing there and trying to figure out what I was exactly, but when I started thinking about it, I got lost. Maybe I had always felt that way, at least a little bit. In between the two countries that were both part of me, I never knew where I was or where I was supposed to be.

The driver keeps his window open a crack to ash his cigarette. Synthetic stuffing spills out of a tear in the seat next to me. Buildings and signs—Panagas, Super 99, Empanadas Don Carlos, Félix B. Maduro, Farmacias Arrocha—pass by in a blur. After a while the driver reaches back and raps his knuckles against my window. "Two minutes," he announces.

We pull up along a street tightly lined with tumbledown shanty houses, their zinc roofs almost flat, their multiple layers of peeling paint stained by water damage. Many of the front doors are open, and people sit in the doorways impassively, their elbows on their knees, thin sandals or worn slippers on their feet.

The driver tosses out his cigarette and rolls up his window as we near. He locks his door. When we stop I pay him, and he looks back at me with bored eyes. "You want that I wait?" he asks, testing his English.

"Please."

He turns off the engine, then props his elbow against the door and ruffles his hand through the back of his hair. He keeps the windows closed.

We're across the street from my father's house. I'm staring at it right now. Maybe he isn't home, or maybe he doesn't even live there anymore, but it almost doesn't matter. At one time at least this was his house, the place where my father cooked his meals and slept and got dressed in the morning and dreamed of me at night. The structure is covered in a faded salmon-colored paint. There is a heap of rusted auto parts in the front yard. A disused woven hammock lies like a dried corn husk on the ground between two trees.

Come on, Mira, I tell myself. This is why you came here. Get out of the car. Go to him. Come on. In one fluid motion, I open the car door and hurry across the street, practically skipping over the pavement as if it's hot and volatile lava. The neighbors are watching me from their stoops. From behind the front door, a clanging noise erupts and then settles, as though someone dropped a pot on the floor. My father. My father is in there. I knock.

Before I got out of the taxi, I remembered being in school the day I learned that the seven continents we take for granted used to be one huge landmass. All the world lumped together in one place. If humans had been around back then, the entire population of the earth would have lived on one gigantic island. I obsessed over it for weeks. Actually, I think I'm still obsessing over it. That single fact is what got me hooked on geology and geography in the first place. Because the idea of it is so compelling. The earth used to be one continent. And over time, that continent, carried on the backs of dozens of different tectonic plates, broke apart. Even now, the plates are moving under our feet. The continents are on a collision course every second of every day. The earth was born and every time a volcano erupts or a plate shifts, the earth is born again. It keeps reordering itself, it keeps trying new patterns, it keeps meshing one piece with another piece, and then another piece, and then another piece. I like to imagine that the reason behind all of that relentless effort is that the continents are yearning to come together again, as they were in the beginning.

Humans try to be like the continents. We stumble and crisscross and stagger all over the world in an effort to find our way back to one another. It seems to be the main business of life sometimes: our disordered attempt to bump into other people. Straining, straining, just to touch.

An older woman holding a dustpan greets me. Her face is long, and her mouth, fixed into a frown, is framed by deep wrinkles like a series of outwardly expanding parentheses. I feel light-headed as a breeze scrabbles at my back.

"What do you want?" she asks.

"I'm looking—"

"Yes?"

"I'm looking for Gatún Gallardo."

"Gallardo?" She repeats the word as if it's a seed she's spitting on the ground, then shakes her head.

"Do you know him?"

"No."

I sneak a look over her shoulder into the dark house. Is this really it? I can make out the edges of a chair and a lamp.

I don't think she appreciates me peering into her house because she takes a step back and puts her hand on the door, making a move to close it.

"Do you know Catherine Reid?" I ask.

"No."

"I'm sorry. I'm just— I'm looking for my father."

"Gallardo?"

"Yes. Do you know him?"

The woman shakes her head. "Amelia Varón," she says, pointing to her chest. "Gallardo no."

I nod.

She tightens her lips and continues pushing the door, the metal hinges squeaking until it shuts.

I'm a levelheaded person. I think things through. I rarely let my emotions get the better of me. I try to keep it all inside. I knew, of course, that there was a very good chance my father wouldn't be there. I wasn't operating under the assumption that finding him could be so easy. But even so, I am unprepared for the sensation, as I climb back into the taxi, that my chest is slowly caving in, that I've been punched square between the breastbones and everything underneath is giving way.

The driver starts off. I can't even pay attention at first to where he's going. Then, vaguely, I assume he's taking me back to the hotel. I don't want to go there yet, though. I don't want to lie in my room by myself with all of that air and space around me and think about what just happened. I ask him to take me downtown instead.

"The hotel is downtown," he says.

"No. Somewhere else, please. Anywhere where I can just walk around is fine."

"You want to go to Avenida Central?"

"What is it?"

"Lots of stores."

"Sure."

He drops me at the mouth of a brick-paved street with stores along both sides, their entire fronts wide open. The street is swarming with a healthy mix of tourists and native Panamanians, many of whom are simply sitting on ledges drinking soda out of bottles or playing dominoes on card tables under the shade of a tree or hanging out in the shop fronts, chatting with the employees. It's the closest thing I have seen to a gathering place here.

All afternoon I walk up and down the street in air so humid it makes my hair frizzy, ducking into shops every now and again to catch a burst of frigid air-conditioning. There are jewelry stores and electronics stores and shoe stores and fabric stores, all overflowing with things for sale, all promising a bargain. In a store that sells Panamanian souvenirs—tiny animals carved out of soap, clay ashtrays with pre-Columbian designs painted in the bottoms, postcards, Panama hats, wood boxes with inlaid Panamanian flags, posters—I buy a wide-brimmed straw hat and four postcards: one of the canal, one of a toucan, one of the Iglesia del Carmen, and one of Panamá La Vieja. I wander into a bookstore that, at first glance, appears to sell books by only three authors: Isabel Allende, Gabriel García Márquez, and Paulo Coelho. Besides a dictionary, those are the only books—stacks and stacks of them—on the table at the front. Toward the back, though, there's some translated fiction, some coffee-table books about Panama, some slim volumes of poetry. It feels more like a newsstand than a bookstore, but I like being there. It's quiet, bathed in the sort of muffled hush that all places having to do with books seem to possess. I graze my fingertips over the spines of the books for a while before I walk out again. When I get hungry, I stop in a busy restaurant and at the recommendation of the waiter order a soup called *sancocho.* It comes with a mound of white rice and boiled *ñame,* which is a stringy vegetable that tastes like something between a potato and cauliflower. The soup is fifty cents per bowl. I order three before I pay. And the whole time while I eat, watching the people on the street and listening to the people in the restaurant, I try to ignore that sinking feeling in my chest, the disappointment that my first best lead didn't work out, and the panic of not knowing where to go next.

A few days before I left for this trip, my mother and I went to a bookstore. I was looking for a Panama guidebook, and she just wanted to get out of the house. She had been saying for months that she didn't like driving anymore. When she had to go to the grocery store, or to SuperCuts for a trim, she took the bus. Otherwise, she usually waited for me to come home from school to take her out. Occasionally, when she was feeling particularly restless, she let George Grabowski take her out. He called her at least once a week to invite her for coffee or for a walk around the Garden Center at Kmart or to a local theater production he had tickets for. She always called me afterward, complaining that George was a bore or that he was too religious or that he had forgotten his wallet again, leaving her to pay for the coffee, which was always—*always*—the most expensive coffee she had ever consumed in her life.

That day at the bookstore, my mother wanted to browse the cookbooks. She asked me for a pen and paper to copy down any recipes she found that sounded good, so that she wouldn't actually have to buy the book, and after I gave them to her, she clomped off in her snow boots.

I headed toward the travel section to buy a Panama guidebook. There were three on the shelf, and I chose the one with a cover photograph of thatch-roofed huts on stilts over the water, a line of them receding into the horizon. As I looked at it in my hands, my stomach tightened. I remember thinking that it was like looking at a piece of myself laid bare. There was something painful about it, the way it was so unfamiliar to me.

I paid for the book, and went to find my mother, who was sitting on a bench in front of a tall window. She was hunched over a thin spiral-bound book on her lap, clacking the end of my pen absently between her teeth—*rack-a-tak-a-tak*—her hat and gloves and coat still on, her untied scarf draped around the back of her neck. She had her legs crossed, one foot swinging in the air.

"What are you doing over here?" I asked. "I thought you were looking at the cookbooks."

She looked up, surprised. "You're done already?"

I held up my plastic bag and swung it lightly. "All done."

"There was nothing good in the cookbooks," she said. "It's all that thirty-minute crap. Listen, sit down here for a second. I need to ask you something."

I sat and waited. I could feel the cold air pressing through the pane of glass at my back.

"Do you know 'Isle of exile'? It's four letters."

The book on her lap was a crossword puzzle book. In the past few months, she had grown obsessed with crossword puzzles. She did at least one, sometimes more, every day. She thought they were good for her, for keeping her mind limber, as she said.

"'Isle of exile'? Maybe Elba."

"Elbow?"

"Elba."

"I don't think that fits with twenty-three across. Unless I have that wrong. Damn it."

"Mom, did you buy that book?"

"Do you know 'Susan of *L.A. Law*'?"

"*L.A. Law* like the television show? No idea."

"You never know the ones about TV."

"That's because I don't really watch TV."

She scribbled a word quickly into a series of boxes. "Tango," she muttered. "I should have gotten that one earlier."

"Did you already buy it?"

"What about 'Last letter in Leeds'? I thought it was *s*, but apparently the answer is three letters long. Then I thought maybe it was E-S-S, but that's stupid, right? You can't spell letters. Letters are what you use to spell other things."

"You can spell letters. One of the final five words in the 1998 National Spelling Bee was the spelling for *h*. A-I-T-C-H."

My mother stared at me in disbelief.

I laughed. "What?"

"How do you know things like that?"

"Come on," I said, trying to get her attention back on the puzzle. "Maybe it's 'zed.'"

"Excuse me?"

"That's how they say the letter *z* in England, where Leeds is. Leeds, England."

My mother shook her head—"Complicated," she said—but she wrote it in. "And no, I didn't buy it yet, but I'm planning on buying it. Don't worry."

"I'm not worried."

"The hell you aren't."

She knew, even though I had never said so out loud, that for the past few months I had been worrying as if it were my full-time job and someone were paying me a multimillion-dollar salary to do it well. At least, that's what it felt like. I worried whether she was getting enough to eat, whether she was getting enough sleep, whether it was good-quality sleep. I worried whether she would pay the bills on time and whether she would write the checks for the right amount, whether she locked all the doors before she went to bed, whether she turned off the oven when she was finished using it, whether she would trip on something on her way to the bathroom in the middle of the night, whether every next time I talked to her she would sound worse than the last.

I got her up, and we waited in a short checkout line while my mother clutched the crossword puzzle book to her chest.

"So what did you buy?" she asked, signaling toward my bag.

"A book."

"What book?"

"Just a book."

"Why don't you want to tell me?"

Behind us, an older man with a beard and ice-blue eyes coughed and looked to the side, but I could tell he was listening to us.

"Maybe it's a gift for you," I said.

"Why would you get a gift for me? Christmas is over."

I shook my head. "You're right. I can't think of a single other reason why I would get you a gift."

"Well, that was mean."

"I was being sarcastic! Come on, don't worry about it." I crumpled the top of the bag—it made an awful crinkling sound—and gripped it in my fist.

A minute later we were at the counter to pay. My mother slapped down her book and started unzipping her purse for her wallet. I watched as the cashier flipped through the book's pages—a routine inspection—and stopped at the puzzle my mother had half filled. I swallowed. The cashier—she was young, maybe in high school—slid the open book to the lip of the counter. Her fingernails were short and bitten.

"Did you know this one's damaged?" she asked.

Still dealing with her purse, my mother said, without looking up, "It's not damaged. I did that."

"You wrote in it?"

She cocked her head at the cashier. "I did. But now I'm buying it."

"I don't think it works like that. I think you're supposed to buy it first."

My mother said nothing.

"Seriously. Because what if you had decided not to buy it?"

"Well, then you would have a book with one half-filled puzzle in it on your shelf."

The cashier narrowed her eyes.

"We were always planning on buying it," I said.

The bearded man behind us craned his neck to see what the commotion was about. I turned my body to block his view.

"I think I should call a manager," the girl said, and took a step back, casting her eyes down the long galley behind the counter.

"You're not going to let me buy it?" my mother said. "I

thought that's what you wanted. And now here I am, ready to do just that." She pinched her lips and stared squint-eyed and unblinking at the girl.

I bit the inside of my lip and waited to see how things would play out. Finally, the cashier sighed and rang us up, although she didn't say another word to us for the remainder of the transaction.

Sure, it was a bit ridiculous, but this was my mother: audacious and gruff and stubborn as steel, doing what was needed to get by in life and dispensing with anything she deemed frivolous. But she was capricious, too, so it was never patently obvious what qualified as necessity and what qualified as frivolity. She was not what anyone would describe as a warm person. She was not only short with cashiers, but with telemarketers, hovering salespeople, bad drivers, and slow pedestrians. Basically, anyone who got in her way. Over the years she had worked as a delivery driver for a pizza restaurant (until she could find something better), a waitress at The Cheesecake Factory (a second job for a brief stint), a receptionist for the Economics Department at Northwestern, a receptionist at a dental practice, and most recently a receptionist at a small law firm in Wilmette. She almost never made more money than she spent. She'd paid rent on the same house for almost two decades. She had $1,236.51 in the bank. She'd once said that if she could have done anything with her life, she would have been an actress. But as she saw it, she couldn't do anything with her life but muddle through it, one day after another, attaching the end of one to the start of the next so that the chain kept extending, until from a distance it was one seamless and winding line that looked like a life. My mother had brown eyes with flecks of gold in them and fine brown hair that she tried her best to plump up with a hair dryer every morning. She wore tastefully brown-hued makeup, except for a phase in the early nineties when she experimented with amethyst. She had freckles that marched across her slender shoulders and over the bridge of her nose. She talked in her sleep. She sang in the shower. She watched public television and prime-time game shows. She liked dressing up and didn't understand the philosophy behind dressing as though you didn't care to impress, dressing with nonchalance—in other words, my philosophy. But she didn't let that inclination interfere with the fact that she was extremely budget-conscious. She trolled for overlooked gems at consignment stores, and once a year she flipped through the whisper-thin pages of the giant JCPenney catalogue for something to splurge on. She cooked meals for us at home, convinced that, as a mother, cooking was one of the obligatory tasks within her purview. Seldom did it seem as though she enjoyed it. She relied on frozen waffles and casseroles and BLTs, which were her favorite. She was stern with rules and discipline. She didn't believe in treating children like children, so she always spoke to me like an adult. She expected me to entertain myself. She had her soft moments, those times when she was tender and bruised—they're inescapable in this life—but mostly she was a plank of wood, braced and erect, weathering anything and everything.

She puffed her chest out to the world and walked through it without taking a breath.

I ride a bus back to the hotel.

As soon as I step off, Hernán advances toward me, waving his arms. "What happened to the taxi?" He looks concerned.

"The bus was fine," I say. Danilo had made taking the bus sound like a challenge, and I thought that if I could do it, I would have accomplished at least something today. I really needed to feel like I accomplished something.

Danilo's painter's bucket is on the sidewalk by the wall.

When Hernán sees me looking at it, he says, "I don't know where he is. I didn't even see him until this afternoon. He was probably sleeping until then. He is not so good with responsibility." He eyes me pointedly.

"It's okay," I say.

"I cannot believe you took the bus!" Hernán tuts. "You aren't worried about getting lost?"

I'm wearing my new straw hat. The brim ripples gently in the breeze. In my life, I tend to worry a lot about getting lost. I like maps because they make it seem possible for every pathway to be laid out, every direction to be marked. But as I stand on a street in the middle of a place I don't know, it occurs to me that this whole trip was about wanting to get lost, about wanting to lose myself.

Loose pouches hang under Hernán's eyes, and sweat glistens where his hat meets his forehead, as he stares at me, waiting for an answer.

"No," I say. "I'm not worried."

I can't sleep that night. Shortly after midnight, I prop up the spongy hotel pillow and crawl to the foot of the bed, leaning out across the chasm between it and the dresser to turn on the television. The only thing on any channel is what appears to be a Panamanian version of *America's Funniest Home Videos.* A woman trips and falls facefirst into her wedding cake. A parakeet plucks the toupee off a man's head. A toddler buries his face in half a coconut, then stumbles around with it suctioned to him before he runs into a wall.

I grab my phone. When Beth answers, she's shouting. "Hello? Who is this?"

"It's Mira. Where are you?"

"Mira! Hi! It's Beth."

"I know. *I* called *you.*"

"We're at Jimmy's." Jimmy's Woodlawn Tap is a local Hyde Park dive, filled with smoke and beer advertisements on the wall and a live jazz band on Sunday nights. It's depressing to think of her there without me. "How are you?"

"I'm okay. Actually, I'm having kind of a crappy day."

"What's that?" she yells.

"Can you hear me?"

"Is the connection bad again?"

"I don't know. You're shouting and I can hear the music in the background. Do you want to just call me later?"

"What? Hold on." Outside my window, the sky is a deep plum color. "Are you still there? I want to talk to you but I can't hear anything. Actually, do you want me to go outside?"

"It's okay. Just call me later."

As soon as I fold the phone and put it on the nightstand, the room feels quieter than before I called her. I wait for it to pass, for the air to recalibrate, but the silence only deepens until I feel as if I'm drowning in it.

I see Danilo right away, in one corner of the hotel bar. Two wiry men sit in the opposite corner smoking cigars and laughing, the air around them a fog. Danilo is playing cards with someone.

"Hey," I say, walking toward him with all the nerve I can muster.

He smiles and scoots back one of the empty chairs at the table with his foot.

"Have a seat," he says. "This is Nardo."

Nardo, wearing a crisp blue button-down shirt with the sleeves rolled to his elbows, doesn't take his eyes off his cards, which he guards in a tight fan held close to his face, the tops of them nearly brushing his nose.

Danilo kicks him under the table. "*Oye,* be polite, man. You could look at the girl at least."

Nardo casts his eyes sidelong, stealing one quick look at me, before focusing again on his cards.

"It's late. What are you doing down here?" Danilo asks. There's a glint in his eyes, as if he wants me to admit that I came down to find him.

"I just wanted to get out of my room. I couldn't sleep."

"You want a drink?"

"Sure."

"What do you want?"

"What are you drinking?"

In front of him is some sort of mixed drink, the glass nearly full, the ice melted into thin wafers that float on the surface like lily pads.

"*Seco* and Fresca."

"What's *seco*?"

"What's *seco*? Nardo! Did you hear that? What's *seco*?" Nardo huffs, but keeps his eyes on his cards. "It's authentic Panamanian shit, Miraflores," Danilo goes on. "Best liquor available anywhere on earth. For sure better than anything you can get in your country."

"But what is it?"

"Sugarcane alcohol." He raises the drink to his mouth and takes a sip, the lily pads swarming in toward his lips as he tilts the glass. When he puts it down, he has a goofy look on his face like he's a little drunk. He yells across the room to the bartender. "Give me two more of these!" Then he picks up his cards, sliding them into view one by one with his thumb. "Nardo, are you going to put something down or what?"

Nardo squints at his cards and after several seconds lays one on the table, letting it snap past his fingertips.

Danilo cackles. "That's the best you can do? Jesus Christ. I don't know why I keep playing with you. I need someone who's a real challenge, you know." He shakes his head and lays down two cards. "Sorry, my man."

Nardo throws his hand down in disgust, the slick cards sliding on the tabletop like brittle leaves skating across a plate of ice. "Fuck." He stands, knocking over his chair as he does, and walks to the bar without bothering to right it. Danilo collects the cards with a smug expression on his face.

"What were you playing?" I ask.

"Rummy. You know how to play it?"

"I know pinochle. And Go Fish. And War."

"Someday I'll teach you this."

The bartender delivers my drink and I sip it, feeling the cool liquid run and burn down my throat.

"You like it?" Danilo asks, shuffling the cards.

If I drink at home, it's usually something more like a hard lemonade, even though Juliette always makes fun of me for drinking something so wimpy. "It's good," I say.

He nods, and for a second it seems we've run out of things to talk about. I take some more sips in silence and then, sensing that it might be best to retreat to my room, ask him how much I owe for the drink.

"Don't worry about it."

"Why? You're buying?"

"One time only. Enjoy it while you can."

"Thanks." I scratch my neck and scoot back from the table.

"Where are you going?"

"To my room."

"Where you don't want to be anymore?"

"I just needed a break from it for a few minutes."

"You missed a nice day today. I mean the weather. If you had gone out, you might have thought it was too hot, but for me, it was very nice. The kind of weather that makes people want to buy flowers. Don't ask me why. I have no idea why."

"What makes you think I didn't go out today?"

"Did you?" He smiles teasingly.

"Yes." I drag the chair and myself back up to the table. Nardo is smoking a cigarette and drinking a beer at the bar. He's standing sideways against it, his elbow on the counter, two fingers circling the neck of the beer bottle. I can smell the smoke mingling with the scent of cigars from the men in the corner.

"And where did you go?"

"I went to Avenida Central and to the address I had."

"The address?" Danilo lets his head go wobbly for a moment, as if it's too heavy for his neck, before regaining his composure. "Your father's house?"

"Yes."

"No!"

"Yes!"

"And?"

"It isn't his house. There was only an old woman who didn't know him."

"He doesn't live there anymore?"

"I don't think so."

"But you went there?"

"I did."

"To Santa Ana?"

"Yep."

"I hope you didn't wander into Chorrillo, though."

"I don't think I did."

"You would know."

He looks impressed. There's a strange satisfaction in knowing that I've surprised him just now and, even more, that I have the ability to.

"So why are you here so late?" I ask.

"Nardo, come on," Danilo yells toward the bar. "Another game. I didn't mean it, man. I love beating your ass."

Nardo holds his hand over his shoulder and gives Danilo the finger.

"What did you say?" Danilo asks, turning back to me before shuffling the deck, the cards spraying like a fountain.

"Why are you here so late?"

"Eh, waiting for Hernán to get off his shift. He doesn't like to walk home alone, so I usually wait for him even on his late nights. He thinks someone is going to rob him. For what, I don't know. He doesn't have anything worth taking. But that's what he thinks. What time is it, anyway?"

I check my watch. "Almost one."

Danilo takes a gulp of his drink before pushing it to the center of the table. He shoves the deck of cards into his back pants pocket. "Old man should be done by now," he says, standing. Then he extends his hand. "I'm glad you went out today," he says. "You can't be scared of your own life, you know. That might be the worst thing."

When I grasp his hand, it's damp from being cupped around the perspiring glass, but it's also smooth and cool against my palm.

"I know," I say. "I'm not." I feel a little indignant at the suggestion.

Our hands are still locked when he says, "So what are you doing tomorrow?"

"I'm not sure yet."

"I could still help you, you know."

"Tomorrow's Wednesday. Do you have time?"

He smiles as he blinks drowsily and says, "Meet me here tomorrow morning," then lets go of my hand.

Five

Infiltration

If anyone had asked me what my father looked like, I would have described a man with thinning silver hair and a blunt silver mustache. I would have said that his skin was smooth and dark, that his eyes were piercing. I would have said that his build was diminutive—neither a wall of corded muscles nor a tower of flesh and blood—and that he walked confidently, with a certain swagger, in tasseled leather loafers. I would have said that he wore a watch on his left wrist and that he had always seemed to me the sort of man who wore a ring, maybe gold and onyx, on his right ring finger.

If anyone had asked me about his habits, I would have said that he had been smoking cigarettes for decades and that he carried a black plastic barber's comb in his back pocket, smoothing it over his silver hair whenever he hoped to light a woman's heart on fire. I would have said that he pulled the skin off fried chicken before he ate it and that he licked his fingers when he was finished. I would have said that he sat alone on the side of his bed every evening and polished his leather shoes to a dull shine using a kit that he kept in a cardboard box on the floor—polish, cotton briefs as rags, a buffing brush, and a nailbrush for the cracks in the soles—rubbing in small circles, his hand like a makeshift foot in the shoe, holding it at arm's length every so often to examine his work. I would have said that he washed his face with soap and scraped the dirt from the undersides of his nails with a small Swiss Army knife that he kept behind the faucet; that he drank water without ice but with a squeeze of lime; that he flashed a brilliant smile at nearly everyone who passed him in a day; that he hummed in the shower; that he snored faintly in his sleep.

Because even though for twenty years I have been mostly okay about not knowing my father, even though for so long I have assumed that he's the sort of person I would be better off without, I would be lying if I didn't admit that I have real and sudden moments of wanting to meet him, little seizures of the heart.

Besides the few other details I gathered from my mother, this is the basic portrait I invented over the years. If anyone asked, that's everything I might say. Or else I would say that I don't know, because, of course, I don't. I can only guess.

The next morning, Danilo is waiting for me. He's drinking a cup of coffee and eating scrambled eggs.

"You want coffee?" he asks when he sees me.

"Please." I sit across from him at the table, as we were last night. It feels strange to see him in the daylight again, as if having seen him last night, in dimmer light, I learned something secret about him that makes him look different—and makes me feel more connected to him—now.

He points to the urn that again has been assembled on the bar top.

"Oh, I thought you were offering to get me a cup," I joke.

"No, but you can get me a refill while you're up," he says.

I don't know the word for "refill" in Spanish, but I gauge his meaning when he holds out his empty mug.

When I return to the table with two cups of coffee, the steam swirling off the tops, Danilo slides a tin can toward me. It's wrapped in a paper label that says "Nestlé Ideal." I pour some of it—a viscous, yellowy milk—onto my fingertip to taste it.

"What do you usually use?" Danilo asks.

"In my coffee?"

"Yes, in your coffee. Of course, in your coffee." Playfully, he rolls his eyes.

"I usually use milk."

"Cow's milk?"

"Yes, cow's milk, Danilo. Of course, cow's milk."

He grins. "This is better," he says, pointing to the can. "It's richer. A better flavor."

"Everything here is better, according to you."

"Of course. This is my country. If I were visiting you in your country, I would expect you to tell me that everything there is better. You have to be like that. You have to be proud, you know?"

I wipe my finger on a napkin before pouring the milk into my coffee.

"So what are we doing today?" Danilo asks. He's wearing what I've determined by now is his unofficial uniform: an old T-shirt, baggy cargo pants, and a pair of Adidas shell-toes, the tongues lapping over the hem of his pants. Today's T-shirt is white with a faded and cracked Esso gas decal on the front, the cotton on the shoulders so threadbare that the shade of his skin bleeds through.

"Where are your flowers?" I ask.

"Eh, I'm off duty today."

"Why?"

"Because we have things to do, no? *Oye,* did you already try the library?"

I don't want to admit that I haven't. I did think about it at some point, but I got distracted by the failure of yesterday.

"Hey, did you hear me?"

"No. I haven't tried the library."

"Wow. You're not exactly a natural-born detective, are you?" He shovels some of the eggs into his mouth. "You want to eat something before we go?"

"We're going right now?"

"Of course right now. If you really want to find your father, then let's find him. There isn't time for waiting around, you know. He's not going to just walk into this hotel and introduce himself. You have to look for him."

"I know."

"Yesterday was one thing, but now we have to keep the momentum going."

"The what?"

"Momentum," he says again, and though I still don't know the word, I figure out the general idea when he rolls his hands one over the other. "You know, I don't believe that you have any Panamanian blood in your veins. Where's your fire, Miraflores? Panamanians have fire. I mean, how sure are you that this man is really your father? I'm not convinced." He's teasing now, although the intimation that perhaps I don't act as a Panamanian would ignites a certain, grazing pain. I wanted to believe that I was doing a good job of fitting in here.

"He's my father," I assure him.

"Okay, then. I'll say it again, if you really want to find him, you have to look for him."

"How far is the library?"

Danilo lights up. "That's what I'm talking about!" He grabs my coffee and gulps down what's left. "Too hot." He grimaces.

I laugh at him, but he ignores me.

"Come on," he says, standing. "We're going to the library." Then he shakes his head. "It's crazy that I'm actually excited about that."

The library takes up the second floor of a concrete office building with tinted floor-to-ceiling windows spaced as evenly as a checkerboard around the outside. It's unassuming, with a narrow strip of parking along the front and palm trees brushing the front wall.

"What's on the first floor?" I ask Danilo as we make our way to the stairwell, my orange bag knocking against my hip.

"A call center. I used to work there."

"Really? Do you know English?"

"It was a Spanish call center. For Latin America. Not everything in the world is about people serving your country, you know." He pushes open the stairwell door and starts up the steps.

"Oh, I know." I'm chagrined that I was so presumptuous. "Our stupid president thinks it is, but most Americans know better."

Danilo swings his head around and screws up his face. "But you elected him, no?"

"Not *me.* But yeah."

"I don't understand that. How can all the people think one thing and the president can go do something else? It's a democracy. That's what you have, right? Why doesn't everyone protest to get rid of him, if they don't agree with him? Here, if people don't like something, they're out on the streets about it. I swear SUNTRACS is out there like every other day." He pauses on the landing, gesturing. "And I'm saying, you know, people are out on the streets here even though there's a history of it being dangerous to do that shit. Like, the government used to have hit men to come and take you out if you were in their way. It's worse in other countries, but

Panamá has it going on, too, you know. The whole system here is so crooked. All of our politicians are corrupt. But even with all that, people were like, 'Fuck it, I'm going to take a stand for what I believe in. I'm going to tell these motherfuckers what's what.' You know? It's not even a risk for you to speak up in your country! Nothing's going to happen to you, right? I mean, not really. But you guys still don't do it." His voice, when he finishes, echoes into the stairwell like the last inch of a bow being pulled across a violin string. He runs a hand over his hair and sighs, then turns to mount the rest of the steps.

"And does it work?" I ask to his back. "When people here protest?"

"Sometimes yes. Sometimes no. But it's the only way."

"The only way what?"

"The only way to live."

When we step inside the library, a woman sitting at a school desk takes my passport and Danilo's *cédula.* She makes photocopies of each before handing us purple stickers that say "*Visitante.*" I stick mine on my shirt. Danilo slaps his onto his thigh. There's a small reading area, magazines with plastic binder covers scattered on a table, and two discrete sections of steel gray bookshelves. Except for the woman at the desk and us, there's no one else in sight.

"We need a phone book," Danilo says.

"I already tried that."

"You have his phone number and you didn't tell me? That would have made things a lot easier, you know."

"I don't have his phone number."

"But you looked in the phone book?"

"Of course. I looked in the one at the hotel."

"Which hotel? Hotel Centro?"

"What other hotel would I be talking about?"

"Those phone books are old as shit. I don't think they've put new ones in the rooms for, like, ten years."

A flush rises in my cheeks.

"Okay, come on," Danilo says. We locate the reference materials, and he pulls the most recent phone book from the shelf. "What's his name?"

"Gatún Gallardo."

"You're joking, right?"

My stomach flutters. "Why? Do you know him?"

"Gatún, like the locks? And your name is Miraflores, also like the locks? Or are you just making a joke?"

"No, that's his name."

"So you two were both named after the canal. That's funny."

I feel a little light-headed at the revelation, as if someone built an instantaneous bridge between my father and me and I can see him clearly on the opposite side from where I stand, gazing back at me. My mother must have done it on purpose. She must have wanted that bridge to exist. I knew about my name, of course. But how was it possible that I had gone my whole life without knowing that Gatún was the name of one of the locks? I wonder whether my mother assumed I knew.

Danilo turns to the G's. I stand shoulder to shoulder with him, staring down at the listings. He's holding the book open with the spine in his palms, the edges drooping like wilted leaves. I scan the names. Just as before, none is Gatún Gallardo, or even G. Gallardo. This time there are two, though, that say just Gallardo, without any first name or initial.

"Those two." I point. "I want to write those down."

I start digging through my bag for a pen and my memo pad. Danilo tears the page out of the book. He flips the rest of it closed with a twist of his wrist and a thud, and hands me the page.

"Here," he says. "Do you have a phone? Mine's dead."

I take the phone book page from him and stare at it, my heart punching insistently at the inside of my chest.

"So?" he prods.

"I have a phone."

"And?"

"I think I want to do this part by myself."

In a corner of the library, I find a cluster of school desks and settle myself into one. It's a challenge to keep my hand from shaking as I spread the torn page on the desktop. Even though the windows are heavily tinted, the sun outside trumpets through. I flip open my phone and dial the first Gallardo. After several rings, a man says, *"Aló."*

My heart is somewhere in the base of my throat, cutting off air. "Hello," I peep, in Spanish. "Gatún Gallardo, please."

"Who?"

"Gatún Gallardo."

"There is no Gatún here. Gallardo yes, but no Gatún. Sorry." He hangs up.

In a daze, I sit with my phone in my hand until the screen flashes off. I take several measured breaths—in, in, out, in, in, out, like I learned ages ago during swimming lessons at the Y—before trying the second number.

The sound of the rings is a solid tone, like a floating period. I squeeze the phone to my ear, mechanically counting them in my head. At twenty-five, just as I'm about to pull the phone away from my ear, I hear a woman's voice.

"Hello? I'm trying to reach Gatún Gallardo," I say. My hand is sweating. I am equal parts hope and hopelessness.

The woman is silent.

"Hello?" I say.

"Yes, who?"

"Gatún Gallardo."

Still she says nothing.

"Is he there?"

"No."

Something about the way she says it makes me ask, "Do you know where he is?"

"Who is this?" The woman's voice is ripe and gravelly, though not unkind.

"I'm sorry to bother you," I say.

"Well."

"He's not there? Gatún Gallardo?"

"No," she says again, and this time her tone is definitive. He isn't there. She doesn't know where he is. She doesn't know him.

"Sorry," I say again before hanging up.

I slide my phone into my bag and stare out the windows. People on the street below are loitering on the corners. Old men sit on benches. Kids zigzag around cars stopped at red lights. Women stroll by themselves, shielded by umbrellas. My father could be anywhere. I could be looking at him that very second and not know it. He could be the man across the street buying a newspaper. He could be the man selling the newspapers. He could be the man sliding neon-colored flyers under the windshield wipers of parked cars. He could be the man driving the Toyota Tercel, his elbow on the open window frame, glowing bronze in the sun. What made me think that I could come here, to a country I knew almost nothing about, and find one person among millions? I wasn't prepared enough. There must have been more I could have done. I never had any sort of real plan. I was an idiot.

"So?" Danilo asks, when I find him. He's in the exact same place, lingering between the stacks.

I shake my head.

Danilo shakes his head back at me. "What does that mean?"

"They weren't him."

"You called both?"

"Yes."

"You talked to people?"

"Yes."

"What did you say?"

"I asked for Gatún Gallardo."

"What did they say?"

"They said there was no one named Gatún Gallardo there."

I'm annoyed suddenly that he's quizzing me as if he doesn't trust that I went through with it or that I asked the right things. "Whatever," I say. "It just didn't work out." I pull my hair off my neck into a ponytail. "Where's the phone book?"

"I put it back."

I sidestep him to find it and pull it from the shelf. Danilo watches me, puzzled, as I thumb to the G's.

"What are you doing?" he asks.

I insert the loose page back where it belongs and shut the book.

"Huh," Danilo says. "So you're like that."

"Like what?"

"Nothing. Listen, I was thinking while you were gone, and I know you're not going to like this idea, but maybe we should try the obituaries."

"Excuse me?"

"You don't know the word?"

"No, I know the word. But are you serious? I don't want—"

"I knew you wouldn't like the idea."

"Of course I wouldn't." Several times over the years I've considered the possibility that my father was no longer alive. Thinking it made an existence without him easier. If there's no chance of something, then it extinguishes the flicker of hope. Thinking of him already gone simply closed a door to a path that was too painful to consider treading down sometimes. I never imagined the particulars, just that he might have passed on at some point, no longer a part of this world. But now, now that I was already on the path, I didn't want to believe that that's what awaited me at the end of it. It's unnerving to hear Danilo suggest it, out loud and so casually.

"But you're not sure, are you, that he's still alive? I mean, I think we need to find out," he presses.

"I know."

When we ask the woman who checked us in at the front desk where to find the obituaries, she disappears into a closed office for a moment before marching out with a librarian whose green eye shadow shimmers teal against her dark skin.

The librarian leads us to two desks in a clearing among the stacks, each equipped with a screen and a drape of black cloth for privacy. Leaning over, she turns a knob, and a roll of sepia images flies by. When she lets go of the knob, it stops. "That's if you want to go fast," she says. Then she presses a small white button and the images move more slowly, like a conveyer belt. She points to a magnifying glass on the desktop. "If you need to look closer," she says. "Wait a minute, please." When she leaves, Danilo takes her seat and taps the screen. "I thought we were going to have to look through a bunch of newspapers," he says.

"You've never used microfilm?"

"I'm not as smart as you," he says.

I presume what he means is that he's not as educated. There's no question that he's smart, and there's no question that he knows he is.

The librarian returns carrying a roll of film, which she loads in the back of the machine. "This is the obituaries," she says. "You can start with that. If you find him, then you know you won't have to keep looking." She smiles as though this is a good thing. "I also brought you the lottery winners for the past ten years. Maybe if the person you're looking for won the lottery, you can find out more about him." She looks at me. "The lottery winners are instant celebrities here."

Danilo says, "No shit?" in a sweetly mock-naïve tone.

"Thank you," I say.

After she leaves, I ask, "So are you going to look for me, or are you going to let me look?"

Danilo is still sitting at the desk. "We can look together, can't we?" He drags over the chair from the adjoining carrel. "Have a seat."

With the black fabric hood over both of us, we peer at the screen together, me operating the controls. I have my orange bag on my lap. Our eyes skim the boldface words for my father's name as the images slide through like credits rolling up a screen at the end of a movie. Twice we stop because one of us thinks we glimpse him. The first time is for Gatún Velásquez, who was eighty-six at the time of his death from illness. That's all it says—illness. My father couldn't have been that old. The second time is for S. Gatún Tiburón, age twenty-two, who died during a deep-sea dive when he ran out of oxygen. We keep going. Scanning, scanning, hoping not to find any Gatún Gallardo.

Three hours later, we've made it through five years and there's no trace of him. Danilo hasn't once asked for the time or complained that the whole endeavor is taking too long. Later he even volunteers to get up to ask the librarian to load the lottery film, but there's no record of my father there, either.

You never know where you might find something. The history of the world is buried in the layers of the earth. My mother has been excavating magazines from the basement, pulling faded back issues out of forgotten nooks and crannies, like tissues from a box, stacking and arranging them all just so and still she complains that there isn't enough order in her life. She complains that she can't find things, that disorganization is tripping her up, that just at the moment she needs something it seems to vanish. "The frustrating thing," she told me once, when she was looking for a spatula, "is that I know it hasn't vanished. I know it's here somewhere. It has to be. I feel like God is looking down on me at this moment and he has X-ray vision and he can see the spatula in a drawer or under a pile of clothes and he can see me spinning around like a moron looking for it and missing it. I almost wouldn't care if I knew it was gone. I mean, if I knew I had thrown it out by accident and there was no way to get it back now. But it's so goddamn frustrating to know that it's here, somewhere, and I just can't find it!" She opened a drawer and slammed it shut. She was so agitated that we searched all afternoon for a spatula we never found. She may have inadvertently thrown it out. It might have been in the attic or buried in the yard. Who knew? In the end, I went to the grocery store and bought her a new one.

The key to finding lost things, though, is knowing where to look. And when you don't know that, sometimes you just have to hope that something will break wide open.

The seam where separate tectonic plates meet, where they kiss beneath the ground, is a fault line. Surrounding every fault line is a mass of country rock that soaks up energy over hundreds of years. It stores as much energy as it can handle, and usually it can handle a lot. But when the supply of energy exceeds a certain threshold, the rock begins to quiver. The fault line slips. It releases all that pent-up energy at once. An earthquake occurs. In an instant, the surface of the earth is remapped. In an instant, everything can change.

Danilo persuades me to go to the canal.

"You said your father worked there, right?"

"He did once."

"Then you know where we're going."

What I know about the Panama Canal is what I learned in school. I had flipped ahead in my world civics textbook and read all about it long before the teacher got to it in her lesson plan—every year I checked the glossary as soon as I got my books to see if there was anything about Panama—but it was still thrilling when she lectured about it in class.

The French were the first to attempt to construct it. A man named Ferdinand de Lesseps, who had been in charge of building the Suez Canal more than a decade earlier, directed their attempt. The French failed miserably. Their equipment was old. They were crippled by disease. When they ran out of money, they sold the project to the Americans. The Americans, thinking maybe geography had been the problem, toyed with the idea of situating the canal in Nicaragua instead. Finally, they were convinced to forge ahead in Panama. But then there was another problem. Panama at the time was still part of Colombia, and Colombia didn't want to let the United States build a canal on its land. So Theodore Roosevelt came up with a solution to that minor inconvenience. If Panama was no longer part of Colombia, Colombia would no longer have a say in the matter, and the United States could build their canal. The Americans encouraged the Panamanians to rise up, stage a rebellion, and demand their independence from Colombia. They sent military support. They fought on behalf of the Panamanians—but really for themselves—for a grand total of three days before Colombia let Panama go to become a sovereign country. The Americans promptly started digging their big ditch. They devised a lock system, which turned out to be a better plan than the French ever had. They discovered ways to deal with diseases like malaria and yellow fever that had killed off the French in droves. And in 1914, after ten years of toil and sweat and innovation and fighting, they unveiled the Panama Canal to the world. There was supposed to be an immense celebration to commemorate the occasion. But the unveiling occurred without much fanfare, since, by then, World War I had started, and the collective attention of almost everyone on the globe had shifted to a very different part of the world.

Maybe it's more than the average person knows. It's just that anytime Panama came up in any context of my life, I paid attention more than the average person.

The bus deposits us in a vast parking lot at the base of a hill. The air is thick and steamy when we step off, and the heat from the sun drips down.

"It's your building," Danilo jokes, pointing.

At the top of the hill is the visitors' center, a modernist concrete building with the word "Miraflores" on the front. For a girl who was never able to find a key chain with her name on it, or a personalized pencil, or a hat with her name stitched in above the bill, it's a shock. But a welcome shock. My name is familiar here. If it belongs here, maybe I could, too.

We start up the long path of steps that leads from the parking lot to the building, my legs burning by the time we reach the top. Inside, the lobby sparkles and gleams with newness. There's a gift shop in the back corner and, to the left of the front doors, signs on placards advertising, in Spanish and in English, a film about the construction of the canal that runs every twenty minutes in the auditorium.

I'm standing in the middle of it all, clutching my bag.

"This isn't it," Danilo says. He pulls me through a wide door straight ahead of us, out into the open air, and leads me to the railing at the front of a broad concrete deck.

"This," he says, "is it."

Two long horizontal waterways stretch lengthwise before us. Across the lanes is a small building, squat and rectangular, with a series of arched doorways and a red-clay roof, and the words "Miraflores Locks" in spaced letters across the front.

"Is that the control tower?" I ask, pointing.

"Don't point," Danilo says. "You look like a tourist."

"I am a tourist."

"You almost seem like you live here. If you don't talk too much, people might believe it."

"If I don't talk too much?"

"You don't talk like a Panamanian."

I look away so that he won't see how that stung. He knows, though.

"It's nothing about your Spanish. Your Spanish is the best I've ever heard from an American. But you don't say things how a Panamanian would."

"Like what?"

"Like you say '*¿Qué pasó?*' but that's textbook. People here say '*¿Qué xopá?*'"

"What's that?"

"'*¿Qué pasó?*' backwards. Sort of."

I scan the smattering of other people on the viewing deck. "I'm pretty sure everyone here is a tourist."

"Sure. Point if you want. Whatever. I was just trying to help."

"I mean, do any Panamanians really come here?"

Danilo takes a step back and looks at me. "I pissed you off, huh?"

I cross my arms and press my fingertips against the sides of my ribs. "Maybe."

"Well, you're right anyway, I guess. Panamanians only come here if they work here."

"Or unless they're showing me around." I smile. My hair flips loosely in the breeze. I wiggle my toes against the canvas backing inside my sneakers. "So where are the ships?"

Danilo walks to the front corner of the viewing deck and leans his torso over the railing. "Out there. You can see them."

Under the beating sun, I lean out, too, twisting my body, and am greeted by a mass of bobbing ships, freckling the expanse of water past the end of the concrete lanes.

"They have to wait for clearance to come in," Danilo explains. "It's always backed up like this."

A flock of birds scatters up from the trees in the hills around us, making a sound like applause. I have to stand very near Danilo in order to see. The faint scent of sweat, delicate and salty, lifts off his skin in the hot air. Once, the front of my thigh brushes the side of his and though I'm sure he'll startle and jolt away, he doesn't.

"It's crazy the shit they have on board," he says. "It's everything, you know, cars and pianos and fuel and food."

He turns toward me. I take a few steps back.

"People swim through it, too," he says.

"Through the canal?"

"Yeah, there's a famous guy. Richard Halliburton. He swam through just after it opened. He hired a guy to follow him in a rowboat and shoot alligators if they got too close. They charged him thirty-six cents."

"I know Richard Halliburton. I mean, not personally. Obviously. But I've heard of him. He died in a typhoon, I think."

Danilo picks at some dirt under his thumbnail as if the topic no longer interests him. "Well, are you ready?" he asks. "*Vamos, pues.*"

I swear we question every single one of the people working at the visitors' center that day about whether they've heard of my father. Every single one of them says no.

"I have another idea," Danilo says. "What time is it?"

I wheel my watch around my wrist. "Eleven-thirty."

"Fuck. He won't be here until one."

"Who?"

"Señor Jaén."

"Who's that?"

Danilo smiles mischievously, flashing his chipped tooth. "So many questions, Miraflores. Well, what do you want to do? Do you want to look at the museum? It's brand-new, you know."

"Is it any good?"

"Let's find out. Come on. If it's too boring, we'll find somewhere to sit and wait."

We walk upstairs, past glass cases filled with taxidermied insects found in the vicinity of the canal and through a life-sized replica of one of the giant culverts that transports water into and out of the locks. There are illuminated maps and charts and timelines. Another case displays a small collection of weathered personal effects—a pair of boots and a pocket watch and a tin flask—that belonged to one of the early laborers. Still another holds the front pages of yellowed newspapers with articles about the construction progress and setbacks. A letter from a young French worker to his parents was translated into English and reprinted in one of the earliest newspapers. The newspaper caption says that the letter was found in the man's shirt pocket after he died in the hospital of yellow fever.

Dear Mother and Father,

I have been entangled and entwined in the most absurd manner a number of times by the curiously tentaclelike foliage on the ground in Panama. The plants are quite like land octopuses. I have also suffered a number of mosquito bites from insects big as hummingbirds, which pierce one's skin until they draw beads of blood to the surface. I should say that not all of the country is so wild. Once or twice, I have made my way to the city, where there are still no modern conveniences (quite a lot of people bathe in the ocean!), but at least it can generally be said to offer a space to breathe in what otherwise appears to be a country entirely and suffocatingly blanketed by jungle. We've not yet had rain, only scorching sun that's left me red as raw clay, but I hear the rain is not to be preferred, either. Tomorrow I trek again through the brush, clearing what I can as I make my way with a machete (a very nice one, too). Say hello to Monsieur Théophile.

Until we reach the end,
I am yours in Panama.

Monsieur Théophile, the newspaper says, was the family cat.

And then we come upon a group of black-and-white photographs housed in glass console cases, each photograph affixed with silver straight pins to a drape of black velvet. Inside the first case is a small sign that reads:

THE FOLLOWING PHOTOGRAPHS WERE TAKEN BY ERNEST HALLEN, OFFICIAL PHOTOGRAPHER OF THE ISTHMIAN CANAL COMMISSION, HIRED TO DOCUMENT THE BUILDING OF THE GREAT ENGINEERING MARVEL OF OUR TIME, THE PANAMA CANAL.

The photographs are wide-angle shots of the same sites over and over, usually taken a number of weeks apart, so that the effect is that of a very slow flip-book. An entire case is dedicated to photographs of Theodore Roosevelt and William Taft visiting the canal.

"Your presidents, no?" Danilo says from over my shoulder.

"Not while I've been alive, but yes."

"This is the one who got stuck in his bathtub?" Danilo asks, pointing at Taft.

"How did you know that?"

"Maybe I'm smarter than you think. They had to break him out of it, right?"

"And then they had to build a bigger bathtub for the White House."

Danilo laughs softly behind me. "At least he fit through the canal."

I smile and stare at Taft, standing on the observation platform of one of the cars, more than three hundred pounds in his blindingly white suit and his pale hat. Mrs. Taft, luminous in white and wearing a dark hat wreathed in flowers, stands next to him. They're both waving.

The rest of the cases are divided between staged photographs of white Americans, the women wearing long white dresses and white hats with netting hung over the brims like delicate waterfalls, sitting at their desks or assembled on their verandas or lined up outside hospitals and clubhouses, smiling for the camera, and more candid, journalistic shots of immigrant laborers with skin as black and slick as oil toiling in the sun. There are photographs of machines like dinosaurs, huge and clumsy, biting into the earth, and men who appear small as ants crawling on them; photographs of men walking up the nearly vertical slopes of rock wall with boxes of dynamite on their heads, their sleeves rolled to their elbows, their boots caked in mud. And then there is a grainy photograph of an injured man, drenched in blood, being carried by a group of workers who are holding him as if they are pallbearers and the man a coffin. I shudder and turn away.

"He probably died," Danilo says. "A lot of them died back then. Those guys carrying the dynamite on their heads? Sometimes it was so hot down there that the dynamite exploded and killed them on the spot. It wasn't just disease, you know. That's what everyone talks about. But it was everything. They were suffocated in mudslides and bitten by snakes and shit. It was hell."

We lounge outside on a set of bleachers until the appointed hour, the aluminum seats scaldingly hot in the sun. We're by ourselves, everyone else gawking at the passing ships from the observation deck we were on earlier. Danilo takes a pack of cigarettes from his pocket, pulls one out, and lights it. He holds the cigarette between his lips, his index finger hooked casually over the top while his middle finger supports it from underneath, before drawing it out and exhaling. He turns his head away from me and pushes the smoke out the corner of his mouth.

"You want one?" he asks, tapping the cigarette.

"No, thanks."

"I didn't think so."

"Why? I've smoked one before."

"One?"

"A few. But I never liked it."

"You didn't give it enough time." He squints and smiles.

In front of us, a green-and-white ship with "Mitka United" painted along the side slides into the first lock chamber. A group of men on the ground scramble around, tossing long cables up onto the deck of the ship. The cables get secured at one end to the ship and at the other end to one of the yellow trams that run on tracks parallel to the water lanes, the heavy lines sloping down gracefully like cobwebs. Once the ship and the trams are connected, the trams will help steer the ship through the water lane. Even though the lanes are perfectly straight, it's tricky because the ships these days are so big they have very few inches of wiggle room sometimes between themselves and the chamber walls. He points out streaks of colored paint along the inside of the canal walls left by ships so big they had scraped through.

As soon as the ship is safely inside the lock chamber, the water drains and the ship lowers as if it's no more than a raft held aloft by floodwaters. When the water level matches that of the next chamber, the gates—two enormous metal double doors that separate the chambers—swing open and fold back into recesses carved out in the canal walls. The ship advances out of the first chamber and into the next. The process repeats once more until at last the ship makes it through the series of water steps and sails out into the Pacific Ocean.

"Beautiful thing, isn't it?" Danilo says.

I nod, wondering whether this is what my father saw every day when he worked here. Under the sun, the surface of the oily water glows an iridescent blue like the wings of a dragonfly.

"Tell me something, Miraflores."

"Like what?"

"Something about you. What do you want to be? What do you like to do? That kind of thing."

"I want to be a geophysicist." I say "geophysicist" in English.

Danilo cocks an eyebrow. "A what?"

"I want to study the earth."

He takes another drag of his cigarette.

"I like to read and draw maps and walk around outside by myself. And I study."

"You're a thinker."

"I hang out with my friends, too."

"Okay. And what else?"

I cross my ankles in front of me and stare at my shoes. The plastic tip at the end of one lace has split and frayed. "I lied to my mother," I say.

"Oh yeah?"

"She doesn't know I'm here. I told her I was going on a

trip for school—I go to the University of Chicago—instead of telling her I was coming to Panamá."

"Why? She doesn't like Panamá?"

"She loves it."

"Then?"

I shrug.

"Does anyone know you're here?"

"My friends do."

Danilo ashes his cigarette over the front edge of the bleacher. "So you go to university?"

"Yes."

He gives me a sidelong glace. "Fucking nerd."

"Hey!"

"Eh, I'm just kidding."

"Aren't you in school?"

"Does it look like I'm in school? Nah. It's not for me." He takes one last drag of his cigarette, stubs it out, then flicks it off the side of the bleachers.

"Why not?"

He spreads his fingers like a starfish, examining his hands for a second, before contracting them into fists. "Did you know that Panamá is the only place in the world where you can see the sun rise over the Pacific Ocean and set over the Atlantic Ocean?"

"That's what I've heard."

"You knew that?"

"I'm studying geology. I know things like that."

"Okay. What's the highest mountain in the world?"

"That's too easy. Mount Everest."

"The shortest river?"

"The D River in Oregon."

"Where?"

"In Oregon. It's in the United States."

"The diameter of the earth in kilometers."

"Twelve thousand seven hundred fifty-six."

"So this is what you do with your friends? You sit around and talk about geology?"

"Not really. I mean, I don't know." I couldn't think of the word for trivia. "We have conversations."

"About what?"

"About whatever. Movies, or school, or books."

"You talk about movies? What's your favorite movie?"

"Have you heard of *Touching the Void*? It's about two mountain climbers. I just saw it. It was incredible."

Danilo shakes his head. "I saw *Terminator 3* last week, though. Do you know that one? It just came out here."

It's been out for ages in the United States and it isn't a movie I would see anyway, but I just say no.

We both fall quiet for a time. All around us a discordant sort of symphony hums faintly—the squawk of birds from the jungle, the strain of machinery. I scratch my nail over the ridges in the bleacher seat. There's still twenty minutes until one o'clock. As soon as we get back to the hotel, I need to call my mother. I didn't call her yesterday.

The minutes stretch out and dissolve until finally I ask, "Do you ever miss being home?"

"What do you mean?"

"I mean do you miss where you grew up? When you were with your parents."

Danilo rubs his chin. "Nah," he says. "I don't even think of that as home. That's only birthplace or something."

"What's the difference?"

"Home is something else. I don't know. Fuck. How can I explain it? It's where you feel most like you belong, I guess."

The sun is high and almost quivering in the sky. The backs of my knees are sweaty.

"I don't know where that is for me," I say.

Danilo appears to think about that for a minute. "It doesn't have to be a place," he says. "Remember, when we were talking in Panamá Viejo? That idea, that geography is an illusion? I think it's true. People live—I mean, really live—in spaces that aren't on a map." He rubs his palm against the back of his neck self-consciously, as though he's worried he just said something sappy. "Anyway, you'll know eventually. You'll just fall into it and suddenly realize that you're there."

This whole time, I've been leaning back, the bleacher behind me digging a line under my shoulder blades. I've been looking at Danilo from an angle. Now I sit up even with him.

"My mother is sick," I say.

"Is it bad?"

"Yes."

"I'm sorry."

"I don't know what I'm going to do without her. I don't know what's going to happen to me."

"You might lose her?"

I can't bring myself to say yes, but I don't need to.

"Then what are you doing here?" he asks.

How can I explain? There's nothing to say that doesn't make me sound selfish or desperate. I tell him about the letters and everything I once believed and everything as it seems to me now. I give him a quick summary of my life growing up with my mother, without my father, all in a more or less factual way. My mother worked hard to support us. My father, and the absence of my father, was not something that consumed me. I had written him off. I defend myself, saying that had been a reasonable thing to do. I recount the story of the three doctors and the diagnosis. I explain that the idea to come here seized me in its impulsive and obdurate grip. And though he doesn't say so explicitly, though all he does is listen patiently without offering any remonstrations or condolences or advice, I think he understands, because at exactly one, he stands up, cups his hands around his mouth like a bullhorn, and shouts in the direction of the control tower across the water lanes, "Hector! *¡Oye!* Hector!"

"Hector!" he screams again when he receives no answer. *"Hector Jaén!"*

Before long, an older man, looking extraordinarily annoyed, thrusts his head through the tower window and shouts in response, "What the hell do you want?"

"Can you let me up?" Danilo asks.

"Danilo?"

"Yeah, it's me."

"Who is with you?"

"This is Miraflores."

"I don't have time for games, okay?"

"That's really her name. We need your help. Can you let us across?"

He glares at us uncertainly before ducking his head back through the window.

"What's going on?" I ask.

"Come on," Danilo says.

We start across the top of one set of closed gates. It's like being on a concrete balance beam three stories high. A few steps in, with my hand gripping the metal yellow railing that spans the length, I stop. Danilo is sauntering on ahead of me as if he's just taking a walk through the park.

"Danilo!" I call.

He turns around. "Holy shit, Miraflores. Don't stop now. They're going to need this gate in a minute. You can't stop."

"I can't go."

He looks at me like he doesn't know what to say.

"Danilo!"

He starts back toward me. And suddenly all I want is for him not to get to me. All I want is for him not to have to pry my hand off the railing and escort me, like a child, across the gates. I want to be able to do this by myself.

"Don't look down," Danilo advises as he nears me.

I look down. My black-and-white sneakers are planted

firmly in the middle of the concrete. Somehow, seeing them helps. The gate has to be about six, maybe seven feet wide, but at that height, it feels more like six or seven inches. I slide one pointed toe forward, move my hand, then drop my heel. Danilo stops. Come on, I tell myself. I want to wipe my sweaty hand against my jeans but I don't dare peel it off the railing. I move again, and again, until finally I'm walking at a halfway decent pace all the way to where Danilo is standing. I wait for him to make fun of me, but he just smiles and keeps on.

As soon as we're safely on the other side, Danilo makes his way to the base of the tower. Hector Jaén is waiting there with the door propped open.

"What is it?" he asks.

Danilo claps him lightly on the shoulder and says, "Long time no see, friend. How have you been?"

"You don't have clearance to come up. I have told you and I have told Hernán before," Hector says.

"That's why I'm down here. If I had clearance, I'd be up there already."

"So what do you want me to do?"

I'm standing by, my body still pulsing with a hundred feverish vibrations, incredulous and optimistic.

"It's important" is all Danilo says.

Hector Jaén rolls his eyes. Quickly, he scans the grounds around the tower, then motions us in.

The top of the tower is one large room, crowded by a replica of the canal and other miscellaneous equipment—reams of paper, binoculars, compasses, maps, tide tables, and at least five clocks mounted on the wall displaying various time zones. Two men sit at instrument panels directly in front of windows that look out over the canal.

I elbow Danilo. "See? I could work at a place like this."

"What do you need?" Hector mutters. "You're going to get me in trouble, Danilo."

"Hernán says hello." At this, a glimmer of a smile passes across Hector's face. "This is Miraflores," Danilo says.

"Again, the same joke?"

"I swear that's her name."

"*Buenas,*" Hector says, dutifully shaking my hand.

"*Buenas.*"

"Miraflores is visiting us from the United States. She's looking for her father."

Hector blanches. "Not me? It couldn't be. I was not with that many women when I was young. I did not—" he stammers, until Danilo laughs.

"Relax. It's not you. It's someone by the name of Gatún Gallardo. He used to work here."

"She's Miraflores and he's Gatún?"

"Yeah, I know."

"Gallardo," Hector repeats thoughtfully.

I feel the electricity in my toes, the tingling of potential.

"It sounds familiar," he says.

"Think hard," Danilo urges.

"Years ago. In the seventies, no?"

"Yes, he worked here then," I say, and in my voice there's a mounting hope, like a kite skimming up through the air.

"He used to work here in the control tower, I think. If I am remembering the right person. He almost caused a big accident here. After that, he moved over to the maintenance crew."

I wonder, for a fleeting second, about the accident, what that means exactly, but I don't want to get off track. "Does he still work here?" I ask.

Hector shakes his head. "I haven't heard about him in a while. I don't know what happened to him. It was a long time ago. He had a small beard, yes?"

"I don't know," I admit.

"Hector, is there any way to find out if he's still here, or if not, where he went?"

"I have access to the employment records, I guess."

Danilo claps his hands. "That's what I'm talking about! Can we look?"

Hector eyes both of us. I can't imagine what I look like then, how eagerly poised my body must be for anything that might come next.

"I'll look and tell you," he says.

For a moment, it appears as though Danilo is going to argue with him, but he takes a step back and raises his hands. "Whatever you want. We'll wait here."

When Hector returns minutes later, Danilo says, "So?"

"He quit in 1987."

"Where is he now?" I ask.

Hector shakes his head lightly. "That was all it said. No forwarding information. He worked here, in a number of different divisions, but he quit in 1987."

Nineteen eighty-seven. Three years after I was born.

"That's all you know?" Danilo presses.

"I'm sorry," Hector says. "That's all I know."

Hernán is at the hotel when we return. I detect a slight frown on his face when he first sees us, but when I look again he's smiling brightly with his arms outstretched.

"Where have you been?" he asks.

"At the canal," I say.

"To Miraflores, yes? Miraflores went to Miraflores." He smiles giddily and watches us as if waiting to see whether he can laugh at his own joke. "And how did you like it?"

"Very impressive," I say.

Without a word, Danilo has walked past us. I watch the slender curve of his back as he leans over to retrieve his flower bucket tucked under the steps.

"Do you know," Hernán continues, stepping into my line of vision as soon as he notices me watching Danilo, "that I used to work at the canal?"

"You did? Danilo didn't tell me that."

"I'm not surprised. He has trouble expressing any pride in me."

"When did you work there?"

"From 1977 to 1987. Ten years."

My breath catches. "Until 1987?"

"Until December of that year, yes. I worked in the control tower at Miraflores, with a man named Hector Jaén, whom I would imagine is still there. He always took his job too seriously. He was the only Panamanian to hold a position of real authority back then, though, so he had a good reason. Mostly, it was the North Americans who ran the show." Hernán shakes his head, remembering.

"Hernán," I say, trying to remain poised, "did you know someone who worked there named Gatún Gallardo?"

"Gatún Gallardo! I haven't heard that name in a long time. He used to bring his lunch every day in a brown paper bag and eat it on the ground next to the control tower. I used to look down and see him, eating by himself and then smoking a cigarette for a long time after. Sometimes he would lie back on the concrete and take a nap, even though that sort of thing was frowned upon. He never seemed to care much about the rules."

My heart races wildly through the cave of my chest. "You knew him?"

"We were not friends. Nothing against him. But we said hello to each other from time to time. He always seemed pleasant enough." Hernán narrows his eyes. "Is that who you were looking for? The other day, in Santa Ana?"

Danilo has plopped himself on the hotel stoop, his bucket between his legs. He's pulling out stems one by one and rearranging them. It doesn't appear that he's listening to our conversation.

"He's my father," I say.

The color drains from Hernán's face and he blinks a number of times in an exaggerated way. "Gatún Gallardo? Your father?"

"Yes."

"Are you sure? I don't understand how . . . But your name is not Gallardo."

Blood is pounding in my chest, in my ears. "My mother met him when she lived here."

"Your mother lived here? When? What is her name?"

"Catherine Reid."

Hernán shakes his head, pale, bewildered. "An American?"

"Yes."

"She must have lived in the Zone," Hernán mutters. "And now you're looking for him? Your father? Gatún Gallardo? Why? He and your mother didn't marry?"

"No. I've never met him."

He looks heartbroken, a series of pained expressions flashing across his face. "I see," he says finally.

"But if you knew him, you could help me find him."

"I didn't really know him," Hernán says carefully. "As I said."

"What you just told me about him, about eating his lunch outside every day, that's almost as much as everything I've ever known about him. Please, Hernán."

He wipes his handkerchief across his forehead and cheeks. "Danilo is helping you?"

"He's trying. But he knows even less than me. I mean, he

knows the city. But he doesn't know anything about my father."

"How long will you look for him?" Hernán asks.

"I have to go home in a few weeks. But I want to find him as soon as I can. I mean, if I found him tomorrow, I would still have some time to spend with him before I have to go back home."

"And you are planning on staying here until you find him?" He gestures toward the hotel.

"I guess so."

"No, Miraflores"—he says it in the same way as Danilo, delicately, liltingly—"I don't think it's a good idea."

"Oh, you don't even know. In a lot of ways, it's a terrible idea. There's all this other stuff going on right now. But I have to look for him. It's sort of now or never. I mean, it's only going to get harder from now on. I don't know when I would be able to come back." I stop when I realize that Hernán has no idea what I'm talking about. I don't feel like filling him in on everything at the moment. I just want his help.

Hernán coughs. He darts his eyes around like an animal that has suddenly realized it's in a cage, trapped. He looks panicked. Then he takes a breath and says, "Of course. What I meant was the hotel. It's so expensive to stay here. Maybe you want to come stay with us, in our apartment. It's small, but that way you could save money, and I would feel better about it, and we could help you, Danilo and I."

The invitation doesn't startle me. Not that I expected it. It never crossed my mind that Hernán would offer to let me stay with him, but it's not surprising somehow. I have a sense by now that Hernán has a decent heart and that, for some reason, that decent heart has a soft spot in it for me. There's something about how he treats me that feels almost like family.

"I don't know," I say, stealing a glimpse at Danilo. He's in a retiring pose on the steps now, his eyes closed against the warm rays of the sun, the shadow cast by a palm tree cutting jaggedly over his body, like feathery claws.

"It would save you money," Hernán says again.

I look briefly at Danilo again and bite my lip.

"Do you have room?" I ask.

"We will make room."

"You really don't have to offer."

"Of course not! But I want to. You can think about it," he says, obviously pleased with himself and the fact that I haven't yet turned him down.

I think he expects me to leave it at that and walk inside, but instead I look him in the eye. "Okay. If you're sure you don't mind."

"You'll stay with us?"

"If you're sure."

"Of course! Good!" He claps his hands together and beams. "We'll clear a space for you. You can walk home with us tonight. You can check out of the hotel right now if you want, and then just tell them that you will collect your things later tonight."

I smile in spite of the fact that part of me wonders why in the world I just agreed to this.

"Danilo!" Hernán cries, turning to his nephew on the steps. "Miraflores is coming to stay with us!"

Danilo sits up, puzzled. "What are you talking about?"

"She is going to stay with us while she is in Panamá."

"Really?" Danilo says, a smile spreading across his face as slow as syrup. He looks at me. "Welcome."

The apartment is on the second floor of a two-story building, above a laundromat and across the street from a bakery. Hernán points out the laundromat, closed for the night, and notes that I should consider taking my clothes there if I need them washed, because they do a good job. "Fifteen cents per pound. They will iron, too, if you want. And if you take your own hangers, they give a discount."

Gallantly, he carries my suitcase up the stairs and heaves it through the front door when we arrive, placing it against a wall off to one side.

"This is it!" he announces. He hasn't been able to stop grinning since I agreed to this arrangement.

It's eleven o'clock—we waited until Hernán finished his shift—but even at night the space has a brightness to it, an airiness so acute that it barely feels like I'm inside at all. All the windows—single-paned, unadorned by curtains or blinds—

are wide open, as are a set of louvered French doors, painted turquoise, that lead to a faux balcony. The front door opens directly into a sitting area with a couch, a wooden rocking chair with a printed yellow cushion, and an old television set resting on a cotton doily. The lamp shades are still wrapped in plastic. The sitting area funnels into a narrow hallway that has three plywood doors along one side. Across from the doors is the kitchen, outfitted with plain wooden cabinets, a gold refrigerator, a stove piled high with aluminum pots, and a small kitchen table. Every wall is painted sea-foam green, and on the one behind the television three diorama-like Panamanian houses, each roughly the size of a clock, hang in a row.

"Danilo's room, my room, and the washroom," Hernán says, pointing in succession to the doors lining the hallway.

Danilo is behind the two of us, leaning against the door frame with his arms crossed over his chest.

"It's really nice," I say.

"Where you live is probably a mansion compared with this."

"Not at all."

Danilo snorts.

"What?" I ask, turning to face him, running my hand along my bag strap.

"You don't have to be nice for our sake."

"I'm not. This is a great house."

"Are you surprised?"

"No. I'm just saying . . ."

"Leave her alone, Danilo." Hernán clears his throat, then advances past me and flips on more lights. "Of course," he continues, "you can sleep in my room, and I will take the couch." He doubles back toward my bag, eager to get me situated.

Danilo, still behind me, says, "She can take my room."

Hernán stops. "You don't even let me into your room."

Danilo scoots past us into the kitchen. He drags a plastic pitcher of water out of the refrigerator and fills a glass almost to the brim.

"Okay," Hernán says, shuttling my suitcase into Danilo's room. When he comes back out, he joins Danilo in the kitchen. "Do you want something to drink?" he asks me.

"No, thank you," I say. I feel stiff all of a sudden, unsure of what I'm doing here.

"You're tired?" Hernán asks.

"Yes, I guess so. Yeah, I'm pretty tired."

"Of course you are," he says, though he looks vaguely disappointed at the idea of a premature end to the evening. "I'll bring a fresh towel to your room for you to use in the morning. We don't have hot water, but it gets warm enough and in this weather I doubt that you would want it hot anyway. I leave by eleven most days. Danilo makes us breakfast."

"Thank you," I say. "I hope I'm not going to be in your way too much."

"We hope so, too," Danilo says, and I gave him a sarcastically amused expression while Hernán swats his arm and scolds, "*Oye.*"

"Come on," Hernán says, ushering me into Danilo's room.

It's small and surprisingly neat. There's a standing fan next to a closet cordoned off by a hanging bedsheet, a simple dresser with nothing but a bowl of change on top, a twin bed with the sheet tucked tidily under the mattress, and a flat pillow slouched against the wall. It reeks of mothballs.

"It looks like he was expecting company," I say.

"He always keeps it like this," Hernán says, brushing past me with my suitcase, which he lays on the floor next to the dresser. "This is okay?"

"The room? The room is great."

"I know it doesn't compare to the hotel—"

"It's great. I promise. I really appreciate you letting me stay here." I still feel strange about it, although I keep telling myself that I can stay just one night and see how it goes. If it doesn't work out, I can always just go back to a hotel. A different one, probably, but there's still that option.

Hernán appears pleased. Then he appears at a loss, standing uselessly in the middle of the room, his hands jammed in his pockets. He's still wearing his hotel uniform, although he took his hat off as soon as he stepped out of the lobby, leaving a dent pressed into his dark, wavy hair. He sucks in a deep breath. "Okay," he says, and gazes around once more. "You want to sleep."

"Thank you again."

He takes a step and, leaning forward awkwardly, kisses me quickly on the forehead, the way you would a puppy or a child. "Good night," he says, and scuttles out as if in embarrassment, closing the door behind him.

. . .

I wonder sometimes how my father envisions me. Assuming that he thinks of me at all, which I believe he does. At least once in a while. I always believed that. Even when I thought he was the sort of person who would cast off his child and his child's mother, I never thought he had entirely left us behind. For some reason I assumed that he must have thought about me from time to time. I think I assumed that, no matter how horrible a person you might be, it would be impossible to have a child, to have a piece of yourself walking around in the world, and not think about that child at least a few times in the course of your life.

I wonder what my father thinks I look like, or what he imagines I do with my days. I wonder whether he assumes that I am in every way like my mother, or whether he lies in bed at night thinking about how much of himself might have blossomed in me.

It's a strange sort of mathematics. I know the ways I'm similar to my mother: we are both humble, determined, serious, resourceful, reserved, and hardworking. I've always thought that if you subtract those traits from the whole of me, everything that's left over must be the ways I'm like my father. Which means that he gave me loyalty, benevolence, patience, an anger that's slow to ignite and that extinguishes quickly, and a heart that, even though I try very hard to hide it, is easily wounded.

Six
Concretion

I wake early that first morning, before either Danilo or Hernán is up. The day feels swollen with possibility, and I'm restless, eager to get going, see them, get dressed, go out, do something. But I don't want to go into the kitchen and make too much noise and disturb them, so I stay put in Danilo's room for the time being. I turn the fan down to low and find my cell phone in my bag to call my mother.

"Mira?" she answers. "How are you?"

"I'm good. What are you doing?" I'm sitting cross-legged on Danilo's bed, clutching the toes of one foot with my hand.

"Nothing. I just had breakfast. It's snowing here, so I don't think I'm leaving the house today. Are you having a good time in . . . shit."

"Washington."

"I've never been to Washington. But I hear it's nice."

"It seems nice so far."

"The only school trip I can remember taking was to Niagara Falls one year. We stood up on the edge of a cliff and white water crashed down around us. I remember we were working on similes in language arts and my teacher, Mrs. Coe, would say things like, 'The water sounds like . . .' and 'The water looks like . . .' and she would wait for someone to raise their hand to fill in the blank. I said, 'The water sounds like a roaring lion.'" She laughs softly to herself. "I can't believe I remember that."

"Nice simile."

"I also remember that I sat with Sally Perris on the bus ride home. In the gift shop, she bought a box of these really fat pencils with the words "Niagara Falls" down the sides in blue. I asked her if she would give me one, but she wanted to keep them all for herself. She was always sort of vicious like that. You know, she came over to the house once."

"Our house?"

"Before I left New York. She sat in the kitchen with me and had tea. I was drinking peppermint tea then. I started with it in the beginning of my pregnancy because people said that it helped curb the nausea. I don't know about that." She lapses into silence, as if she's forgotten her place in the story.

"Sally Perris and you were drinking tea," I say.

"What?"

"Sally Perris and you were drinking tea."

"Yes, and she told me that she couldn't associate with me

any longer. She said that my father had gone to her and all the rest of my friends and told them that I had shamed him and my mother, and that unless they stopped associating with me, he would have their husbands dismissed from the military. He could have done it, too. He was very big in our town. He taught at the academy. Did you know that?"

"Yes, I knew that," I say delicately. I did know that her father taught at West Point. I'm not certain whether she understands what else she's telling me, but I want her to go on.

"He threatened them. And they caved. Every last one of them." Then, "That's enough about that. I'm going to have my breakfast now."

By the time we hang up, there are noises coming from the kitchen. I walk out to the sight of Danilo making eggs. He's standing in front of the oven in the same T-shirt he had on yesterday and mesh shorts that hang to his knees, his hair sticking out at the sides and flattened in the back.

"They'll be ready soon," he says when he sees me, and a minute later he delivers to the table a plate of eggs scrambled with cubes of ham and shredded cheese. I sit at the table and eat silently while he continues cooking, the sounds of sizzling cheese and popping grease filling the kitchen. I'm about to ask where Hernán is, when all of a sudden the sound of his singing floats down the hall. At first I think it's coming from outside, but the longer I listen, I realize that the warbling voice is coming from the bathroom. I laugh.

"What?" Danilo asks.

"Is that Hernán?"

"Singing? Yeah. Dude loves to the sing in the shower."

"Is he singing Shakira?"

"He fucking *loves* Shakira. He has videotapes of her concerts that he watches when he's feeling depressed." I laugh again, and after giving the eggs a quick turn in the pan, he says, "You think that's funny?"

"Sort of."

"Oh, it is. It's funny as shit. A man his age sitting around watching Shakira. His eyes get all big and he leans forward on the couch. I hope you get to see it while you're here." He pushes the eggs around again and turns down the flame on the burner. "Although you probably won't. He's so happy you're here that I don't think he even needs Shakira."

"I'm better than Shakira?"

"That little thing? Flicking her hips around? Any day, Miraflores. You're better than her any day."

His back is toward me, so I can't read the expression on his face, but I have the sense that he means it.

Hernán goes on singing, and I go on listening, amused. Danilo opens the shuttered window in the kitchen and pours us both glasses of orange juice that tastes vaguely like Tang, before joining me at the table.

"These are good," I tell him after several bites of the eggs.

He doesn't respond.

"So what are you doing today?" I ask, trying to sound casual.

"I'm meeting up with Nardo later. He wants to get some new sneakers, so we'll probably go to La Onda or somewhere to look for something cheap. This afternoon, I'll be out with my flowers. And tonight we have a hot card game set up." He picks at something in his teeth. "What are your plans?"

I don't want to tell him that I was counting on him to provide me with plans. "I guess I'm going to try to find an Internet café so I can get on the computer and maybe find out something more about my father."

"Those places are a rip-off."

"What?"

"They're too expensive."

"It's okay."

"Why? You're rich? You probably are, right? All Americans are rich."

"Who says that?"

"Everyone. You're all driving your Mercedes-Benzes and living in your big houses."

I can't tell whether he honestly believes that or whether he's just baiting me. "I don't think so," I say. "I told you last night my mother and I don't have a big house. And we definitely don't drive a Mercedes. We have an old car that doesn't want to start when it's too cold outside."

He looks like he doesn't believe me. "Danilo, come on. You're not that . . ." I don't know the word for "naïve." "You know better than that. It's just like anywhere. There are people who don't have much, people who have some, and people who have a lot."

"But in the United States, there are way more people who have a lot than anywhere else."

"Maybe," I say. "But I'm not one of them. I have enough. Definitely. More than enough. But I'm still not one of those people you're thinking of."

Hernán walks into the kitchen a few minutes later, dressed and freshly scrubbed and smelling of talcum powder. He plants himself opposite me at the table.

"Eggs, please!" he says, winking at me. Grudgingly, Danilo heaps some onto a plate. From a lower cabinet within reach, Hernán produces a book, then drops it with a thud onto the table. "Don't mind me," he says in a way that makes it obvious he wants nothing more than for us to pay attention to him.

Danilo snickers. "I've never seen you read."

"Just because you have not seen it, doesn't mean that it does not happen."

"Okay, then," Danilo says, playing along. "What are you reading?"

"If you must know, I'm reading *Don Quixote.* The Man of La Mancha. Besides the Bible, it is the only book worth reading."

"You know, in order to say that, you would have had to read every book ever written."

Hernán narrows his eyes. Danilo is ruining his performance. "You know, in order to say *that,* you would have to be a real smart-ass."

"Oooh, such language!" Danilo teases.

Hernán makes a harrumphing sound and opens the book, the spine cracking as he turns to page one.

I stand and smile at him. "I've always wanted to read *Don Quixote*," I say. "I'm studying Spanish in school, but I won't take that class until my . . ." I hesitate. I don't know how to say "junior." "My third year. You'll have to tell me how you like it."

"I thought you were studying geology," Danilo says.

"I am. But my minor is Spanish."

"I told you she was smart," Hernán says. "Just like me."

I expect Danilo to say something sarcastic, but he settles for rolling his eyes.

I didn't know why I stood up, but now that I'm standing, there seems like nothing to do but excuse myself from the table and go to my room. Who knows what I'll do there, but I'll figure out something until both Danilo and Hernán leave for the day and the coast is clear for me to emerge again and figure out my next move. Which is exactly what happens. I sit on Danilo's bed, my heels digging into the mattress, my chin balanced on my knees, and watch a gecko, its skin so thin it's nearly translucent, dart out from behind the dresser and scamper across the wall. I attempt to braid my own hair and then let it all unravel. I listen for the sounds of them leaving. But after a while what I hear instead is a knock on my door. When I open it, Danilo is standing in front of me with his arms crossed.

"Nardo can find his own shoes."

"Excuse me?"

"Do you want me to go with you?"

"Where?"

"I don't know," he says. "Let's find somewhere."

. . .

The next few days are a blur, a pinwheel spinning in the wind. Danilo and I spend our waking hours together, devising plans over breakfast each morning for places where we can search for my father, teasing out any lead that seems even halfway viable, poring over maps and Internet printouts and my father's old letters over and over again. Every day, we start out serious in our mission, though we're rarely able to sustain our determination for more than a few hours. We abandon our plans in favor of going to places or doing things that Danilo suddenly decides I need to experience instead. Always, Danilo totes along his flower bucket, though he seldom makes a sale. He hardly even tries half the time beyond calling out to someone we happen to be passing on the street, asking the person, usually a woman, if she wants something beautiful in her day.

In the evenings, Danilo leaves me on my own. I hole up in his room and read, or else I talk to my mother or my friends. Girls call the house for him sometimes, and Danilo ventures out in the middle of the night to meet up with them. I always hear him. Even if I'm sleeping, I somehow wake up at the precise moment that he shuffles past my room and closes the front door with a soft click behind him. He joins his friends for card games or at clubs sometimes, too, I know, but he never invites me along. I don't know whether he's embarrassed by me, or whether he assumes I won't want to go, or whether he just needs a break from me, but I don't bring it up either way. He still has his own life to attend to, a life that was going on before I got here and that will go on after I leave.

Even so, when we're together I talk to him in a way I've never talked to anyone. Not even my friends at home. He doesn't ask anything of me, and yet I find myself telling him everything. Part of it, I'm convinced, is the fact that I have to speak in another language. It's more Spanish than I've ever spoken with anyone. But with limitations comes freedom. I don't have the luxury of relying on the automatic expressions I have at my disposal when I'm speaking in English. There's no default mode of communication, few standby phrases and ready-made sayings. I have to *think* about how to express myself. I have to be creative and take roundabout routes to get across what I want to convey. Which means that I say things I never would in English. Ideas occur to me in ways they never have before. Which makes the world seem just that much different, and makes me think of myself a little bit differently—a little more imaginative, a little more spirited, a little less ordinary. Because while for most people the experience of having to measure out what they're going to say might draw them inward, make them more pensive and cautious, it seems to be drawing me out instead, giving me access to some part of myself I didn't even know was there.

If that was the whole story, though, I would speak to Hernán and anyone else I met with similar ease. But I don't. I can't. So I know that being forced to communicate in Spanish is only part of it. The other part of it is Danilo himself.

There's something about him. I love how he teases me, fishing me out of myself, casting and recasting his line, tugging gently, holding on tight, reeling until he dredges up something real. I love his inclination for rebellion and how flippantly he uses language, as if words are something to be tossed around like confetti rather than laid out like a stone path. I love catching glimpses of his vulnerability, too. When everything else has melted away, I can see it, uncovered and raw, filled with rare and piercing sorrow. But mostly I love how stubbornly he demands life from himself and from everyone around him. Life explodes off him the way snow lifts off a speeding car and showers everything in its wake. And the more I'm around him, the more I fall under his spell.

We have solemn talks about my mother and Alzheimer's, Danilo discussing it with a frankness that other people have trouble mustering about a topic so big and so heartbreaking.

"Explain to me how it works," he says.

"It's in a person's brain. There are these plaques—"

"What?"

"Like sticky blobs. And wherever they show up, they start killing brain cells. They're like little thieves. They just sneak in and take memories and knowledge from people. And they lock the door behind them, because after a while people can't put any new information into their minds, either. The brain starts to shrink."

"Nothing new?"

"So part of it is forgetting. That's the part everyone knows about. Information that people had stored in their brains vanishes as their brain cells die off. But yeah, the other part of it is that people with Alzheimer's can't get any new information in. So if my mother puts her fork in the sink, that's new information. When I ask her later where her fork is, it's not that she took that information in and can't remember it now, it's that the information never formed an impression in her brain in the first place, so the information isn't there at all when I ask her to rely on it."

"That happened?"

"No. She's not like that yet. I mean, once in a while. I don't know. She told me once it was like someone had taken an ice cream scoop to her head. Like there were just empty spaces all through her mind."

I tell him one day, "I'm afraid it's going to happen to me."

I've had that thought and tried not to think it a hundred times since my mother announced her diagnosis, but saying it out loud is like a lightning rod shooting straight through my bones.

"I can't tell you it won't," Danilo says.

"I know."

"But you shouldn't live like it will."

"People lose themselves."

"Yeah."

"It's like if you were a bridge and pieces of you just started crumbling off and dropping down into the water and sinking and you could never reach them again."

"And after enough pieces fall off, the whole thing collapses. You're not anything anymore."

"Exactly. I just don't want to forget everything."

"I don't think anyone would want that," he says.

Although, I think, maybe my mother is an exception. She tried so hard to bury the past and erase her own history—moving from New York, keeping undone the ties she was forced to sever, relegating my father to one brief episode in her life. Now, in a strange way, she's getting exactly what she wished for. All of it is leaving her piece by piece. Even though—and this is the cruelty of it—I'm pretty sure that while she acts like she wants to forget, she has all along silently and secretly been holding tight to those memories.

Any discussion about Danilo's parents is off-limits, but he confides in me about the strained relationship between Hernán and him. Hernán is angry and hasn't forgiven him for dropping out of school, because he believes that Danilo is making a mockery of the life that Hernán worked so hard to give him after his parents left.

"He used to make jabs about it all the time, which was annoying as hell. Hernán's soft, though, so he still tries to be nice to me, but things with us were never the same after I told him I was quitting school."

We're at a food stand called Donde Iván, sitting at a picnic table while I eat a shrimp *empanada* and Danilo drinks a beer—one called, simply, Panama. Every so often he picks at the edges of the paper beer label with his fingernail, tearing off the pieces. I have the thought that he's doing the same thing with himself—peeling back a layer to show me what's underneath, making himself as transparent as glass.

"Hernán doesn't know everything, though," he says.

"What do you mean?"

"He doesn't know that I have other shit going on. Haven't you looked around in my room?"

I smile. "Did you want me to?"

"I just figured you might have." He takes another swig of beer.

"Maybe I'm not that interested in you," I say.

Danilo shrugs. "I keep my drawings in my bottom dresser drawer."

"What drawings?"

"I've been doing them for a long time. Just pencil and paper. They're like comics. But not kid-stuff comics. Nicer than that. More sophisticated."

I don't know the word—*tebeos*—so I ask.

"Like Spider-Man," he says. "But more adult. Even though I guess I know plenty of adults who like Spider-Man." He finishes the beer and puts the bottle down on the table. The glass bottom half covers a rusty nailhead in the wood. "I'm going to get that shit published, though. One day. And when I do, I bet Hernán won't give a fuck that I dropped out of school."

"Can I see them?"

"What? The drawings? You know where they are now," he says, and leaves it at that.

Of course, I do look for them later and find more than a dozen lined notebooks filled with sketches and doodles and illustrated panels that, stacked next to each other, tell a story.

On some pages, handwritten notes cascade straight down the margins like ivy. His handwriting is like I knew it would be: wide, flattened O's and angular S's and stylized F's, all of it in thick graphite marks. It looks like graffiti.

Once, on the bus, Danilo asks whether I have a boyfriend at home. I tell him no, and then admit that I've never had a boyfriend, even though, as it's coming out of my mouth, I can't understand what would possess me to say such a thing, especially to him. But that's how it is. I want to give up every inch of myself to him. I want to hand myself over and say, Here, this is me, this is all so you'll understand me, and even though I've never offered all of this to anyone before, I'm giving it to you because I trust you to hold on to it and take care of it and handle it gently.

I'm elated to talk to him about nothing, too, having conversations that unravel haphazardly and that make little sense. I mention once that I like the way the roosters in people's yards sound in the morning. "They sound like this: *pío, pío.*"

"Don't know what you're talking about," he says.

"*Pío, pío.*"

We're on Salsipuedes, a street crowded with dozens of makeshift markets, people selling enormous baskets, pottery in the shape of animals and miniature huts, sterling-silver jewelry, Guayani dresses in bright colors, wood carvings made from cocobolo wood. It's noisy with the conversation of everyone around us, so I'm not sure he heard me.

"*Pío, pío,*" I say again.

"*Guau, guau,*" Danilo replies.

"What's that? That's not how they sound."

"That's for the dogs—*guau, guau.*"

"So you do know *pío, pío*?"

"I know *pío, pío.*" He's ambling with his particular confident strut. "Haven't you seen those chicken restaurants all over the place? You know, with the yellow signs? Pío Pío."

"In the United States the dogs say *woof, woof.*"

"'*Woof, woof*'?" Danilo repeats, wrinkling his nose in distaste.

"*Woof, woof.*"

"*Woof, woof!*" he barks loudly, and when people turn to stare at us, I crack up, covering my mouth with my hand.

Over the weekend, I ask him to take me to a bullfight.

"Where do you think you are? Spain?" Danilo asks. "We don't have bullfighting here. Well, I've heard about it in Los Santos, I guess, but it's just a bunch of farm workers in a little pen playing games with a bull. It's nothing official."

"I thought I saw a photograph once of a bullring here."

"A long time ago, maybe. But not anymore. Now we have cockfighting. You want me to take you to a cockfight, I will."

We're in the kitchen in the morning. He's wearing a gray T-shirt, long navy blue mesh shorts, and the rubber flip-flops he always wears in the house. He's standing with his hips against the counter, his ankles crossed.

"I don't think so," I say.

"You'd go to a bullfight, but not a cockfight? What's the difference?"

"Is that even legal?"

"Yeah. People set up fights in the streets. No one stops them."

"Have you been to one before?"

"Once. I had a bet on one of the birds. I lost, so I figured it wasn't my thing. I have better luck with cards, but I could go again if you want me to take you."

I scrunch up my nose.

"I'm not saying you'll like it. I can almost guarantee you won't like it. But it's something you'd never do at home, right?"

"Definitely not."

"Okay," he says, as if I just agreed to something, and the next thing I know he's pulling his phone off the counter and calling Nardo to find out whether there's a fight today and what time it starts.

When we arrive at the one-story concrete building, people, mostly men in hats and blue jeans, are filing in the door. Inside, the air feels superheated and stagnant. A concentrated bubble of noise—people talking and shouting and catcalling—echoes off the walls. There's a small dirt-floor ring surrounded by five circles of stadium seating that incline out toward the back row. By the door are tables crammed with plastic cups of beer for sale for fifty cents, and another table swarmed by men handing off thin slips of paper and placing bets.

Danilo leads me to the back row, to wooden folding chairs

numbered 131 and 132. When it's time to begin, two birds—one brown-feathered and one white-feathered—are placed in the ring and someone in the front row rings a bell. Everyone rises to his feet and starts waving his arms and shouting at the birds. I keep hearing one man's voice in particular screaming, "*¡Dale! ¡Dale!*" The only other woman I see in the place, a woman wearing a striped shirt so tight it shows off her fat rolls, stands in the second row clapping.

The birds alight sporadically, beating their wings once or twice, and then come down on each other, darting their beaks at each other's neck and head and chest. They have razor blades tied to their feet, and if they jump high enough, they slice the other bird upon landing. When the birds were first dropped into the ring, Danilo lowered his head and kept his gaze down between his knees. But now, even though he, like me, is one of the few not standing, he's craning his neck to glimpse the action. It doesn't take long before the blood blooms on the feathers of the white bird. I cringe. His head is covered in the dark red stickiness.

"How much longer?" I ask Danilo.

"You're ready to go?"

The white bird crumples to the ground and then, shakily, tries to stand again. I feel like I might throw up. "Yes," I tell him.

"Good," he says. "I was right the first time. This shit isn't my thing."

We fight through the cheering crowd to make our way

outside, where the city, which I usually associate with so much noise, suddenly sounds almost quiet by contrast, and where the sun, even though it's still pulsing its heat at us, feels like a welcome relief from the thick air inside the stadium.

"You okay?" Danilo asks, pulling out a cigarette as we walk.

"That was horrible," I say, as he stops and cups his hand around the cigarette to light it.

"You're right. I'm never doing that again. The whole scene was fucking sick."

I don't know where we're going now, although I don't ask, either. I assume back to the apartment, or for something to eat.

"The bullfights aren't as bad," Danilo goes on. "You know, earlier when I asked you, What's the difference? I really think they're not as bad. Still sick. But at least there's some majesty about it."

A soft breeze scampers up my back, under my shirt, and I start to feel a little bit better. We amble on, toward a bus stop, and when we get there, I ask, "Would you ever be a bullfighter?"

"You want me to?" Danilo says. He's smoking his second cigarette in a row now, something I've never seen him do. I take it as a sign that the cockfight unsettled him as much as it did me.

"I'm just asking if you would do it."

"If you wanted me to be a bullfighter, Miraflores, I would do it."

"I don't want you to be."

"What *do* you want me to be?" He tilts his head back and exhales.

A block away, the bus stops with a squeal. Plumes of diesel exhaust filter up into the air.

The world seems wide open at that moment. I could say almost anything. I want you to be a salesman. I want you to be an artist. I want you to be my tour guide. I want you to be my confidant. I want you to be my friend. I want you to be in love with me. The way he asked makes me think he's angling for one answer above all others, or at least that he's testing the waters to gauge the depth of my interest in him. It's too much pressure, though. The bus trundles up.

"Nothing," I say. "Just how you are is fine."

The night after the cockfight, I call Beth, Asha, and Juliette, in that order, but not one of them answers. It's Sunday. Nine p.m. I imagine them all out together, probably at Doc, watching a movie, as we usually do on Sunday nights. They're probably in their seats already, their winter coats crunched up behind their backs, their boots dripping snow onto the floor. Asha is probably pinching the skin around Juliette's wrist to signal that she really, really needs to stop talking now that the previews are over. Beth is probably sneaking Raisinets out of her bag and slipping them into her mouth one by one.

I run my fingers through my hair and shake my head. Then I pull out the postcards I bought earlier that week and start writing.

Dear Beth,

I just tried to call you guys but you didn't pick up. I know I talked to you yesterday, so I'm sending this for historical purposes, just so you have a record of my time here. Ahem . . . Herewith writes Mira Reid from an apartment in the Exposición neighborhood of Panama City, Panama, to where she has traveled to find her father, whom as of this day she still has not met. It is with much sadness that she misses her friends, who she assumes are currently watching a movie, although she is having a good time here and has been fortunate to make new friends.

Okay, that was lame. But whatever. I just wanted to send you a postcard and I don't really have anything to report that you don't—or won't by the time you get this—already know.

Much love,

Mira

Dear Asha,

I'm in the postcard-writing business tonight and I chose this one of a toucan especially for you (no, this is not because I think you have a big nose!). You've probably been getting updates from Beth. Not a lot has happened, though. I've just been hanging out with Danilo and sort of looking for my father. We went to a cockfight today, which was horrible. I don't know why I thought I'd be able to handle it.

Did you ever find my notes for Intermediate Mechanics? That class is ridiculously hard for the first few weeks, but it gets easier toward the end. I'm sure you're doing fine. Anyway . . . As they say, The weather is here, wish you were beautiful.

Much love,

Mira

Dear Juliette,

Heellllloooooooo! How are you? I'm still here in Panama, obviously. I'm sure Beth has been keeping you apprised of my goings-on (such a weird word). I don't want you to get too excited about the Danilo thing. I'm pretty sure we're destined to just be friends. He seems to have a lot of girls already, and I don't think he's into me like that.

No progress yet on my father, although I do feel like I'm learning a little bit about him. I'm getting a sense of what his life growing up might have been like here. Which has had the unintended effect of making me realize how little I know about my mother and *her* life before me. What am I going to do, though? Go to Highlands (in New York, where she's from)? I think one trip for now is plenty.

I'm running out of room. I hope you're okay, and I'll see you soon!

Love,

Mira

. . .

A week later, Danilo and I are no closer to finding my father. We keep trying new places and asking new people, but we don't have any real leads. In an act of desperation, Danilo draws flyers that say, in stylized block letters in the middle of the page, DO YOU KNOW GATÚN GALLARDO? In smaller letters underneath, he writes, "If so, call 227-0497," and sketches a mazelike border around the edges. He makes dozens of photocopies and takes them everywhere he goes with his flowers. He claims it actually helps business. "People are kind of over the flower thing. They've seen it before. They think they've seen it all. They're waiting in their cars and they can buy flowers or dish towels or fruit or watches or newspapers or cassette tapes. But to see someone walking around waving a piece of paper that I'm going to give them for free? They don't know what's up with that. Curiosity gets the better of them. So they roll down their windows and I give them the paper about your father and sometimes I manage to tack on a flower sale, too."

But no one ever calls.

I press Hernán for anything he might remember about my father, even the smallest misplaced detail, but over and over he reiterates that all he knows is what he told me the first time my father's name came up. Anytime I try to ask, Hernán steers the conversation to general recollections and reminiscences about his time on the canal and, beyond that, the history of the canal itself. He likes to sit with me at the breakfast table and regale me with tales about what the whole adventure was like. Danilo typically leaves the room when Hernán starts, and I have the distinct impression that he already tried out this same material on Danilo over the years, but now, in me, he has found somebody willing to listen.

He tells me about the first successful passage through the canal and about the hundreds of frogs that gushed in with the water the first time the lock chambers were filled. He tells me about how the men who built it were imported by the boatload mostly from the West Indies and how, as soon as they stepped off the ships upon arriving, they were pulled aside one by one and measured for their coffins. "That's how probable death was," he says.

"You know," he goes on, "they were cutting the world in half. But the land was not happy about it. All the landslides! When I worked there, it was always a threat. You don't know because you haven't seen it rain in Panamá. But when it rains here"—he grimaces—"it is as if God himself has torn the sky in two. And working in it? It is like being trampled by elephants.

"Even so, the whole thing is very beautiful. The ships sliding from ocean to ocean, over and over again, like someone working a sewing needle back and forth through a piece of fabric—the precision, the rhythm. And there are mountains under the water because the engineers flooded the land to make the canal. If you take a boat out onto Gatún Lake and look down, you can see them. You can see fish swimming around the tops of mountains."

Hernán looks entranced by his own account, as if he just came up with a particularly fantastic fairy tale to tell a child, except that it isn't fantastic at all. "It's true," he assures me. I have no reason not to believe him.

Seven

Saturation

There's a famous story about Archimedes, bearded and gaunt, stepping into his tub to take a bath one day and noticing that the water level rose as he settled in. It was simple enough, but we only notice things sometimes when we need to. Archimedes had recently been charged with the task of figuring out whether a new laurel-wreath crown commissioned by Hiero II, the king of Syracuse, was made of pure gold or whether, as Hiero suspected, a devious goldsmith had used an equivalent weight of silver to forge it instead.

This is what Archimedes knew: Silver weighs less than gold. The crown weighed the same as the amount of gold Hiero had given the goldsmith. Therefore, it seemed clear that the crown was indeed made from pure gold. If it had been made from silver, it would have weighed less. Except that Archimedes realized something else: The goldsmith might simply have used much *more* of the silver to bulk the crown up to the same weight, to make it *seem* as though it were gold. Weighing the crown was not proof enough. What Archimedes needed to figure out was the crown's volume.

When he stepped into his bath that day and saw the water rise and overflow, he had a moment of clarity. He realized that the amount of water displaced was equal in volume to what had been submerged. He could dunk the crown in water to determine its volume. And if the volume was greater than the volume of the gold Hiero had supplied, he would know the goldsmith had cheated the king. Archimedes' mind reeled. He was so overcome with the thrill of discovery that he jumped out of the bath and ran into the streets naked and shouting.

There's a similar idea in geology, known as isostasy. It explains how the layers of the earth stay balanced and how different topographic elevations and depressions exist. The earth's crust is a seesaw. If one part of the land gets heavier, it pushes down the crust beneath it, and other areas of the land rebound. When part of the world is sinking, another part bobs up.

On Sunday, a week before I'm scheduled to leave, Danilo suggests over breakfast that we go to Taboga.

"It's an island. It's less than an hour from the city," he says. "A lot of Panamanians who live in the city like to go there for their vacations. People here get four weeks off and they take them all at once, you know."

"You think my father might be there?"

"I don't know. I just think it's one place we haven't looked. And if he's a city guy, it's possible. I mean, anything's possible, but maybe."

The way his voices snags on uncertainty betrays his concern that this, too, will bring us to yet another dead end. I know he feels a particular responsibility for the fact that we seem to be running into so many of them. But the idea of getting out of the city and continuing our search in a whole different locale makes me hopeful, so I tell him we should go.

We board a ferry called the *Calypso Queen Panamá* and sit on the upper level on one of ten or so painted wooden benches lined up like church pews down the middle of the boat. Danilo stretches his legs out in front of him, crossing his ankles and holding himself erect with his hands planted on the bench as he gazes out past the nose of the vessel, the wind streaming against his face. I sit beside him in plaid shorts, Converse, a T-shirt that says "I Rock, but Don't Take It for Granite," and the enormous straw hat I bought on my head. I hold my orange bag on my lap.

The humid sea-salt air whispers by as the ferry chugs along. Flocks of white birds dip and dive overhead, skimming their bodies across the surface of the water. In the distance, through the burnished haze, I can see the Panama City skyline, like a bar graph of shimmering silver buildings, as it recedes. We sail under the Bridge of the Americas, and a white couple, sipping orange soda from glass bottles with straws, points up at it in awe as we glide along. Every so often, the ferry rocks awkwardly and Danilo's body bumps softly into mine.

Forty-five minutes later, Taboga comes into view. I glance at Danilo, who is picking at a scab on his knee. He must have seen it a dozen times—green hills, like the rounded backs of hulking monsters; pastel houses built into their sloping sides; an arc of beige sand at the front; a huddle of rocking wooden boats docked by the pier; tiers and tiers of trees and plants so lush they're all just a mass.

"That's it?" I ask, pointing.

"Good eye," he says sarcastically.

When we step foot on land, Danilo starts off toward the left while the rest of the passengers move collectively to the right.

"Should we be going that way?" I ask.

"They're all going to the hotel. It has a private beach and a place to shower, so people like it. But we're going into town."

We wend our way through narrow cobblestone streets with dogs ambling lazily along the edges of the thick green foliage. We pass a dance hall and a church and a makeshift soccer field where someone has rigged up an old pink shower curtain to serve as a goal at one end. We ask random people on the street and people resting in hammocks on their patios for information about my father, but all we get in return is shaking heads and blank stares. Finally, when we come to a small house that's been converted into a restaurant, we stop.

"I think we should ask here," Danilo says. "I know the

waitress. She's been here forever, so if anyone would know, she would."

We take a seat inside at a small round table under a ceiling fan. When the waitress approaches, I expect Danilo to make his customary inquiry, but instead he orders food: plantains, rice, and a Panama beer.

"Do you want anything?" he asks.

"We're going to eat?"

"I'm hungry."

I order a tutti-frutti soda, a flavor found everywhere here.

"What are we doing?" I ask after the waitress leaves. A bell rings outside, presumably from the church we passed earlier.

Danilo leans across the table. "She's not the one we're looking for."

"Shouldn't we ask her anyway? She might know something."

"You want to ask her? Be my guest."

When she comes back with Danilo's food on a bright blue plate and my soda in a sweaty glass bottle wrapped halfway up the sides in a thin napkin that looks like a cast, I say, "Excuse me. We're looking for somebody. A man named Gatún Gallardo. Do you know him?"

The waitress—she's young, and she wears large gold hoop earrings and a delicate gold necklace with the letter B hanging from it—shakes her head. Her earrings twist and sway, hitting her jaw. "I don't know him," she says. "But I just started this job last week. If he lives here, then I wouldn't know." She looks at Danilo. "Do you live here?"

"Taboga? No."

"The city?" She smiles, then coyly bites her bottom lip.

"Yes," Danilo says. "With her." He points to me. "We live together."

The waitress glances at me as if she has forgotten I was there. "Her? I thought she was, like, your little cousin or something."

Without missing a beat, Danilo says, "That's funny. I thought you were, like, going to get a tip or something." He smiles sweetly and cocks his head.

The waitress stands stunned for a moment before she walks away.

"What was that?" I ask.

He doesn't say anything. He seems annoyed suddenly, maybe at the waitress, maybe at having to defend me, maybe at the fact that my presence interfered with the possibility of hooking up with her, maybe because I wasted time asking her about my father even after Danilo told me she wasn't the one we needed to talk to, maybe some other reason altogether. He gulps down the rest of his beer, then wipes the foam from his mouth with the back of his hand. When he sees the waitress again, he beckons her over.

"Changed your mind?" she asks, standing with her back pointedly toward me.

"Where's Gloria?" he asks.

"She doesn't work here anymore. You get me now."

"Since when?"

"I told you. Last week. She got married and moved to Paraguay."

"She got married? She was, like, eighty."

The waitress turns up her palms. "Love." She looks at me. "You can't explain it, right?"

I take Danilo's lead from earlier, letting impudence get the best of me. "*You* probably can't. You're right," I say.

Danilo snickers.

"Fuck you," she says, and turns on her heel.

"Weak," Danilo says under his breath, smiling as though the whole thing was a game. "But you," he points his fork at me. "That was good."

My heart is pounding from whatever's gotten into me. I can't believe I said that to her. And I can't believe what she said to me. No one's ever said anything like that to me before. Oh God, wait until I tell Beth. But for now I just nurse my soda and feel an unfamiliar sort of euphoria about it all.

By the time we walk out of the restaurant, though, euphoria gives way to disappointment once again beating its wings against the insides of my bones. I really did think—and maybe it was naïve—that all we needed was a change of scenery, that coming to Taboga would somehow break open our search and reveal something new. Danilo must sense my frustration, because after a few paces outside, he says, "Come on!" and starts running, kicking up dust as he goes.

I have no choice but to run after him, the humid air like a web I have to fight through in order to move. My bag bounces even as I try to hold the strap firm. My skin tingles with dissolving sweat.

"Where are you going?" I yell after him, but he doesn't answer.

Soon enough, though, I realize that he's running toward the water. I'm a fair distance behind him and I watch as he bounds over the uneven sand and does a belly flop, fully clothed, onto an incoming wave. Then he stands up and, after shaking his head like a dog, beads of saltwater spraying, turns to see whether I followed him in or whether, as he must have known I would, I planted myself in the sand far from the lapping water.

"What are you doing?" he yells.

"What are *you* doing?" I yell back.

I want to have followed him—impulsively, foolhardily, without any inhibitions. Every time I think I am becoming that sort of person, there's some reminder of how fundamentally I am not.

"I'm swimming," he says. "Do you want to come swimming with me?"

"I don't know."

We're still shouting at each other. A young girl carrying an inflatable raft under her arm is staring at us. She and a slightly older boy whom I take to be her brother are the only other people on this stretch of shore.

"It feels great in here!" Danilo says.

I take off my hat, then pull my bag off my shoulder, over

my head. I look at the kids. They wouldn't steal it, would they? I bend down to untie my shoes.

"Miraflores, I swear to God!" Danilo yells.

"What?" I say.

But I know. I stop untying and walk toward him. When I get to where the sand is darker and packed firmer from the water, I keep going. A film of foam skates over the rubber toes of my sneakers. I take another few steps and feel the water seep in through the eyelets in my shoes. Then the water is to my ankles. To my knees. I bend down as it rises to my waist. It flows under my shirt and when I stand up straight again, my shirt sucks back against my body, clinging to my ribs.

Danilo says, "You know how to swim, right?"

I duck my head under and stroke out to where he is.

When I come up, he says, "I guess you do."

"I took swimming lessons as a kid."

"Oh yeah? So you're good?"

"Not really. But I know how."

"You think you could beat me out to that buoy? See it? Floating in the water?"

"The orange ball?" I rake my wet hair back with my fingers, wondering how I must look to him.

"Come on. Ready?" he says. "Go."

We make it out to the buoy at about the same time. I think I would have won, but anytime I got ahead of him, Danilo grabbed my ankle under the water and dragged me back so he could pass me with a vigorous surge of kicking. It's deep enough by the buoy that we have to tread water. Danilo's T-shirt balloons up around him like the body of a jellyfish. His wet hair, glistening in the sun, sticks up in sharp, separated points like the scales on a pinecone, and he looks off toward the horizon as he works his arms just below the surface. The water is so clear that I can see all the way down to our shoes. I can see his bare waist. I can taste the saltwater on my lips. My nose is a little runny.

"Hey," I say. "Did you know that if it were possible to extract all the salt out of the ocean and dump it over all the land on earth, there would be a layer of salt more than five hundred feet high?"

He dips his head and blows a parade of bubbles across the surface of the water.

"The salt in the ocean is the mineral . . ." I don't know the word for "residue," so I say it in English. "Residue from rocks that . . ." I don't know the word for "eroded," either. "Never mind," I say.

We rise and fall with each passing wave, close enough to each other that when I scull my arms under the water, my fingertips occasionally brush his. Then Danilo shoots up like a rocket, sucks in a deep breath, and drops down, pulling me under the water with him. I flutter my eyes. Danilo smiles and waves. And for a few seconds, we're just floating there, goofily, under the pale aquamarine water, weightless, holding our breath. I don't know what we're doing there. I don't really care. There's just something about it that feels good.

Like a cord has been cut. I'm completely untethered, unconnected, free. Just for a moment.

We sit on the pier afterward, our dripping clothes blackening the wooden slats underneath us as we wait for the ferry. I can see, though I try not to make it obvious that I'm looking, Danilo's every line and curve under his wet clothes. The hair on his arms perks up little by little as it dries.

"I don't know what else to do about your father," he says after a time.

"Maybe we could ask the police or something."

Danilo recoils. "In this country? You think the police are going to help you?" He shakes his head.

I grab the hem of my T-shirt and twist it into a rope, squeezing out the ocean water and watching it plop onto the pier. I run my hand over the rough straw dome of my hat sitting atop my wet hair.

"What?" Danilo says.

"What?"

"You want to say something. I can tell."

I sigh. "Danilo, do you remember when we went to the library and I called all those people in the phone book?"

"Sure."

"One of the women I talked to acted strange when I mentioned my father." I didn't want to bring it up before now, because it seems like it so easily could be just a figment of my imagination or wishful thinking, but I haven't been able to get her out of my mind.

"Strange?"

"I don't know. For some reason I remember thinking that she knew him."

Danilo furrows his eyebrows. "Really? But why? She said she didn't."

"Right. And then I got off the phone thinking that she was a little bit crazy, anyway. I mean, that she was just kind of . . ."

"Fucked up?" Danilo tugs his thumbnail against the chip in his tooth, taking in the information. "Maybe she *was* just fucked up," he says.

"I know. Maybe. But what if she wasn't? Or even if she was, what if she knows something?"

"I don't know, Miraflores. We've asked almost fifty people in this country whether they've heard of your father and no one has any details. I mean, I got you some with Hector Jaén, and I know Hernán told you a little, but I don't know what else you want to do. We could keep asking around, but the way it works here, everyone knows someone who knows someone. Everyone in this country is, like, connected. So if no one knows anything by now, we probably won't find anyone who will."

"I think we should call that woman back."

Danilo looks pained at the suggestion, but the more I think about it, the better an idea it seems. "It couldn't hurt," I say. "You call her this time. Ask her for Gatún Gallardo. See what she says. You can see how she sounds to you. That's all you have to do."

"Do you even remember which woman you called, or do we have to go through all the listings again?"

"She was the second person listed as only Gallardo. No first name."

Danilo runs his thumbnail along his teeth again, then sighs deeply. "I don't know," he mumbles.

"Danilo," I say. I know it's just that he doesn't want me to be disappointed again. "Let's try one more time. Just this one other person. I'm leaving in like a week. There isn't that much time left."

As he stares at me, something in his face, something behind his eyes, crumbles.

"If we can find her number," he says, "I'll give her a call."

We return from Taboga in the late afternoon, our clothes dried to a crisp. Danilo is hungry again, so we stop at KFC for chicken. I think he chooses KFC because he believes it's food that I, as an American, will like. I don't want to disappoint him or spoil the effort by telling him otherwise. We bring it home with us. I'm too exhausted to eat, though, so I go to my room and lie down for a while. Through the wall, I hear Danilo call Nardo and arrange to meet him at the batting cages. After he leaves, I have the apartment to myself, the sounds of halting traffic from the street below drifting in through the windows and the French doors. For the rest of the day, I lie curled up on the bed, my hands pressed between my knees, my hair damp against the pillowcase, as the light outside grows dimmer. I think about my mother for a little while, and about this ridiculous goose chase I'm on, and about sinking under the water with Danilo earlier that day and how crazily much I wanted to reach my hands out and touch his waist and drift closer to him while we held our breath.

I nod off for a time and open my eyes again to pitch blackness. I'm on top of the covers, still in my clothes, my shoes tied on my sockless feet. I sit up slowly, drawing away some strands of hair stuck to my cheek and rubbing my eyes. When I turn on the light, my watch shows it's two-thirty in the morning.

I'm starving, so I get up and find in the refrigerator the cardboard bucket of chicken, a piece of aluminum foil curled around the top, and take it to the kitchen table. I flip on the soft, peachy light above the table. Ants are climbing over the mangoes in the fruit bowl. Two one-liters of Coke stand on a folded paper towel on the floor beside the refrigerator. The chicken is cold and clammy in my mouth, the fried skin knobby and hardened, but I'm so hungry that it tastes like the best thing I've ever eaten. I've finished two legs and a wing when Hernán, dressed in boxer shorts and a V-neck undershirt, walks out from his room.

I don't see him too often these days. He's taken to staying in his bedroom while Danilo and I eat breakfast, emerging only after I've moved on to the bathroom to shower and dress. Even with the shower water running, I can usually hear him pulling plates out and sliding pans around in the kitchen as he prepares himself a meal. By the time I come out of the steamy bathroom, he's usually tucked himself into his bedroom to eat his food behind a closed door. He stays there either until Danilo and I leave or until it's time for him to report to work.

Now Hernán looks surprised to see me. I lay the chicken—my second wing—down on a napkin. Hernán clears his throat.

"I was hungry," I say softly.

He nods.

"Do you want some?"

He appears exceptionally uncomfortable, hanging his hands low over his groin and not moving from where he stands. "I did not know you were awake," he says apologetically. When he speaks, he sounds different from how he usually sounds. It isn't until he opens his mouth again—"I was going to watch television," he says—that I realize he doesn't have his dentures in.

Hesitantly, he makes his way to the small couch at the front of the apartment. From where I sit, I can see him. He takes a pair of headphones from the drawer of an end table and plugs them into a jack at the back of the television. He slides the headphones over his ears, settles himself on the coffee table, and turns on the television. With his hands on his knees, he watches a black-and-white western. I can't tell whether it's a movie or an old television program. Hernán keeps shifting himself into good posture, holding his back and neck perfectly erect for a time before he starts slumping again and then, when he notices he's wilted, straightening himself.

I wrap the bones and bits of skin from my chicken in my

napkin and throw it away. I don't want to go back to bed, so I walk over to Hernán and tap his shoulder. He startles and jerks his body back. He exhales when he sees it's only me, and slides the headphone off one of his ears.

"I didn't mean to scare you," I whisper.

He curls his lips around his gums.

"Can I watch with you?"

"Television?"

"I'm not tired."

He looks distressed at the request, so I'm about to tell him that I'll just read in my room instead when he holds out his hand toward the chair and motions for me to sit. As soon as he unplugs the headphones, sound rushes into the room. He scrambles to jab the volume button on the set until it's just loud enough to be heard. He puts the headphones away and sits on the couch. We watch for several minutes—a group of men tie up their horses and unfurl their bedrolls in an open field—but it's clear he's ill at ease, glancing at me every few seconds then staring at his hands. I think maybe he's embarrassed to be seen in his underclothes or to be seen without his teeth. Maybe he'll relax before long. But at the first commercial he stands up and says, "I think I am tired after all." He makes a show of yawning and stretching his arms overhead.

"I didn't mean to bother you," I say. "I can go to my room. You should stay out here."

"No, I think I'm tired." Then he gazes at me, as if something in my face is causing him immeasurable grief, before grimacing and padding out of the room, back down the hall, to his bed.

All of a sudden, I just want to go home. I'm sitting here cross-legged in an armchair, in someone else's house, in someone else's country. Belonging halfway doesn't make it mine. Belonging to someone who belongs to it all the way doesn't make it mine. I feel like a fraud. And like a failure. And like I'm in everybody's way.

The front door clicks. Danilo walks in and, when he sees me, grins, evidently unfazed that I'm awake in the middle of the night, fully dressed, watching television. He heads for the kitchen, grabs the bucket of chicken, kicks off his sneakers, and comes out to join me, plopping himself on the couch.

"What are we watching?" he asks, pointing a drumstick at the television.

"I think it's an old movie. I don't know what it's called."

He blinks heavily. He's drunk.

"I'm sorry it didn't work out today, in Taboga," he says.

"Yeah."

"You don't look good."

"Thanks."

"Something happened?"

I don't respond. I don't know the answer. Or maybe I do. No, nothing really happened, but I feel misplaced, unwelcome, homesick, hopeless.

"Hey, Miraflores, tell me something about him. Something good."

He's trying to pep me up. "About my father?"

"No, about Michael Jordan. Yes, about your father!"

I've already told him everything I know. What else is left to say? "He loved my mother."

"Of course he did."

"I mean he really, really loved her. I don't know if many people get love like that."

Danilo chomps on a thigh. Then he rubs his eyes and says, "Miraflores, can I tell you something?"

I tense. "Sure."

"It bites ass that we don't have a maid. Everyone else in this fucking country has a maid in their house, but Hernán insists—*insists*—we don't need one. And frankly, that's bullshit. I'm eating chicken out of a bucket because we don't have a maid. I want, you know, like homemade *arroz con pollo* for dinner. I want fucking *corvina* cooked up the way I like it. Is that too much to ask?"

"I guess not."

"You guess not? I'll tell you. It's not."

"You could make those things, couldn't you?"

He shakes his head. He has one whole arm around the bucket as if he's holding a child. "I do breakfast, but that is all that I do." He closes his eyes. I have an urge to climb on top of him. When he opens them again he says, "Why are you all the way over there?"

"I'm like four feet from you."

"You should come over here. Come on, we'll watch television together."

Something's going to happen, I think. How could it not? Not too quickly, but not too slowly, I move over to the couch, narrowing the distance between us from four feet to about four inches. I can feel every atom in between.

"Did you eat?" he asks.

"Yes."

"You ate this?"

"I ate two legs and one and a half wings."

"Impressive. Listen, though, maybe you don't know because you've never had it . . . Have you had it? But I am telling you that real fucking Panamanian *arroz con pollo* like everyone else gets in their house would have been better than this shit."

He's so drunk and so energetically angered by it that I just smile. The lights from the screen flicker in the dark and the sounds from the television, distant voices and riotous laughter, seem to float weightlessly somewhere miles from us. I try to look as casual as possible. I tuck my hair behind my ears and skirt my bangs across my forehead lightly with my fingertips. Danilo sits slumped into the cushions. He laughs after a few minutes, wheeling his upper body around like a wobbly bowling pin and, at one point in the rotation, casting himself toward me. I think, This is it. He's going to kiss me. But instead he tilts his head and puts his mouth to my ear. His hair smells sweaty.

"Don't tell Hernán, but this show kind of sucks," he whispers. Then he reels back. "Hey, where is the old man, anyway?"

"He's in bed."

"What did you do to him?"

"What do you mean, what did I do to him? I didn't do anything. I was eating in the kitchen and he came out, so I offered him some chicken but he said he was going to watch TV, and then I asked if I could watch TV with him. That's all."

"You're sure?"

"Why?"

"I just think it's weird that he's in bed. He's usually up watching his shows now."

"He usually watches TV in the middle of the night?"

"Just since you've been here. He made me go with him to buy those headphones so the sound wouldn't wake you up."

"Why doesn't he just watch TV during the day, when I'm awake?"

"What?"

"Is he trying to avoid me?"

"Did I show you my bruise?"

I wrap my hands around my ankles. "Hmmm?"

Danilo rolls the sleeve of his T-shirt up over his shoulder. "Motherfucker Nardo hit me with his baseball bat."

There's a spot the size of a plum on his arm. It's pink, giving way to brown.

I touch it gingerly with my fingers. "Did he do it on purpose?"

"Yeah, that's a good question. You ask him that."

My nails are short and unpolished. They look so strange to me, running over his skin. I just keep staring at them, afraid to look up at his face. I'm waiting, waiting. I circle my fingers around the perimeter of the bruise. I drag them up to the peak of his shoulder, just under the edge of his cotton T-shirt.

All at once, Danilo drops his sleeve and hands me the bucket of chicken. "Anyway," he says, and flips open his phone even though I didn't hear it ring. "*Aló.*" He smiles. "*Emelinda. ¿Quiúbo?*" He pads away with the phone to his ear.

The cardboard tub is on my lap. I squeeze the rounded rim in my fingers and listen for a time to the sound of his voice, of him making plans to meet up with yet another girl, as it drifts softly through the air.

Eight
Friction

My mother wants to know where the hell the Judean Plateau is. She's been cursing more lately.

"How many letters?" I ask. I've embargoed myself in my room, afraid to come out and face Danilo after the embarrassment of last night. Maybe, I think, he's even repulsed by me, the way I was acting like an obsequious little hanger-on when all he had tried to do was be nice to me. He's probably already complained to Nardo about the fact that I somehow got the wrong idea.

"Six. Is it Judean like Jewish?"

"Exactly. So where do you think it might be?"

"New York."

"'New York' is seven letters."

"Did I tell you that Lucy made homemade strawberry jam yesterday?"

Earlier, she said it was blueberry.

"Save some for me. I'm going to be home soon, you know."

"I know. I have it on my calendar." She hums absently for a moment. I hold the phone away from my ear, straining to discern any evidence that either Danilo or Hernán is awake yet, but there's nothing. Why do I want to see him? I want to explain myself. No, not really. I don't want to revisit last night. Well, then, I just want to make sure everything's okay between us, that I didn't ruin a friendship or whatever other sort of "-ship" we have going on.

"Israel?" my mother asks.

"Yep. To the east is the Transjordan Plateau, which has almost the same topography in reverse."

"More than I need to know, Mira."

"Sorry."

"So everything's good? What are you doing today?"

"Just more research. About volcanoes."

"Tell me where you are again?"

"I'm in Vancouver, Washington."

"Those are two different places."

"Well, there's a place in Canada called Vancouver. And there's a place in the United States called Washington. Actually, there are a lot of places in the U.S. called Washington. Okay, but that doesn't matter. I'm in Washington state, and there's a city here called Vancouver."

My mother gasps. "There's a bug on the window."

"Mom?"

"It's a really big bug."

The front door clicks. Someone going out or coming in?

Or did I imagine it? The air folds into silence again. I wish it were him, knocking on my door like he did that first morning, standing there with his arms crossed, inviting me to go somewhere even if both of us had no idea of the destination.

"Mom, I think I need to go."

"Time to get on with the day!"

"I'll talk to you soon."

Danilo isn't at the hotel. I haven't been back to it since Hernán offered me a place to stay, and as it comes into view now, it's like glimpsing a structure I haven't seen in decades. It's part of another lifetime, one in which I didn't know anyone in Panama and believed that finding my father would be much, much easier than it has turned out to be.

Dressed in his uniform, Hernán is standing stiffly at the foot of the front steps, his hands clasped behind him, his hat pulled low on his forehead. He seems lost in thought, and when I first wave as I approach him, he appears not to recognize me.

"Hernán," I call.

He swings his head in confusion, like someone awoken from a dream, and when he spots me, forces a smile. I wonder if he's still upset that I intruded on his television viewing the night before.

"You're at work early," I say.

He unclasps his hands and gives a firm tug to each of his shirtsleeve cuffs. “Not really.”

“I’m looking for Danilo.”

Hernán rolls his eyes. “You are always looking for him. I do not know where he is.”

“He’s not here at the hotel?”

“No.”

“Have you seen him today at all?”

“I saw him last night, but he wasn’t there when I woke up this morning.”

“What time did you wake up?”

“Seven.”

“And he wasn’t in the house?”

Hernán shakes his head. “Your mother, at home. Doesn’t she miss you?”

The question catches me off guard. “What?”

“Your mother. Doesn’t she want you to come home?”

“How do you know about my mother?”

“What do you mean? I was only asking. I was wondering how much longer you’re planning to be in Panamá.”

His tone is innocent enough. I don’t think he knows about my mother’s illness or that I left her behind like I did. Nonetheless, I can tell—I can see it in the uncomfortable expression on his face—that he hopes I’ll leave soon. I doubt he’s mad at me, but maybe I’ve stayed too long, or maybe I’m just in his way, or maybe he regrets ever inviting me in the first place.

. . .

Danilo isn't at Mi Pueblito, where we went once even though he deemed it a huge swamp of quicksand for tourists. It took us a long time to struggle through the language of that one. But eventually I got his meaning: It was a tourist trap. "Even so," he said, "there's something cool about the fact that people are trying, you know, to hold on to something." He told me he liked going there sometimes when he needed to take a step back from his life.

Mi Pueblito is the Panama City version of Colonial Williamsburg, an assortment of replica buildings—an old town store, a gazebo, a church, residential huts where life-sized clay people are hunched forever over a fake fire—made to reflect what life in Panama was like in earlier days. When we went, Danilo shepherded us past all of it and led us up Ancon Hill, through the dense and overgrown grass and foliage, until we reached a reasonable plateau where we could sit in the heat.

"There's a Kuna Village down there," he said.

I didn't want to tell him that I had read about it in my guidebook. He made fun of me anytime I said that.

"I know. You already know. But what you *didn't* read"—he smiled—"is that they build the floors of their huts so that they're creaky. It's kind of like a tradition, you know. When a man wants to be with a woman in their tribe, he's supposed to sneak into the hut in the middle of the night when the woman and her whole family are sleeping. If he makes it all the way across the floor without waking anyone up, he gets the woman. If he doesn't . . ." Danilo made a slicing motion across his throat with his hand.

"They kill him?"

"They kill him."

"Shit," I said, and Danilo sprang up.

"Miraflores! Such language!" He looked positively gleeful, amused by my transgression.

"What?"

He shook his head. "I don't know."

"I'm not always good," I said.

"Yes you are."

"Well maybe I'm not anymore, then," I said.

We spent nearly four hours that day at Mi Pueblito, and of course, we asked everyone we laid eyes on about my father, and of course, no one even recognized his name. Now, when I don't see Danilo anywhere on the premises, I ask some of the employees if they remember him, but they offer no recognition of him, either.

He isn't at El Dorado, the mall where he took me the one day it rained since I've been here. It wasn't supposed to rain. I had learned that during the dry season in Panama, no matter how threatening the sky looked, no matter how low and full and dark the clouds, rain would not actually tumble from the sky. I knew that because of the myriad times I, glimpsing a purplish-gray sky, remarked to Danilo, *We should bring an umbrella with us*, and Danilo, with a lifetime of experience to back him up, would tell me not to worry because there was absolutely no way it was going to rain. Not until April. I would eye him skeptically and he would say, "Trust me. It's not going to happen."

But it did. One morning I woke to a minor cacophony composed of the sound of rain spitting against the windows and Danilo banging on the bedroom door.

"Miraflores! Are you awake? It's raining."

I was groggy in bed.

"Get dressed," he ordered. "We're going out."

I should have known he wouldn't bring an umbrella.

"I swear to you," he said, "this is the only time it will rain for you in Panamá. You could stay here for the rest of your life and it would never again rain during January for you." He shook his head. "I can't believe it's fucking raining now!" He was giddy about it. "So there's no way you're going to stand under an umbrella for it. This is a historic event, Miraflores. You need to experience it."

The sky outside was perfectly blue and clear, slender needles of rain lit by the sun.

"So that means getting wet?" I asked.

"Exactly."

I wiped my soaked bangs off my face and twisted my hair into a rope that uncoiled almost as soon as I let go.

"Look, you can always dry off later and you'll be good as new. Humans are well designed that way. We have this thing called skin, and it's fairly waterproof. Not waterproof like a fish, because you know when you stay in the bath for too long, your skin starts to wrinkle. That shit is crazy. But waterproof enough, you know, so that when you dry off your skin just goes back to how it was before. So there's no harm in getting wet, okay? I wouldn't do this to you if it were dangerous."

I smiled sarcastically. "Thanks."

We walked four blocks, the rain pattering down on us. We looked ridiculous, strolling as if immune to the fact that long dashes of water were falling from the sky. Other people walking by with their umbrellas hoisted in the air or plastic grocery bags tied over their heads looked at us with puzzlement or derision. But Danilo didn't seem to care or notice, and after a time, neither did I. Maybe he was right. Maybe this was the only time in my life I would get to experience Panamanian rain soaking into my skin and drenching my hair and the fibers of my clothes. Maybe that was something.

"So this is what we're doing?" I asked, after we had passed several more street corners. "Walking in the rain?"

"This is what we're doing first. But we're also going to the mall."

We ended up at El Dorado, a fairly typical-looking mall, not terribly unlike one in any town in the United States. As we cut across the parking lot, I saw a McDonald's and a sporting goods store and something called Collins that looked like a department store. The hallways were covered, but there were no doors, blurring the division between inside and out. At the mouth of each corridor opening, elderly people sat behind wooden folding tables lined with small square papers that, I later learned, were lottery tickets. The papers were in rows, secured by long rubber bands that had been snapped around the tabletop. Each time a breeze swept through, the bottom edges of the tickets fluttered up like a swarm of butterfly wings.

Danilo and I walked inside and sat on the ledge of a fountain in the middle of the mall. Surrounding us were shoe stores and clothing stores and a store that sold embroidered linens being billed as authentic handicrafts, a fluorescent-orange piece of posterboard in the window advertising a sale, "*Venta.*" I looked at Danilo. He was sitting with his hands folded in his lap, an expression of contentment on his face. His soaked T-shirt clung to the slender contours of his chest. His wet hair was sideswept over his forehead. I remember I wanted to lean forward there, in the middle of the mall, and nuzzle my face against his slippery neck, but I turned away instead and stared, through a passing group of girls in flimsy dresses, at the neon Gran Morrison sign down the way, the rose icon blinking every few seconds. Then I noticed it: how loud it was in there. The longer I sat, neither Danilo nor I speaking, the louder it seemed to get. I looked back at him and pointed toward the ceiling. He nodded. I understood why he had brought me there. Without his having to say anything, I understood. Covering the mall was a zinc roof, which was high and spread over an area as large as a cavern. When the rain pounded down on it, the inside of the building thundered so deeply that I swore a herd of horses was stampeding over the roof. The sound swelled and boomed and echoed and reverberated in my chest, and unless it had rained and unless Danilo had brought me there, it was something I wouldn't have experienced.

On one of these outings, I can't remember which, Danilo had, out of nowhere, claimed that there were eight continents spread over the earth.

"Are you trying to sound stupid?" I asked. We'd fallen by then into a sort of teasing camaraderie.

"I usually don't have to try."

"Come on. There are seven continents," I told him. "You know that."

"List them."

"Asia, Australia, Antarctica, Africa, Europe, North America, and South America."

"And what about Central America?"

"What about it?"

"Central America is the eighth."

"Central America is part of South America," I said.

He balked. "What? Here we learn in school that Central America is its own continent. Everyone here thinks that. And if we all think it and we live here, then it's true."

"I don't think that's how it works."

"People here believe it in their hearts, Miraflores, and the heart is a fucking stubborn thing. It makes true what it wants."

"I'm pretty sure there are only seven continents," I said again, and he let it drop after telling me that I was being narrow-minded.

But the heart is a stubborn thing, I think now. It must be or else I should have given up by now. I should go back to the apartment and start packing my things. I should call the airline and book a return ticket back to Chicago. Because I'm tired of looking for people—of looking for Danilo, and for my father, and for my mother underneath everything, and for myself. But something won't let me stop.

The only other place I can think to check is Panamá La Vieja.

I wait at the bus stop for half an hour. Everyone—nearly twenty people have gathered by the time the bus arrives—grumbles in the heat about the wait. I sit toward the front, next to a bald man with a gold lightning-bolt earring in his left ear. He glances at me, then turns away. As the bus growls away from the stop, he swivels his head back around. I'm staring straight ahead, but I can feel his eyes on me.

"*Buenas,*" he says.

"*Buenas.*"

The bus is crowded, packed with people of all ages, and steaming hot despite the fact that nearly every window is open. A woman standing at the front flicks a paper fan in front of her face while she gazes impassively at the city as it slips by.

"You ride this bus a lot?" the man asks.

My neck tenses and I clench my toes in my sneakers. "Not usually."

"I'm trying to get to a restaurant called Firenze. Do you know it?"

And all at once, I think I might laugh. He wants directions? And he looked at me and thought I could provide them?

"I'm sorry. I don't know it."

He squints. "You're Panamanian?"

"Yes."

The man rolls his eyes. "Even Panamanians don't know what's happening in our own country anymore. There's so much that's new!"

And then, as if to prove his point, the bus drives by a construction crane hovering over a new high-rise, like a colossal metal flamingo.

"I know," I say, playing along and smiling. "It's crazy."

"It's a madhouse!"

I'm the only passenger who gets off at Panamá La Vieja. At first sight, no one besides me is on the grounds. If Danilo was here, he would be in one of two places. Except that he isn't in the hollow cathedral when I check. In the small square space made of molded stones, there's nothing but a gray bird pecking at something in the corner. Which leaves only one other spot I can think of.

I see him before he sees me. He's sitting with his legs dangling over the side of the bridge, fiddling with a blade of grass between his fingers. My throat tightens. He looks so serene. Something about the way his shoulders are rounded and the way his fingers fumble with the grass makes him seem inexpressibly forlorn. I feel an aching tenderness toward him that I've never felt for anyone, not even my mother, who at various moments invokes her own sort of tenderness and ache from me. But standing there watching Danilo is different. He doesn't seem small or pitiable or lost, as my mother does more and more. He seems entirely himself, only sunken in an odd sort of gloom.

He peels the blade of grass into two thin strips and then peels those strips into even finer ribbons until the ribbons turn into little more than threads, and gathering them all in his hand, he tosses them out over the edge of the bridge. The strands float down to the water like feathers lit in the breeze. He's rubbing his palms along the thighs of his pants when he turns his head enough that he sees me. He furrows his brow, then scrambles to his feet, brushing his hands hastily against the front of his pants again.

"Were you looking for me?" he asks when I reach him.

I don't know what to say. *Yes, I've been looking for you* makes it sound like I won't leave him alone. *No, I haven't been looking for you* sounds like a lie, because what? I just happen to be stopping by Panamá La Vieja on my own for no good reason?

"I hadn't seen you all day," I say.

There's no one else around. From the bay, I can hear the rush and swell of the water as it brushes up onto the shore and crashes against the rocks behind the seawall. A sewage smell lances sharply through the air. Danilo pushes his hands into his pockets and starts walking past me, up the slight hill I just came down, his strides long and assured. "Come on," he says. "I want to show you something."

The bus rumbles down Avenida Balboa under a cloudless sky. A woman sitting in front of us is wearing over her head a scarf with a purple diamond print, and she hums as we lumber along. Not ten minutes later, as the bus slows, Danilo stands and announces, "This is it. On your feet, Miraflores."

We step off onto a street teeming with traffic. There are a handful of businesses—an auto body shop, a travel agency, a nail salon—but we pass them all and turn onto a side street, into an area that very quickly becomes residential, the houses small and squat, well kept.

Danilo stuffs his hands back into his pockets, keeping them there for the half-mile or so that we walk until we come to the lip of the land hanging over the bay.

The water is brown and foamy, riddled with tiny pieces of debris where it laps at the shore. Farther out, though, toward the horizon, it appears placid, glittering in the fiery late afternoon sun. There are several sailboats with their masts raised bobbing not far off and, in the very far distance, the shadowy smudge of larger vessels lined up in anchorage to pass through the Panama Canal. It's the way all of Panama City seems: a place where the sidewalks are cracked and broken, where people live in buildings that look as structurally sound as if they were built with toothpicks, where the storefronts are soiled from polluted air, where abandoned cars sit on the side of the road and sometimes in the middle of it, where armed guards perform random street checks and stand menacingly in front of even the drugstore, where mangy dogs roam free, and where bits of garbage are caught in every patch of overgrown grass throughout the city, and yet, for all the grit, there's a sublime sort of beauty, too, the way the whole of the city shines in the gracious, broad rays of the sun, the smile—welcoming and sincere and full of life—on people's faces as they walk down the streets, the brilliant flowers blooming in even the most unsuspecting nooks and crannies, the ebb and flow of the bay against the land, the black iron sand swirled into the shore, the songs of birds—like birds I've never heard before—coursing through the morning hours of every single day. It's the kind of discord that exists everywhere, or at least in any place that's large enough to be more than one thing. But it's different here. The beauty and the disarray are everything. They are the edges of Panama, the borders that define it, and there is nothing else in between.

"This is where I used to live," Danilo says.

"Where?"

"Right here."

The nearest house is half a block behind us. We're standing on nothing but dirt studded with pebbles.

"There used to be a house here," he says. "Hernán sold it when he was sure my parents weren't coming back." I'm surprised to hear him bring up his parents. "He thought he'd made us a lot of money from it that he could use to help take care of me. But we burned through it in about two years."

"So what happened to the house?"

"Hernán sold it to a contractor. Guy tore it down after a few months to make way for some condo project, but then the condo project fell through. Anyway, this is where I used to live when my parents were around." He says all of this while keeping his eyes fixed on the water in the distance.

"What was it like?"

"What?"

"The house."

"Nothing special. It was just one floor. My bedroom was in the back. When I was a kid, I used to kneel on my bed and watch my mom through the back window, hanging clothes out on the line. We had some roosters that used to come up and try to eat her ankles, and she had to kick them away. My father killed one of them, once, for being such a pest. He took me out there with him and showed me how to chop the machete through its neck. He told me you had to do it quick. And you had to believe it would die, you had to do it without pity, or else it wouldn't die right away. It would only suffer." He crosses his arms. "My parents' room had air-conditioning. Just a shitty window unit. It fogged up my mom's mirror all the time, and she would hit it with her slipper like she thought she could get it to behave better. I don't know. It was just a regular house."

"It sounds nice."

He turns to me, and if I have ever seen wistfulness etched in another person's face, it's then. "What's your house like?"

"It's just a regular house," I say, smiling.

"Come on. Tell me."

"It's one story, with two bedrooms. One for my mother and one for me. They're right next to each other, so I can hear her sometimes on the other side of the wall. We share a bathroom. The toilet seat is padded."

Danilo turns up his palms and shakes his head.

"Um, it's like . . . it's not hard like a normal toilet seat. It has this padding on it, so it's comfortable when you sit down."

"Most houses in the United States have that? It's popular?"

"Ours is the only one I've ever seen."

"So you and your mother are just weird?"

"A little bit."

Danilo smiles. "Yeah, a little bit."

"There's a small kitchen. And a basement, too. So I guess that makes it a two-story. I'm not sure how that works. But it's nice. It's the only place I've ever lived."

"That's what makes it nice," he says.

The day is darkening, the cover of dusk descending like a veil.

Danilo says, "I think about them sometimes. I don't know whether they ever think about me." He kicks his heel against the ground.

"They do, Danilo."

"You don't know that."

"You're right. I don't know that. But that's what you would say to me in the same situation. And besides, I believe it. I don't think any parent gets through life without thinking about their child, at least sometimes."

"You believed your father didn't think about you."

I shake my head. "No. I believed he didn't care about me. But I always thought that every once in a while he remembered I was out there and wondered about me."

"Hernán used to pester me to call them. Every day he would say, Call your parents, they miss you."

"And did you?"

"I thought that was up to them. The one who gets left behind is the one who deserves to be found. That sort of thing."

I tuck my hair behind my ears, trying to think of what to say.

After several more seconds, Danilo says, "Tell me something else. Tell me about the music in the United States."

"What do you want to know about it?"

"What's popular?"

"I don't really know. I don't listen to what's popular."

"Do people listen to reggaetón?"

"Some people probably do."

"They listen to it at the clubs?"

"I never go to clubs."

"But other people go to clubs?"

"Sure, some do."

"But you don't." He smiles kindly, then peers out again across the water. "Do you see those ships out there?" he asks, gesturing toward the queue of vessels barely visible in the dimming light.

"The ones getting ready to go through the canal?"

"They'll cross from one side of the world to the other. Just like that. That's fucking insane, isn't it?"

I don't say anything at first. "You could go to Brazil. You could visit them."

"I know."

"You should. You could have them back. At least in some way. God, I would take any way at this point, to have my father. I know I have those letters. And what he said in them . . . well, knowing all of that is a lot more than I had before. But if I could just talk to him, even once, my whole life would be different. Come on, Danilo. You could go to them. They're out there. You know how to find them at least."

"Yeah."

"It wouldn't be that hard."

"Was it hard for you when you came here?"

"Sure. At first it was. But then it wasn't. After I met you, it got easier."

Danilo is quiet. I want to tell him more: how much he matters to me, how he makes me feel boundless and switched on, how I'm afraid that I'll go home and go on and never again meet someone like him.

He says, "But if I went to Brazil, you wouldn't be there. I wouldn't have anyone to make it easy for me."

"You might meet someone else."

"I don't think so."

From the house half a block away, a dog yelps into the muggy air and a woman runs out onto the patio to scream at it.

"Lovely country, isn't it?" Danilo says.

"I like it."

"Every year they say we're going to be discovered. We've got cranes up everybody's ass, building condominiums for all the people who are supposedly going to invest here. But I don't know. I don't see it."

"My mother liked it, too. I think it was probably the best time of her life, being here."

"That's what you said."

"I already told you that?"

"Well, you told me she loved it. She should come back."

"I don't think she can now."

"Because of the Alzheimer's?"

I nod. "I mean, I guess she could, but it would be so complicated"—I rub my forehead in my palm—"just all the traveling and everything. I don't know. Plus, I don't know if it would mean anything to her anymore."

Danilo draws a cigarette out of a pack in his pocket and lights it. The two of us are side by side, not meeting each other's eyes, just watching the surface of the water bob and sway, occasionally building up into an undersized wave.

"And what about you?" he asks. "Are you ever coming back here?"

"I don't know."

He kicks his heel again, tamping the dirt. "That's a shitty answer. I mean, if you like it so much, you should just decide now that you're going to come back sometime."

"I didn't say I wouldn't."

"You didn't say you would, either."

I don't want to argue with him.

He takes a few quick drags of his cigarette, the singed odor melting into the air. "You know, Miraflores, if you don't come back, you'll be just like your mother."

I know he says it because he's going to miss me when I leave and he can't bring himself to tell me directly, but it's impossible not to feel upset with him for playing on what he knows is one of my deepest fears.

"I can't believe you said that," I tell him.

"Why?"

"I'm not going to end up like her. I'm not going to *be* her."

"She came here, right? She met someone. And then she went back to her life and she forgot all about him. She acted like she had never even known him."

I set my jaw. "You don't know what she did."

"You told me all of that! And now you're going to do the same thing, aren't you?"

"It was different for her, Danilo. You know that."

"I can't believe you're not, like, more pissed at her."

"I am pissed at her."

"You don't act like it."

"What do you want me to do? I mean, yeah, I'm pissed. I'm fucking mad as all . . . Jesus! She kept everything from me. She took *everything!* But she's sick now, Danilo, and she did what she did, and I'm not going to yell at someone whose mind is slipping away for letting her whole goddamn life slip away!"

"And yours," Danilo adds.

I take a deep breath and lower my voice. "It's not the same."

"But she did take a part of your life from you. A really big part."

"I know."

Danilo throws his cigarette, like a shooting star, ahead of him over the edge of the rocks. "Well, that's very magnanimous of you."

I sigh.

"Look, I only said what I did before, about you becoming like your mother, so you can make sure it doesn't happen. You *can* make sure, you know. You can decide to make it different for yourself. You can be a different sort of person from her."

There's a quivering tension, taut and persistent, skimming somewhere under my skin.

"So are you going to come back?" he asks.

"I don't know."

"Just decide."

"Danilo, I don't know. My life, in case you haven't noticed, is all up in the air right now. I have no idea what's going to happen to me after I get home. I don't even know what's going to happen to me in the next hour."

"So you don't have plans. So you could make plans."

He's trying to be funny, I know, to impart some levity, but it's only annoying. I sigh again, this time louder.

"I'm just saying, how hard can it be to make a decision? Think about what you want. Come on, Miraflores!" Unexpectedly, he stomps his foot. Loose particles of dirt fly up in the air. "See, that's the problem with you. Since I met you, that's been the problem with you. I mean, you like geology and geography and you look at all these fucking maps all the time, and that's cool, but you're not going to get directions for your life from a fucking map."

"I know that!" It's strange to hear myself scream out, into the air, into nothing, and then to hear the scream recede again into silence.

Danilo spits in the dirt. "Whatever, Miraflores."

He walks away.

Nine
Crystallization

There are at least fifteen hundred active volcanoes in the world. There are dozens of variations: shield volcanoes, composite volcanoes, ice volcanoes, mud volcanoes, submarine volcanoes, subglacial volcanoes, supervolcanoes, and on and on. Some geologists dedicate their entire lives to studying them—how they form, how they behave, the chemical makeup of what they spew, what they signify about the shape of the earth as it was before and the shape of the earth to come. But for the average citizen, the most interesting thing about a volcano is in the story of its eruption. People are fascinated by the idea of a fiery swell building underneath the surface of the earth for millions of years only to one day tear through the crust, flaring it open like a bullet shot through the skin of a peach. They imagine the restless lava disgorged into the air like a heavy and tired geyser, globs of superheated rock and ash rising upward and upward as if all the fury and energy amassed within the earth can't be stopped. And they imagine it dropping back down, slugging against the slope of the mountain until gradually, very slowly, it begins to cool.

I was never as interested in volcanoes as other geologists seem to be. But there is something about the process of a volcanic eruption that always strikes me as both beautiful and sad. It's the pain of the earth bubbling up through the surface and ripping it apart. It's the earth's ineluctable heartbreak.

I lie in bed in the morning listening to the frustrated gurgle of the coffeemaker percolating in the kitchen. Chair legs scrape against the floor. A drawer opens—there's the rustle of silverware—and closes.

I have to force myself to go out there. I'm going to tell him that I'll call the airline today. I'll change my reservation. I was only supposed to be here a few more days anyway, but I'll leave now as early as I can. I know he doesn't want to see me, that I've disappointed him, angered him, frustrated him, whatever. But I'll just tell him, *You won't have to see me anymore,* and then slink back into my room. It's so stupid, really. I got too optimistic—about him, about this trip. Two days ago we were on an island, looking for my father. It all feels hopeless now, though, as if the ruse has come to a close. The curtain has dropped.

Danilo is bent over a cup of coffee, his head in his hands,

when I walk out. There's a second mug on the table. I sit and brace myself for whatever he might say. Danilo gets up and walks to the counter, where half a pineapple, already cored, lies on a cutting board. He starts cutting it into chunks.

I'm about to tell him about contacting the airline when, with his back to me, he says, "You know, I called her."

"Excuse me?"

"The Gallardo woman. I talked to her on the phone."

"You did? When?"

"Last night."

"When last night? I didn't hear anything."

He turns and holds up a hand. "Okay, wait a second. That isn't what I wanted to say first." He takes a deep breath. "First, I wanted to say I'm sorry about yesterday. You know, how I talked to you."

"I didn't mean to get you so mad at me."

"I wasn't mad at you. Well, maybe I was. But I'm not now. I just . . . Listen, I hope you know that I've never exactly been friends with a girl. Not once that I can remember. Girls are usually something else to me. But I feel like I can talk to you, or like you understand me or something."

I have a sinking feeling undulating down through my chest and into my stomach.

"I think that's why I got so pissed off yesterday," he goes on. "Now that I know what it's like to have you in my life, I don't want you to, like, step right back out of it again. I wanted you to tell me that it was like that for you, too, I guess, and that we'll still see each other or at least talk to each other sometimes even after you leave."

The sinking feeling bobs back up and is replaced by something else. Joy. Gratification. Wonder.

Danilo butts his hand against his chin and pushes his head from one side to the other. He looks unusually nervous.

"It's like that for me, too," I say.

Danilo looks at me. Surprise registers on his face, but he only says, "Good. That's good. Now we don't have to get in idiotic fights again."

"Yeah," I say, aware of a vague sadness somewhere inside me that whatever I hoped might happen between Danilo and me won't. But it feels light and far away and almost precious compared with the elation of knowing I'm apparently more to him than that. Things don't need to happen between us. Nothing needs to be rearranged or activated. Everything between us is already in its right place.

"But the woman . . ." he starts again.

I'm in a bit of a daze, but I try to focus.

"Just so you know, I tried calling her when we got back from Taboga. I went to the hotel that night and looked her up in the phone book."

"I thought the phone books at the hotel were old."

"The ones in the rooms are. But they keep a current one at the front desk. Anyway, when I called, she didn't answer. I was going to let it go. I mean, I thought if we were supposed to talk to her, she would've answered."

"But you tried her again?"

"Yeah, last night. I just . . . fuck, I don't know. I don't know why I did it."

"What did she say? How did she sound? Did she sound weird to you?"

I readjust myself on the chair, tucking both legs underneath so that I'm sitting on my heels.

"Miraflores, I don't want you to get too excited."

"I know. I'm just asking. How did she sound?"

"She sounded a little off. I mean, yeah, she sounded fucked up."

He looks like he's going to say more, but he turns back to the counter to continue slicing blocks of pineapple and dropping them one by one into a ceramic bowl.

"What did she say?" I ask again.

Danilo holds the knife still against the cutting board. I watch the angles of his shoulder blades through the back of his thin T-shirt, today a heathered blue. They don't move.

"What?" I ask.

"She has a box."

"What does that mean?"

"She told me she has a box of his things."

"My father?"

Danilo nods silently toward the counter.

"What kinds of things?"

"I don't know."

"How did she get it?"

"I don't know."

"Do you think she knows him?"

Danilo spins around. "Miraflores, I don't know. I'm telling you, she's an old lady and it sounded a little like her head was cracked."

I don't know what to say. I stand up, and then I sit back down. I can't stop smiling, and yet I can feel my natural defenses trying to rein me back. "We should go see her."

"I thought you would say that."

"Well, don't you think so?"

"I told her we would come later today, sometime after lunch. She lives in Costa del Este, which should take us about thirty minutes to get to with traffic, but I asked Nardo and he's pretty sure there's a bus that will get us there."

"We're going there today?"

"Don't start freaking out. Let's just see what happens when we meet her."

"She'll know something," I say. "She has to."

Danilo sighs. "Yeah, we'll see."

Her house is a wide, two-story structure faced with vanilla-colored stucco in a gated neighborhood filled with wide, two-story structures faced with vanilla-colored stucco. A black iron fence runs around the perimeter of her property. There's professional, exuberant landscaping—a crowd of bushes and trees and a freckling of aloe plants—and a large, imposing front door made of riveted dark wood. The windows are covered with the sort of horizontal frosted-glass blinds that open and close like gills on a fish.

"Nice place," Danilo says as we approach.

"Is she rich?" I whisper.

"Everyone in this neighborhood is rich."

We don't even have a chance to knock when the door opens, just a crack. A woman with stylishly done short hair and heavy makeup thrusts out her face. "You're the boy?" she asks. The scent of her perfume floods out the door.

"Danilo Pittí."

"And where is the girl?"

Danilo nudges me into the woman's line of vision.

She gasps and throws a hand to her mouth. She has on a set of gold bangles that slide down her arm and tinkle as she does. Then she composes herself and, with her fingertips clinging to her chin, asks, "Your name?"

"Miraflores," I say.

"May we come in?" Danilo asks, laying his hand on the door as if he has every intention of pushing it open even if she says no.

Slowly, though, she opens the door wide enough for us to pass.

Inside, the house is dark, filled with black lacquer furniture and heavy drapes. The sun cuts in at harsh angles through the slits where the drapes fall away from each other or don't quite reach all the way around the sides of the windows. The air smells strongly of onions and of the woman's perfume. I pinch Danilo's arm, but he ignores me. He won't acknowledge how bizarre this is, like I want him to. The woman shuts the door behind us and, without a word, points to a cardboard box on the floor next to an empty silver birdcage with newspaper lining the bottom and an old stereo.

"That's the box?" I ask.

"You speak Spanish?" She looks surprised.

"A little bit."

"No, not a little bit," Danilo says. "She's good."

"Who taught you Spanish?" the woman asks. She has a hooked nose and, even under all her makeup, a smattering of dark beauty spots on her cheeks and along her hairline. Her lips are drawn like pleats. She's wearing a black dress that grazes the tops of her calves.

"I learned it in school. And from my mother."

"Your mother?"

"She always liked Spanish. She wanted me to know it."

The woman turns from me, crossing her arms. I glance at Danilo, as if to say, What's going on with this woman? He widens his eyes and shakes his head so slightly it almost looks like a shiver.

"Do you mind if I look inside the box?" I ask.

"I've had it for years," she says. "I haven't shown it to anyone."

I don't know if that means I can or can't look at it. Is she saying she hasn't shown it to anyone and doesn't want to start now, or that she hasn't shown it to anyone but is ready to break with tradition? And why hasn't she shown it to anyone? Does she know what's inside?

Danilo hands me his house key. "I think it's okay," he says. "Go ahead."

I kneel and put my bag down next to me. Tape stretches across the seam of the box flaps. There's no writing anywhere on the cardboard.

"Where did you get it?" I ask, gazing up at the woman, who is hovering over me, twisting her bracelets around her wrist.

"I found it."

"Where?"

Danilo coughs.

The woman frowns. "I guess I don't remember."

There's something going on between them, some sort of silent communication that I'm not privy to.

"Danilo?" I say.

"Go ahead," he urges.

I tuck my hair behind my ears. "Do you remember when you found it?" I ask the woman.

She rests her eyes on Danilo, then on me. "No."

Something is definitely going on. "You're sure?" I press.

The woman nods unconvincingly. "You should just take it if you want it. Take it and go."

But earlier, when Danilo told me he talked to her, he said that she had a box of my father's things. He said that specifically. How did she know what was inside if she never opened it? Did my father give it to her? Did someone else, upon handing it to her, tell her, This is a box that belongs to Gatún Gallardo?

I stand and look the woman in the eye. Her face is cast in the shadows thrown by the drapes. "Did you know my father?" I ask. "Did you know someone named Gatún Gallardo?"

She blinks several times in rapid succession. Then she cranes her head around me and looks at Danilo, who is still on the floor. "What do you want me to say?" she asks him.

He won't meet my gaze. And suddenly, I understand that he knows. He knows something, and has known whatever that something is since before we stepped foot in this house.

Then, to my back, the woman says, "Yes."

I whip my head around. "Yes, you know him?"

She sighs. "I'm his sister."

Ilsa Gallardo. At one time Ilsa Gallardo de Toro, but when she was widowed she dropped the de Toro. She instructs Danilo and me to sit on the couch, a small tight-backed piece of furniture upholstered in the kind of black velvet that makes it seem as though it belongs in a room called a parlor. She sits in a wooden chair she pulls from the dining table and places in front of us. Stiffly, she offers us both sodas, but she does it only as a matter of civility. I wouldn't be surprised to learn that she doesn't even have any soda in the house. Danilo waves off the offer. He's uncharacteristically quiet, though I can tell by the way he keeps angling his head that he wants me to look at him. I refuse. I can't deal with him right now. There will be time later to think about him and why he brought me here and what he knew and how complicit he was in this setup and to what extent he orchestrated it. Right now, though, I need to concentrate on Ilsa.

"We weren't always close," Ilsa explains. "I'm his half sister, to tell the truth. Our father had an affair, and from the affair had me. It was very painful for Gatún to be around me for a long time. I was a reminder of something he didn't want to know about. Even after his mother learned of the affair, she stayed with our father. When I look at the whole situation now, she should have left him. If a person cheats you that way, they're telling you they don't want you. But Gatún's mother was the sort of old-fashioned Catholic who believed that marriage meant staying no matter what. She lived unhappily with our father for the rest of her life. Gatún and I only became close after our father died." She speaks gently and with a measured cadence. "I'm sorry," she says. "I'm going on."

"It's okay," I tell her.

"I always wondered what you looked like," she says.

"You knew about me?"

"Of course. Gatún told me. He wondered, too."

"What I looked like? He never saw a picture of me?"

"When you were a baby, your mother sent one. But after that, no." She draws her lips tight, the pleats deepening. "It would have been nice."

"I never saw a picture of him, either."

"No?"

"I came here to find him," I say. "I have an old address and I went there, but I guess he doesn't live there anymore. Does he still live in Panama City? Or did he move? Do you have his phone number?"

"No."

"Do you still talk to him?"

"No."

"Do you know how I can find him? Please, I'm running out of time. I'm not going to ask him for anything. I just want to see him, have him see me. If he never wants to meet again after that, it's okay. Please, you have to help me."

Danilo pushes his hand through the top of his hair and grips it, hard.

"I'm sorry," Ilsa says. "He's dead. He died ten years ago."

The back of my neck tenses like someone is squeezing it. My lungs drain. I shift my eyes to various points in the room before, through a doorway, they lock on a gas knob on the stove.

Ilsa says, "I didn't know that it was you on the phone that day. The boy told me when I talked to him that you had tried to call. I thought perhaps it was your mother. She called once before. But as soon as she gave her name, I hung up the phone. I was"—her voice quiets—"very angry with her."

Everything and everyone in the room is perfectly still. It's a symphony of the most immaculate silence. Around the black gas knob, rust spreads like a disease along the stove's porcelain veneer. The surface of the knob is dull, though not worn. It's oblong with a slim fingerhold running vertically down the middle. Like a cat's eye.

"Miraflores," Danilo says. He prods my leg with the tops of his fingers.

I blink and close my mouth purposefully. My lips are dry.

"I'm sorry," Ilsa says.

"Is he really dead?" I whisper.

"I got what's in the box when I went to his house to clean out his things. I didn't keep much. But when the boy said it was you, I told him what I had. I put it in a box and taped it shut for you. I hoped perhaps you would simply come here and take it. I'm sorry. I didn't want to tell you."

The word "eclipse" comes from the ancient Greek verb *eklei-pein,* which is generally taken to mean "to omit," or "to fail." The earth falls into the shadow of a total solar eclipse only once every few years. I know that. The next one isn't due for months. And yet, as I sit there taking everything in, it's as though the moon has made an unscheduled move into the path of the sun. For a moment, the world feels lost in darkness.

First, there are the photographs. Polaroids mostly, ten in all, some of them caked and cracked like plaster, whole chunks of the images missing or dissolved into dust that has settled into the bottom of the frame. They are pictures of my mother, and of my mother with him, and one wallet-sized portrait with rounded corners of me as a baby, lying on my back on our green shag carpet, wearing a lemon-yellow bunting, my mouth in the shape of an O. On the back of that one, in my mother's handwriting, is written: "Miraflores Catherine Reid, 5 months, 1 week." And underneath that, in my father's, only my name—"Miraflores."

I sift slowly through the rest of the photographs. Even though I am seeing my father as he was more than twenty years earlier, it's the first time I've laid eyes on him, the first time I have anything more tangible than my own invention to fill out what he looks like. I want to see myself in him, the resemblance of our features or expressions, but it's hard to tell whether those connective threads are there. In the two photos where he appears, he is slender to the point of looking lanky, the flared bottoms of his dark brown pants emphasizing the narrowness of his knees and thighs. In both photographs he is wearing a printed button-down shirt tucked into his pants, which are held up by a wide leather belt. He is smiling wide, an irrepressible joy bursting through the seams of his features. His teeth are white and straight. He has a neatly trimmed mustache. His hair is wavy, pure black, parted deeply on one side, and giving way to sideburns. In one photograph he has aviator sunglasses; in the other I can see his eyes, shining with the same sort of ebullience that defines the rest of him. He looks, I think to myself, like a man in love. With my mother, I assume, but also with the world, with the whole crazy tangle of life. In one photograph he is standing next to my mother with his arm slung over her shoulder, and in the other he is demurely holding her hand. Both were clearly posed. I imagine them asking a passerby on the street to take a photo of them, and then the two of them huddling together eagerly over the glossy Polaroid paper, waiting for the result to crystallize into being.

The images of my mother, in photograph after photograph—my mother's back as she walks down a street in Panama City; my mother sitting on a step outside a small shop, her legs crossed; my mother posing sidesaddle in a hammock with her arms thrown up in the air and a triumphant grin on her face; a blurry close-up of my mother's smile and imperfect teeth; my mother in a navy blue bathing suit, displaying in her cupped hands an assortment of seashells she must have collected from the beach; my mother waving at the camera; my mother curled up and sleeping in her dress on a couch as the sunlight drapes in through the windows—are in a way more astonishing to witness. She looks familiar enough; I have seen other photographs of her from the early eighties, the mid-eighties. Her hair was darker then, parted in the middle, falling straight down past her shoulders. She wore polyester dresses with exaggerated collars and platform sandals that crossed in an X over her toes and buckled at her ankles. But in another way, looking at her in these new pictures throws me off kilter even more than seeing my father for the first time. Because in all the photographs I've seen—not only from that time, but ever—she has never looked so carefree, so utterly and unabashedly happy, so perfectly radiant as she does in these. In all my life, I have never seen her look like this.

Then the letters. The ones from my mother are on top, the airmail envelopes stapled to the upper left corner of each.

Gatún,

I'm so sorry—really I am—that I didn't say good-bye to you before I left and that I didn't tell you where I was going or anything of the sort—I was just so confused—and so much has happened—and I didn't know how to tell you about it. I needed to figure some things out on my own first. I hope you'll forgive me. But here is the news—I hate having to give it to you in a letter like this, but I don't think I could bear to call you and hear your voice and hear your reaction—I'm so afraid for what it might be—and you'll have questions I don't know how to answer yet. But here it is: I'm pregnant. I'm going to have a baby—and it's yours—I'm sure—it's not Brant's—there's no way it could be—it has been too long between he and I—but you don't need to know that, I suppose. I'm having your baby. Maybe you can understand now how my head got all turned around. I've come back to my parents. I haven't told them about you yet—but I will—I swear it—and together we'll figure everything out—but for now I just wanted you to know. Part of you is inside me. Part of you will always be with me.

Your little bird,

Catherine

Gatún,

So much has happened—and I've been thinking it over—and perhaps it would be best for me to stay here and have the baby here and live here with the baby on my own. I know you *said* you were excited—but I also know that a child right now was not exactly in your plans—and I don't want it to become a burden for you—you shouldn't feel any responsibility. Besides that, it's just not a good time here—you don't understand how people here can be—their attitudes, their judgment, that sort of thing. I'm going to stay here for now—and you should stay there for now. Maybe in the future something can change.

Catherine

Gatún,

We have a baby girl—you have a new little bird. She's a week old now—with the most perfect feet and elbows and nose—the most perfect everything. We are staying with my parents—they've insisted—no visitors. I'll write again soon.

Catherine

Gatún,

It's the hardest thing—you can't imagine—I can't believe—but you have to stay where you are—it will just be better for everyone—and you should try to forget about me—about the baby—it's no use—it wouldn't be good here for you—I can't think straight but I know that—and it would make her life more difficult—and yours—and mine—so you should just go on—and we'll go on—and you shouldn't worry—there are lots of single mothers—and I'll just be one more—but whatever you do you should pretend that I never happened—and I'll do the same about you—and life can continue without all the complications—we'll just release each other—just like that—we'll let each other slip away—and it will all just be like a dream that we've woken up from now—that we walk out of without looking back. It's best that way.

Catherine

Gatún,

I'm sorry.

Catherine

The rest are stacked loosely, unencumbered by envelopes or paper clips or staples. Page after page on onionskin paper, written in the same handwriting that graced the letters I found in my mother's room more than a month earlier. All of them undated, all of them unsigned, and all of them for some reason unsent.

Dear Catarina,

I wonder sometimes whether you really know how I feel about you. I have trouble putting it into words, so I probably didn't tell you as often as I should have or as well as I wanted to. I'm not a poet. I'm only me. But I do want you to know, if you didn't know it before, that you changed my life. When I met you, you were a spirited, funny young girl who couldn't stop talking. You ordered *seco* in the bar and smoked cigarettes on the street. You drank Coca-Cola straight from the bottle and I remember you always wanted to keep the bottle when you were finished. You would slip it into your pocketbook to take home with you. Why? What did you ever do with all those bottles? I always wondered. And do you remember our first kiss? In my kitchen? I was cooking *plátano* and you were humming at the table and then you walked up behind me and laid your hands, like two soft paws, on my back. Catarina? I said. Gatún? you said. And I laid the fork down and turned to face you, the palms of your hands skimming around my body until they stopped on my chest. You started humming again, and then you smiled and rose up on your toes and kissed me. I never knew the name of that song.

I remember how you kept your shoes on the first time we went to the bed together. You giggled when I unbuttoned your blouse. You breathed against my neck in the dark. And that one night, you fell asleep afterward with your hand resting so gently on my thigh.

I was in love with you. I'm still so in love with you. It seems like it should be fading by now, but it only gets stronger. I can't stop thinking about you and remembering you. On the street, I don't see anyone else. No one else registers. I could live a hundred more lives and a hundred years in all of them and never again find another person besides you.

I don't know what to do now without you. I feel like I'm on a carnival ride, spinning around and around, dizzy, unable to see anything clearly. My life now depends on being with you. My life! You'll think I'm exaggerating, or that I sound too desperate to be taken seriously, or you'll be frightened because I never told you all of this, even though I should have.

Please write to me. I don't have a phone number for you in the United States, even though I tried to find one though the administration offices on your base. They produced one that rang in a small town in New York, but the woman who answered told me it was the wrong number. I only have these letters. I'll wait for your handwriting. I'll wait for you, *mi pajarita,* however long it will take. I'll be loving you exactly like this every day for the rest of my life.

Yours

Dear Catarina,

Thank you for the photograph. I can hardly stand to look at it, although it's all I want to look at. She looks so . . . No word, in either English or Spanish. It is cold there? Please send more. Take one every day so I can see how she's growing.

Dear Catarina,

I don't know why I write to you anymore, except that I can't help myself. I feel compelled to share my life with you, even if you don't want to receive it. I haven't heard from you in months. The girl is nearly a year old now. I still think of her as "the girl." It's too painful, her name, what meaning it has. I wonder all the time what she looks like now. I see children on the street and have to duck into shops sometimes to weep.

I'm still working at the canal, although I'm on the maintenance crew now. Today we started cleaning and repairing one of the gate leaves. It was quite an operation, watching the crane barge lift the gate from its slot and take it to the dry dock at Mount Hope so that it could be laid down for us to work on it. One of the men on my crew told me that each gate weighs twelve tons. It's all new to me.

I was moved from my previous post at the Miraflores control tower because of a stupid mistake. In all of canal history—forty ships passing through every day!—there's never been a single collision, but I almost caused precisely that because of my carelessness. I was managing the log and somehow, because I was not paying close enough attention, I radioed to two separate vessels that they could enter the locks at the same time. I didn't know what I'd done until the operator on the ground starting blowing his whistle frantically. Hector Jaén (do you remember him?) and I both ran to the window of the control tower to see what was going on. The operator was pointing toward the two oncoming ships and doing what, to be truthful, looked like a vigorous jumping-jack routine. When I looked, I saw one container ship and one coaster ship both headed toward the entrance of the locks from opposing angles. Hector Jaén grabbed the nearest radio receiver from the wall and called the captain of the coaster ship (it was smaller, so it could stop more quickly). The captain asked what the hell was going on. Hector Jaén implored the captain please to stop his boat. There were a few prolonged minutes of arguing, in which the captain tried all manner of threats and reasonings ranging from that he didn't see why he should be expected to stop, to that he had been traveling for a week already, to that he knew the governor of California, and finally, to that his ship was carrying human hearts for people awaiting transplants in Africa, a falsehood which Hector Jaén didn't even dignify with a response since both of us could see from the log that the ship was clearly headed to Asia and that it held 75,000 pounds of onions. When Hector Jaén told the captain of the coaster ship to stop, or else he would risk imperiling the crew's life, the captain finally agreed. The container ship went through the locks and, an hour later, the coaster ship passed as well. I don't think I exhaled once during the whole ordeal.

The *Panama Canal Spillway* ran a front-page story about it. Hector Jaén asked me what I could have been thinking. I didn't tell him that I was distracted because I'm depressed. I think only of you. He wanted to fire me. I begged him to let me stay. I told him my job was all I had. It's true. After you left, it became the last thing that mattered to me. I told him I would do anything. He took pity on me and recommended me for a job in the maintenance division.

Still yours

Dear Catarina,

All day at work I hear the shrieks of the howler monkeys echo throughout the rain forest. When I first started working at the canal, I hated that sound—I heard the shrill bursts in my dreams—but now I find that if I go too long without hearing it, I almost miss it.

Yours

Dear Catarina,

It's the rainy season. You remember it well, no? The way the sky is given to fits of rain that pound down for a few minutes and shut off again. I walked you to the bus stop that night from the bar when it was raining and neither of us had an umbrella and your blouse clung to your skin.

The streets in the city flooded today.

Maybe you're sitting on the other side of the ocean, writing letters to me, too, that you'll never send. Maybe you still think of me. Is there a chance for us?

Dear Catarina,

This morning for breakfast I ate an overripe mango smothered in honey. I had a cup of coffee and then I went to work. Sometimes I go even on Sunday when I'm off. I stand around and watch the lumbering ships pass by in front of me. I stay until dusk and watch the sun set, the orange glow spreading out against the sky. After the lights in the water lanes and control towers flicker on, I return home. I wash my clothes. I have a drink. I sit in the dark and remember you.

Dear Catarina,

It's been another year, and still I've heard nothing from you. I feel crazy still expecting to.

I've been transferred to the canal's dredging division since I last wrote. We scan for abnormal deposits of silt and mud on the floor of Gatún Lake—conditions that could lead to a mudslide. Every day, I ride in a little tugboat with four other men and drag a tool through the water that beeps when the floor levels are off. There are fish gliding through the water, too, and we place bets on whether one of us can catch a fish with his bare hands. Every time I try, I pull my hands up with nothing but water streaming through my fingers. Last week one of the men (Mario) did nab one (a big one!) and we took it to the cafeteria and had the cooks fry it for lunch.

Also last week I learned that one of my crew had made an arrangement to receive some baseballs from one of the ship captains who come through the canal often. Did you know that the New York Yankees visited Panamá once? I've never seen it, but at Balboa High School, in the Zone, there is a shattered window from when Joe DiMaggio hit a home run through it. That probably doesn't impress you. In the

United States, I imagine you see baseball stars all the time. But here, for us, well, you know how important baseball is. When the captain of the ship was lined up in anchorage, we steered our tugboat alongside and a young sailor came out onto the deck and tossed baseballs—one for each of us—overboard as we caught them. I put mine in my kitchen cabinet for safekeeping.

I hope you're well.

Yours

Dear Catarina,

I was walking down Avenida Central this afternoon, looking for a new brown belt, when the rain roiled up out of nowhere. I stepped into a fabric shop to keep dry until it passed. In the front of the shop was a young woman, she couldn't have been much older than you, sewing on a machine. I watched her as she pulled pins out of what had just been sewn, as she made folds and measurements in what still needed work, as she held the needle between her lips. I thought of your lips. And then, feeling like a creep, I moved to the back of the store. Bolts of fabric were propped up and leaning against the walls, one in front of the other. Where the fabric ran off the end of the roll, it hung down over the bolt behind it, as if in an embrace. I thought of you again. It seems there's nothing in this world that doesn't remind me of you.

Yours

Dear Catarina,

I went to a *quinceañera* for a friend's daughter. Actually, I don't know him so well. He's the bartender at El Cuarto Paitilla, but he's fond of me (probably for the money I spend there) and invited me to the celebration.

It was quite an event. When I arrived, the boys were in the driveway playing jacks, but they were all dressed in *montunos* with striped *chácara* bags slung over their shoulders and fine *ocueño* hats on their heads. Do you remember when we saw the men in the parade dressed like that? The girls wore *polleras,* and the bartender's daughter wore a *pollera de gala* that he told me cost fifteen hundred dollars to have made. She wore another three hundred dollars' worth of gold jewelry on top of that.

Nearly a hundred people were in the backyard, walking around in their finest clothes and perfumes. I wore starched pants and my best *guayabera.* And of course my hat. They must have spent a lot on decorating, too. Strands of colored bulbs were strung from beam to beam all the way around the perimeter of the yard, like walls of light. Round tables draped in pink tablecloths had been set up, with enough space left over for a dance floor. At the front was a head table with flower petals sprinkled over the length and an arrangement made from birds of paradise in the center. As soon as enough people were settled, waiters charged like bees from a nest with flutes of champagne for everyone. I didn't know anyone there, so I sat at a half-occupied table with a few people who clearly didn't know anyone, either.

The girl's grandfather made a toast, telling us that he paid a lot of money for the party, enough that he could have bought a new car. He asked the crowd if we'd seen the new Alfa Romeo Quadrifoglio Verde. When no one answered, he said, "It's very nice. Of course, not as nice as being able to celebrate my granddaughter in grand fashion. Of course! There is no comparison. Of course. But I paid a lot of money nonetheless, so I hope you enjoy yourselves. *¡Salud!*" Then he thrust his glass high above his head and finished his champagne, licking his lips when he was done.

When the girl made her entrance, she strutted slowly, holding the corners of her long *pollera* skirt up like a crescent, showing off the intricate appliqué. She turned on the dance floor while people took photographs. The boys poked one another when they saw her. I clapped politely.

Later, after he had drunk too much champagne, the girl's grandfather tipped backward in his chair and fell into the wall of lights behind him, pulling the whole thing to the ground like a bedsheet from a laundry line. After the initial shock, everyone broke out in laughter, but I didn't have the heart. By then, I was lost in my own champagne and my own head, quiet and alone at the table.

Do I have to tell you that I missed our daughter? Is it possible to miss someone you've never met? And I wondered, as I often wonder, what she must be like. I believe she must be prettier and, I hope, far humbler than this girl was. I know it will be the great regret of my life that I'll never meet her. I feel delirious with anger at you sometimes because of it.

Dear Catarina,

I don't know why I didn't think of it sooner. But today I had the idea that I could jump aboard one of these ships passing through and ride it to the United States, to see you. I looked at a map and Chicago's in the middle, no? I could take a ship that docks on the eastern coast and then take a train from there. Is that possible? Will you want me to? I know you told me not to, but can that still be true? If I were to arrive, and there was nothing you could do about it, I think once you saw me again

I stopped this letter in the middle of writing it, because I scared myself. All of a sudden, anything seemed possible. What if I did it?

I got Hector Jaén to let me back up in the control tower to look at the log. There's a ship sailing through to Savannah, Georgia, that leaves tomorrow. Tomorrow! I might see your face again! I want to lie next to you and hold your face in my hands. Listen to this! Me, getting so carried away. All is forgiven for never writing me back. I know your energy has been spent on other matters, like raising our daughter. Look for me soon.

Until then and always

Dear Catarina,

God must be watching over me. I didn't board the ship. What a fool I would've made of myself! I promised I would stay away and I will.

I am yours.

Dear Catarina,

The comet Halley is supposed to pass tonight. People are gathering on the sandbank of the bay to watch the sky catch on fire. The newspaper ran an interview with a woman who was alive the last time it passed, in 1910. She said that back then there had been paranoia because everyone thought that the gas in the tail of the comet was a poison that would shower down. Of course, that did not happen. She said it was like an electric peacock flashing across the black sky. I can hardly imagine. Everyone is so excited. Everyone keeps talking about how spectacular it will be.

Yours

Dear Catarina,

I learned today that I'm sick. My lungs and liver are damaged and failing. I knew it was something, although I would've guessed it was my heart. The doctor said it was too much drinking and too many cigarettes. But then he looked at me and said, "Depression has taken its toll, hasn't it?" He knew. I've been drinking and smoking for a reason.

Not that it matters. In the end, it doesn't matter whether it's my liver or my lungs or my withered heart. God has a stubborn will; He takes each of us when He wants.

Off and on for five years now I've been writing you these letters. I woke each day with the dim hope that I would somehow hear from you. I've thought about you all this time. Are you still in Chicago? Are you in New York? The fact that I don't know breaks my heart. I always thought that, after enough time had passed, I would find you again. I always thought that you would finally allow yourself to be found. I wonder sometimes what I meant to you, and whether I was only one in a parade of men, a lover easily eclipsed by others. I try not to think about it too much.

The doctor says that if I start to take care of myself, I could go another few years still. He says if I toss out the alcohol and cigarettes (and cigars!) and if I start exercising, I'll improve for a time. I don't know whether he's telling the truth or just trying to make me feel better. No matter how long I can extend it, though, my time is limited.

Either way, with the news has come the urge to collect the pieces of my life, remember them, and soothe myself with them, like a baby with his blanket. Only I've found that there aren't many pieces to gather—in my life there were my parents, there was the canal, and there was you. It seems pathetic to admit. Then again, I had real happiness once. A blinding, burning happiness. It was because of you.

I still love you, Catarina. I wanted to at least write those words down on paper one last time, to have a record of them in the world.

There's nothing else to say.

I lay the last letter down slowly and straighten the edges of the pile with my fingertips. I stack the photographs on top. There is nothing else in the box. Danilo stares at me with a blank face. From the floor, I peer up at Ilsa, who has perched herself on the arm of her sofa and is moving her mouth in tiny motions, as if she were eating birdseed.

"Can I keep them?" I ask. I don't know whether it's appropriate. It feels a little like walking into someone's house and seeing a teapot you like, or a television, or a rug—an item that's patently not yours—and asking if you can just take it. But I feel desperate to own the letters, to take them with me, and be able to look at them again and again.

"They're more yours than mine," she says.

Even though the box is bigger than it needs to be for a handful of photographs and sheets of paper, I don't know whether I should leave it behind, so I drop everything back in and pick it up, light as a hat, as I rise to my feet.

"I remember when he met her," Ilsa says. "He didn't say anything, but I could tell something was going on with him. And eventually I got it out of him. He had been waiting to get his shoes shined and he saw her walk by with a roast pig in her arms. She had come from the butcher. She dropped it and he went to help her pick it up. He was never the same again."

"He used to get his shoes shined?" My voice sounds weak.

"Every week. Until he couldn't afford to any longer. Then he did it himself. He was a bit of a dandy, your father."

I nod.

"I could tell you more," Ilsa says, "if you want to stay. And if you want to know."

I want to know everything.

"Come on," she says. "Sit back on the couch."

Danilo is still there, and I drop myself beside him, resting the box on my lap.

"What can I tell you?" Ilsa asks. She crosses her legs and stacks her hands atop her knee. The skirt of her dress hangs like a gaping mouth.

"What did he like?"

"What do you mean?"

"What were some of his favorite things? His favorite food or music or something?"

"He very much liked strawberry ice cream. Since he was a boy. And there's something here called a *carimañola.* Do you know it? It's a fried yuca roll stuffed with meat. He would have eaten that every day if he could. For music, I don't know. He liked Tito Puente. Do you know him?"

"I've heard of him."

"And that North American singer with a Mexican name—Joan Baez. He had cassette tapes that he recorded from friends' albums because he could never afford to buy the originals at the store. But he didn't listen to them that much that I remember. He would rather have been walking through the neighborhood, stopping to chat with people outside."

"What neighborhood?"

"He grew up in Río Abajo. I only saw him when I was sent over to his house to visit my father. Their house always smelled of menthol ointment." Ilsa makes a face.

"Did you ever meet my mother?" I ask. "When she was here?"

"No, I never met her. I saw her once. She had long hair and a blue dress. Very pretty. I was at his house, dropping off some pants I had hemmed for him, and she arrived, fresh off the bus. He was waiting for her at the window. I remember because he had told me that when she came, he was going to go outside to meet her and that he would take her for a walk. He wanted me to slip out before they returned."

"Why?"

"Oh, Gatún was so self-conscious. Not because of her. But because he was so much older, I suppose, and because he was *un panameño* and she was *una gringa.* He didn't care, of course. But he was always afraid of other people's judgment. He knew how cruel people could be and the kinds of things they might say."

"You wouldn't have been like that, would you?"

"No. And he knew that. But he was just so protective of her by then. He was always nervous about upsetting the equilibrium of her life and about making her life difficult for her."

"She did that for herself."

"Excuse me?"

"Nothing." I change course a bit. "Did you know she was married?"

Ilsa's eyes widen. "Later, you mean? She married?"

"No, while she was here. That's why she came here."

"She was married? When she was with Gatún? To whom?"

"A Marine. He was stationed in the Canal Zone."

I'm twisting my fingers together. What must Ilsa think of my mother now?

"She was married to the Marine?"

"Did you know him?"

"The one . . ." Ilsa shakes her head. "But no. She was married to him?"

"His name was Brant."

Ilsa appears confused now, squinting and holding the tip of her tongue between her teeth as she focuses on something on the wall behind me. "I think . . ." she finally says. "Maybe I have the story wrong. But I thought the Marine was a homosexual. Only a friend."

My eyes widen involuntarily. "Brant Strickland?" I whisper.

"Strickland. Yes, that was his name. Gatún told me he was only a friend to your mother. Maybe he meant . . ."

"But they were married."

"Maybe he meant it was only *possible* for him to be a

friend to her since he was . . ." Ilsa gazes at her lap and murmurs, "I'm sorry. . . . I probably have it wrong."

I fix my eyes again on the gas knob and try to sort out the thoughts in my mind, but everything is crowded and knotted like a bramble of thorns. He was gay? Surely my mother didn't know that when she married him. Although maybe she suspected it. What was it she'd told me once, "It wasn't right from the beginning or the middle or the end"? And it made sense, then, how she had allowed herself to have an affair, how she would even have been receptive to the possibility. My head is pounding. The box of letters is at my feet, my bag slumped on top of it. My bangs are getting too long, hitting my eyelashes each time I blink. Out of the corner of my eye, I see Danilo's knee, cloaked in olive cargo pants.

Ilsa says again, "Maybe I'm wrong."

I shake my head. She's right. It all fits.

She realizes it, too, because she goes on. "It's probably why . . ." She turns the bangles on her wrist, then lets them hang. "I doubt he cared very much that your mother was with Gatún, then. Assuming he knew. It would have been ridiculous to stop her. He couldn't have expected loyalty from her in that circumstance."

Danilo sighs and falls back against the couch in apparent disbelief at this twist to the story.

"It probably made things worse when she got pregnant," I mumble.

"Why?"

"It was one thing for her to carry on an affair. He probably thought no one would find out about it, anyway. No one from home, I mean. But there was no way to hide having a baby that wasn't his. I mean, there was no way it was going to look like him. It was like a very public fissure"—I say the word in English—"in their relationship. Everyone would know that they weren't working. And then people might start to wonder why. They might have started asking questions." I'm unspooling everything almost as if I'm just talking to myself.

"Maybe I should have known they were married," Ilsa says, regaining her voice. "Why else would your mother have been here, in Panamá? I just didn't think about it. Gatún never made it clear."

I take a deep breath. I'm going to need some fresh air soon. "Did he find someone again, after my mother?" I ask.

"No."

"No one?"

"There were women. They came and went. But no one who meant anything to him. Your mother was the only one for him, I think. He never recovered from her."

"I don't think my mother ever recovered from him, either."

Ilsa frowns. "It would have been nice if he could have known that. You can't imagine the sadness that lived in him after she left. It dislodged part of his soul. He carried that around with him every day. It was always there. If he had known, if she could have at least told him, that she still cared about him, what a difference it would have made."

"She couldn't."

"What?"

"She couldn't tell him. I mean, she wouldn't let herself." I sigh. "I didn't know her then, obviously. And I'm just putting everything together now, but that same sadness that you say my father had, for my mother I think it turned into anger."

Ilsa makes a fist and holds it in the air. "Like this? She grew hard?"

"Yes. She grew hard."

She opens her hand and sinks her other thumb into her palm. "What's inside?"

"The sadness is still there, too."

She adjusts the hem of her dress and straightens in the chair. Next to me, Danilo straightens, too.

"Your father wasn't alone, though," Ilsa assures me. "He had me. And people liked him. Everyone liked him."

"Did he talk about me?"

Ilsa shakes her head. "Not often. I knew about you, of course. But I think it was too painful for him to talk about you openly. And what did he know? What was there to talk about? He could only wonder what you must be like. To see you now! Here! In his country! He would have been overjoyed. Very astonished and very pleased. You look like him. The roundness of your nose. The way your mouth curves."

"I do?"

"He would have been very happy to see that."

"I thought he abandoned us," I say. "I didn't know . . ."

"It wasn't your fault."

I know what she's insinuating. "My mother did love him," I say.

"Maybe."

"She did. You don't know her."

"I know enough. I read her letters. I know how she broke him."

But Ilsa is wrong. I know, like my father knew, that my mother didn't want to write the things she had. She hadn't meant them. The words on those sheets of paper weren't her. They were the words of someone who had become hardened, her emotional self calcified, by the kind of heartbreak that happens when someone—not you or the person you love—forces your heart to break. It was her parents. They got to her. And my mother, no matter how strong she liked to seem, was like anyone else—weak and scared and pliable. I recognized that when I read the first batch of letters, but there's a new force behind knowing it now. It rolls up like a wave and crashes over me. Out of nowhere, I realize it: I came here for her. I thought I came here for me, to find my father. I thought I came here because I wanted to meet him, and because for so long my mother has been all I've had and now there was this possibility that there could be someone else. And I did come here for those things, but—and I see it so, so clearly now—I came here for her, too. Because even though I've been walking around feeling angry and confounded and cheated and resentful, underneath that mess is still the simple bit of knowledge that she loved him. Guilelessly and hopelessly, she loved him. She still loves him, I'm sure, even if she'll never say it. When everything else flees, every other memory and experience that made up her days, I think my father is the last thing she still wants to have. She pretended to let go of him because it was the only way to hold on. In a heartbeat, it all becomes clear to me. I came here because I wanted to deliver him back to her. I wanted to give her back the best part of her life before she forgot she ever had it in the first place. I was trying to reclaim a past I never knew until recently that I had, and I was trying to reclaim for my mother a past that too soon she would never be able to find her way back to again.

I stand up with the box pressed against my abdomen. Danilo stands, too. I feel dizzy.

"I'm sorry," Ilsa says. "I didn't mean to offend. I try to believe that she was doing what she thought was best, or at least what she thought was easiest. The two often masquerade as the same thing."

"I need some air," I say, making my way to the door.

Ilsa follows behind saying something about how I can call her if I have more questions and something about bus fare and again how she's sorry, but I can only concentrate on getting outside to clear my head.

For the next three hours, I walk without breaking my stride. I can't stop. I can hardly feel my legs, and yet they keep making the motions they're supposed to make, one foot in front of the other, leading me forward. Each time I near a dead end, I make a quick right or left turn and keep going. Danilo follows behind me at a distance, kicking through the gravel.

The day is pallid and humid, as if it's sick. It takes a while, but eventually I make it out of Ilsa's neighborhood and back into the heart of the city. My arms are wrapped tightly around the box, the cardboard corners digging into my biceps. I walk past storefronts, some sealed off with corrugated aluminum gates covered with graffiti, and past a row of residences with openwork concrete-block fences at the edges of their yards. On one corner, a young boy ties a rope around a bundle of newspapers in preparation to walk through busy intersections with the papers in his arms, trying to sell them to motorists stalled at red lights. And the entire time, I feel so extremely aware of myself slicing through the world, of the largeness of everything around me, and of myself, charged like a lightning rod in the middle of it all. I feel electrified and peculiar and crushed by sorrow.

If, at some earlier point in my life, someone had described this situation to me, everything that had happened, and asked me to guess how I would have felt at this moment, I think I would have imagined myself pacing around in a state of disbelief, not knowing how to take it all in. But as I walk that afternoon, that isn't what I feel at all. I believe that my father is dead. I think perhaps some part of me believed that, or at least suspected it, long before Ilsa told me. It's been so difficult to find him, after all, and at some point I sensed the futility of the search. So that's it. He's dead, and I never knew him. I thought I knew him once, what sort of man he was, only to learn that he was a different person entirely, one I think I would have liked if I'd gotten the chance to spend even one minute of my life with him. But I won't find out now. It's over.

As I walk, thoughts drift toward me from every direction, their edges overlapping like playing cards. Ilsa's house. How dark it was inside. The birdcage on the floor. The revelation that Brant, my mother's husband, was actually gay. And how overt had he been about it? How had my mother known? The letters. My mother. How complicated she seems to me. How much she has endured and made herself endure even when she needn't have. How furious I am with her. Furious anew. About what she did to him. My father! And at what she had done to me, denying me him for the few years we shared on this earth. He was here in Panama, lovelorn, broken by the thought of her, hopeful and bitter, obedient and scared. It's amazing how much he loved her. It's amazing that she didn't let him. And at the same time, that idea, that I came here for her, too. Isn't there a tacit forgiveness in that? Or at least a willingness to try and understand my mother, what she must have been going through? Has this whole trip been about understanding her?

Compulsively, I start tracing everything—the letters, the years. My mother was twenty-five when she had me. Which meant that he was forty. Which meant that he was forty-five when he wrote that last letter to my mother. If he died ten years ago, he died when he was fifty. Which meant he gave up writing to my mother for only the last five years of his life. Maybe he tried to forget her. I doubt he succeeded.

But I start tearing up not because of my father. Not because of my mother or Panama or myself. Because of Danilo. And Hernán. They lied to me. They betrayed me. They strung me along, and like a fool, I fell for all of it. All that time I spent following Danilo around the city, when we were supposedly looking for my father, and all that time he knew it would result in nothing. He knew it was a goose chase. How long had he known? Since the beginning? He didn't know right away, before the library, before he even knew my father's name, right? But then, when he heard it, did he know? Or did he find out later? Did he and Hernán sit around together at the end of the day and talk about me and conspire? This whole time I was the butt of an elaborate joke. How stupid I must have seemed to them. How ridiculous Danilo must have thought I was, insisting that he call Ilsa and getting excited at the possibility that it might lead to something. They must have thought I was so fragile, so goddamn fragile, if they felt they needed to protect me like that. How stupid and gullible and—

My cell phone rings. I stop and fumble for it in the bottom of my bag.

"Mira, is that you?"

"Lucy? What's wrong?"

"She had an accident. I don't know how it happened. I was outside shoveling the walk, and by the time I had come back inside, it had happened."

"What happened?" I am standing on the side of Avenida de La Paz, facing the traffic as it zooms by, my phone tight against my ear.

"There was a fire. It was only a small one, a kitchen fire, but she burned her arms. We're at the hospital right now. I haven't seen her since I brought her in. I don't know what they're doing to her, either. They won't tell me."

The tears that were welling in my eyes, wobbling hesitantly along my bottom lids, spill over now, one after another, streaming down my cheeks. I breathe through my open mouth as Lucy goes on about how the doctor wants to give specifics only to family and how she tried to convince him that she was family, even though to look at the two of them, of course, she might as well have been saying she were related to a giraffe. After a while her voice fades away, but like a statue, I keep holding the phone to my ear. I shouldn't have come here, I keep thinking. I shouldn't have come.

"Lucy," I finally say, stopping her in mid-sentence. "I'll be home as soon as I can."

When I turn around, Danilo is standing in the middle of the sidewalk, his hands in his slouchy pants pockets, as people make their way around him like a stream around rocks.

"I have to go home," I say.

We stand next to each other at the bus stop. A thin elderly man dressed head to toe in chocolate brown sits on the bench. He's eating potato chips from a bag that crackles each time he digs his hand in for more.

After a time, Danilo says softly, "She told me not to tell you."

"I don't want to talk."

"I need to tell you this."

I bite my lip and run my fingers along the underside of the box. "You had a lot of time before. I've been here for more than two weeks, Danilo. You could have told me anytime."

"I'm sorry."

"Great."

"She wanted you to read it for yourself. She said one of the letters would make it clear. She said that it would be like he told you himself."

I can't speak. Cars and trucks rush by in front of us, making a sound like they're being sucked into a vacuum—*whoooooosh, whoooooosh*—again and again.

"I guess that sounds stupid now, but I don't know, when she suggested it, I thought it sounded okay, you know?"

"How long have you known?" I finally ask.

Danilo sighs and scratches his head.

"You knew all along?"

"I don't know. Hernán knew kind of early, I guess. He said he thought he knew the first time you mentioned your father to him, but he wasn't one hundred percent sure so he asked around to find out, and it was true. He didn't want to tell you, but it was because, well, Hernán is many things. You know he and I don't always get along. But he's not malicious."

"What?"

"Mean. He's not mean. He was trying to protect you. He thought—well, his feeling was that you were just so hopeful that he didn't want to extinguish that hope. Those were his words. You know how he talks. He said that would be crueler than lying to you. Even though he was convinced it wasn't lying, you know. He said it was just that he was letting you go on believing, and that people need to believe in things that are impossible." Danilo takes a deep breath. He pulls a cigarette from his pocket and lights it quickly.

"So you knew."

He shakes his head. "I knew Hernán's theory about it. But look, I didn't want to believe it. It's not like he had papers to prove it or anything. I thought maybe we really could find him. I wanted to find him for you. I swear."

"You knew."

"I don't know what you want me to say."

Dusk is settling. Several streets over, in what looks like an apartment building, perfect little boxes of yellow light form a grid against the sky. The old man on the bench balls up his potato chip bag and tosses it on the ground.

"I didn't know for sure until I talked to Ilsa. And that was just last night." He clears his throat as if even dredging up the explanation is painful. "Before that, I really thought it might have been possible."

After a few minutes, I turn to him. He gazes at me achingly, ruefully. I don't have anything to say.

Ten

Erosion

The view from the window is beautiful. I don't want to think that. It doesn't seem fair that anything should be beautiful anymore, or that I should think of it that way, but there's no denying it. As the plane nears Chicago, the snow is spread over the ground like frosting. The sun shines down on it like a blessing.

We fly over Hyde Park, over the Midway and the campus buildings and 55th Street bowing around an apartment building at the eastern end. The Metra tracks run like a scar along the edge of Lake Michigan. Once, in a life that feels far away, my mother and I walked underneath those tracks on our way out to a sidewalk where she confirmed a diagnosis I had suspected for some time.

The plane soars gracefully around the Sears Tower and the Hancock building, over the lake with giant S-shaped scales of ice, its arms straightening as we close in on the airport. I pull the waxy bag from the seat back, holding it on my lap, fingering the tabs along the opening as I force myself to breathe through a surging bout of nausea. As the plane drops further, my stomach rises like a buoy. I hold the bag over my mouth. We're close. Only another hundred feet or so. If I can just hold on. Saliva gathers in my mouth. I spit into the bag. Then comes the jolt. The wheels hit the tarmac. The plane screeches as it decelerates and the world on the ground—gray, listless, full of concrete—speeds by.

I go to the house first, even though I know very well that she's in the hospital. From the airport in Panama, I spoke to Lucy on the phone again and she gave me the details: they're at Cook County; they're on the fifth floor, in the burn center; my mother is sharing a room with another woman; there's an ice machine in the hallway that makes too much noise; fresh flowers are forbidden; the bed pillows are too thin and the sheets are too rough.

"You're on your way?" Lucy asked.

I told her I was. I called the airline on the bus back to Danilo and Hernán's apartment. They charged me a hundred dollars to change my reservation.

"I feel awful that you had to leave your trip," she said. "Did your teacher understand?"

My teacher understood, I assured her.

I talked to Beth from the airport, too, to tell her I was coming home.

"I thought you weren't scheduled to come back until Sunday. I have it on my calendar."

"I know. But Lucy called me. My mother's in the hospital."

"Oh God, Mira! What happened?"

I told her everything I knew and to pass the word along to Asha and Juliette because I didn't have time to call them. She promised she would.

The first thing I notice when I get off the plane is what a relief it is to hear English again, to understand immediately everything someone says, to eavesdrop without concentrating, to decipher signs at a glance. I'm struck, too, by how contained everything is: lanes of traffic are perfectly orderly, grass grows in even plots, trees thrive in mounds of mulch, building faces are austere. The air smells cleaner.

I take the el from the airport and walk the seven blocks from the train station to our house, my suitcase bumping along behind me over patches of ice and snow. I'm dressed in the same outfit I left in nearly three weeks ago—jeans, Converse, a navy zip-up hoodie, and a hip-length brown jacket with a pocket on the sleeve. Because I didn't want to crush it in my suitcase, I'm wearing my straw hat. The wind stings my cheeks. My scarf, which has been balled in the corner of my suitcase, is wound around my neck and over my mouth. The wool smells like Hernán and Danilo's apartment, like mothballs. It makes me want to cry.

As I walk up our street, our house in the distance looks

the same as always, the flagpole in the middle of the front yard surrounded by a doughnut of snow. Inside, though, things have changed. Along the wall, my mother has apparently piled more collections. When I left, there were only magazines. But now there are magazines; restaurant menus; a stack of LPs, their covers feathered at the edges; cassette tapes in cracked cases; matchbooks; a mountain of different-sized envelopes arranged from largest to smallest; a milk crate filled with empty glass soda bottles; and a tower of shoe boxes alphabetized by brand. As if providing some counterbalance, the rest of the living room has been stripped to the essentials—our couch and television set, a pair of lamps.

I drop my suitcase inside the door and wipe my wet shoes on the dingy green carpet. There's a message on the answering machine from George Grabowski. "Catherine, it's George. I'm just calling to make sure you're okay. I haven't seen your light on in a few days. Maybe you went out of town? Call me when you get back. I'd like to take you out for a coffee if you would like to go." He coughs. "Okay. I'll talk to you soon, I hope."

I don't delete it, even though I understand now that George never stood a chance. My mother made a decision, a choice hardened into stone long, long ago, that she would cut people off. She would shut them out. She did just that, after all, to a man who loved her for who she was, a man who loved her persistently and truly, a man who loved her without asking for anything in return except that she remain open to him. And she couldn't do it. She closed. Not only to him, but to everyone.

In the kitchen, the smell of scorched air lingers. The oven, a double-decker range built into a wall of cabinets with old, wrought-iron handles, is caked with soot along its glass fronts. The cabinets are charred, streaks of black running up them like stalagmites seared into the wood. I slide my fingers over the indentations left by the flames, imagining how the fire slithered its way up after bursting in an awful pop inside the range, how it must have fed out through the edges of the doors, and how my mother must have just stood here, watching it, dumbfounded. I imagine it all unfolding as Lucy shoveled the sidewalk, unable to hear or know what was happening until my mother started screaming. Or maybe she never made a noise. Maybe Lucy didn't know that anything was wrong until she smelled the smoke.

When I was in junior high, my mother attempted to make duck confit. Looking at the stove, I remember that. It took her two days and thirty-six cloves of garlic, among other ingredients, to do it. She's never been a big reader, but apparently she read in a book somewhere that only forty-seven people in the world still partook in the glory of actually making confit, a number that struck her as dismally, abominably low. It was like an endangered species of the culinary world, something akin to a bald eagle or a Sumatran tiger, and she was single-handedly going to save it. We went to the meat market together and bought three ducks. When the man behind the counter, in a bloodstained white apron, asked her whether she knew what she was doing, she said, "I'm buying three ducks."

"But do you know what you're going to do with them?" he asked, smiling. He must have thought she was flirting with him.

"I do. I'm going to take them home with me," she said. "Is that okay?"

His smile dropped. He understood that she wasn't teasing with her first answer. "Whatever you want, ma'am," he said, and hauled three wrapped pale duck bodies up onto the gleaming metal counter.

In the car, with the ducks lined up next to one another in the trunk as if they were sleeping, she complained. "Why would he have thought that I didn't know what I was doing?"

"I don't think people usually buy three ducks," I said.

"I should have told him I roasted a pig once."

"You did?"

"A long time ago."

At home, I positioned myself at the kitchen table to watch as my mother pulled out little glass jars of cumin, coriander, cinnamon, ginger, nutmeg, cloves, allspice, and thyme, as well as a bay leaf. She steadied herself with her hands on the counter and surveyed the spread. Our salt and pepper shakers were rooster-shaped porcelain figurines with holes drilled into the tops of their heads, and I remember thinking that they, too, were watching. She sifted everything together in a cereal bowl. She wrenched the legs off the ducks, sprinkled all six of them with a generous amount of salt, and lay them in a dish with the thirty-six cloves of garlic. She put the dish in the refrigerator.

"Don't touch it," she told me. "It needs to stay in there for two days. It's going to cure."

Two days later, I watched as she heated the oven, drained the dish, covered the legs with duck fat, baked the whole thing, strained the fat through a cloth, and stuck the legs in a jar, which she sealed and set on the counter.

"Aren't we going to eat it?" I asked.

"It stays good for six months."

"We're not going to eat it for six months?"

"I want to see if it keeps. That's the whole point of confit."

"But what about dinner?"

"Casserole?"

She always made casserole. I didn't want casserole. I made a face.

"You want the duck?" she asked.

"Yes."

"You can't wait six months?"

"Mom!"

"Six weeks? Can you wait six weeks?"

She was funny sometimes without intending to be.

"I want to try it."

She gazed with anguish at the freshly jarred duck legs. "No, I'm making a casserole."

I don't know why I was so outraged about it, but I summoned a tide of defiance, more than I typically showed my mother, and said, "Casserole sucks!"

My mother spun toward me. "Casserole sucks?"

I nodded, the tide coursing out already.

"Duck sucks," she said.

She must have known how it sounded.

I cracked a smile. She snorted a laugh. I giggled. She laughed harder. And for the next ten minutes solid we were both losing it over nothing, a kind of wild joy that was rarely present in our house, pulsing beneath our skin and issuing from our hysterical open mouths. When she had regained herself, my mother said, "Oh, it's too short, Mira. Life is too short. Let's eat the duck."

I wonder whether she remembers that.

She's sleeping when I see her. She's on her back under a pink waffle blanket, her arms, wrapped in gauze up to her elbows, perfectly straight along either side of her. Her face is pale and sunken. Her eyelids are mauve. Silvery roots have grown in at her scalp. Even under the blanket, she looks thinner than when I left.

The room itself is dreary, with light gray walls and rubber baseboards. My mother shares it with an elderly woman, who lies in her bed, holding a plastic cup as big as a pitcher and sipping water through a straw, her blue eyes wide open. The two of them are separated by a gray cotton curtain that hangs from a track on the ceiling. My mother is on the side of the room with the window, the aluminum blinds closed, some of them bent and drooping at the ends. A piece of framed needlepoint—a kitten pawing a ball of yarn—hangs on the wall next to her bed. It's terribly depressing.

Lucy stands when she sees me walk in. She has on a yellow gown, just like the one I and everyone else are required to wear as long as we're in the burn center. When she hugs me, we crinkle against each other. "She's okay," Lucy says. She smiles sheepishly. "No, I'm lying. She's not okay. She'll recover from the burns. But she's not okay." Her look is stern. She wants to make sure I understand. Then she says, "Why do you smell like mothballs? They have a lot of mothballs where you were?"

I could tell her, and I probably should, too, but I want to tell my mother first.

"The person I was rooming with had mothballs in her suitcase. The smell got over everything."

"Where's your suitcase?" she asks.

"I dropped it off at home first."

"I cleaned everything up the best I could. I went back there after she was settled. I think you'll have to get an inspection, though. Have someone over to take a look at the oven. I don't know if it's still usable. You might need to buy a new one."

"Okay." I'm hardly listening. My eyes are locked on my mother. Looking at her, I feel a constriction, a tightening around my heart, as well as a drowning guilt—the strongest sense of it I've ever had—over leaving her like I did.

"It would have happened even if you'd been home," Lucy murmurs. "I'm a trained professional and I wasn't able to stop it. It's like having a child. No matter how much and how closely you mind them, every mother I know has a story about how their child fell off the bed at least once. You can't be there all the time." Lucy puts her hand on my arm in a way that makes it feel like absolution. "You can talk to her. She probably won't wake up for a while still because of the medication they've got her on, but I've been talking to her anyway."

I stay still.

"Go on," she says, nudging me a little. "I'm going to take a little walk in the halls. Been sitting down for too long now."

I sit on the side of my mother's bed, balancing awkwardly so as not to disturb her. I don't know what to do next. A minute later the door to the room opens, and though I can't see beyond the curtain, someone shuffles inside. I wait, thinking maybe it's a nurse coming to check on my mother. But then there's a murmuring from the other side of the curtain.

"Elizabeth," a man says. "Elizabeth, how long have we been married?" His voice is thin. "Is it forty-eight years? Forty-eight years, is that right? I have to fill it out on this form. They're asking how long we've been married. I think it's forty-eight years, but I can't remember." The man makes a sound like scribbling. "Does anyone in your family have trouble clotting blood?" he asks. There's no sound. "I'll put down no. Is there any mental illness in your family? Did anyone have a stroke?" He goes on and on in his fragile way. Every so often, the woman in the bed, his wife, Elizabeth, makes a noise of consent, but mostly the room holds only the man's voice, searching, trying with desperation to take care of his wife, groping for answers.

When he leaves, I look over my shoulder at my mother, still sleeping.

"I didn't go to Washington," I whisper. "I went to Panama." Her face is still. "I found his letters to you. In your room. I knew you wouldn't want me to go there, but—"

She stirs.

"Mom?"

"Mira?"

"I'm here."

As soon as my mother is back at home, I call Dr. Herschel's office and tell him that I need more time. I explain that my mother had an accident. We make a plan that I'll return to school the following fall quarter. Dr. Herschel assures me my scholarship will carry over.

The day we return from the hospital, there's a potted bouquet of yellow flowers wrapped in cellophane on the front step.

"What is that?" my mother wants to know. "Did I already die and I don't know it?"

"They're flowers. Daffodils, I think."

She sighs. "Well, bring them in the house. We'll put them on the ledge next to George's plant, I guess."

The flowers are from my friends. A plastic spear stuck in the soil holds a note that says, "Let us know if you need anything."

I call Beth as soon as I get my mother settled inside, watching television.

"You didn't have to do that," I say.

"We had to do something. I mean, we wanted to do something. We were going to come there sometime this weekend, too, if you want. We don't want to be in your way, but if we can help, you know we'll come."

"I know."

"Are you okay?" Beth asks.

I draw a deep breath in and hold it for a second, feeling the pulse against my ribs. "Tell me something else. What's going on over there? All we do is talk about me these days."

"Well, the big news is that Asha got a terrible haircut yesterday. It's longer in the back than in the front."

"It's a mullet?"

"That's the thing. It's not exactly a mullet. But it's definitely not good."

"What was she doing?"

"She got into a huge fight with her parents the other day, and she decided that they were too obsessed with her being a perfect Indian girl and that she was tired of being a perfect Indian girl, so she went to Art and Science and told them to chop it all off. I don't know. It's bad, though. She skipped all her classes today because she doesn't want anyone to see her. I'm supposed to take her my red knit hat this afternoon."

"It's going to take forever for her to grow it out again."

"I know."

It feels good to be talking about something meaningless.

"Oh, wait. This is even bigger news. I forgot because it happened a few days ago and the Asha hair debacle was just yesterday, but Ben Linwood called Juliette."

"No, he didn't!"

"Well, I wasn't actually on the call, so I can't say for sure, but she said he did. They're meeting up after his shift tomorrow night."

And then, as if I stepped in quicksand, I am sucked back into a lonely desolation.

"That's great," I say. "It's great for her."

Before we hang up, Beth says, "I don't know if I should ask. I mean, I think I know the answer since you haven't said anything about it, but did you find him?"

"I found his sister."

"But not him?"

"He died. Ten years ago."

"Oh, Mira. I'm sorry."

"It's okay."

"I kept worrying that you would see him and he would reject you. Maybe this is better than that. No, that's stupid. Forget I said that. It's obviously not better. I'm so sorry, Mira."

I ask Lucy to stay on with us for a while, and fortunately it's not difficult to convince her. We establish a tag-team routine of sorts where at least one of us is no more than a few feet away from my mother at all times. We entertain her, start the shower water for her and sit in the bathroom while she washes herself, pour milk in her cereal, knot her freshly laundered socks, find the radio station she likes in the car, escort her on short walks through the neighborhood, blow-dry her hair, read her the mail, tell her again and again that her black beaded necklace is on the dresser. My mother seems fine at times, and at other times gets excessively frustrated, and at still others simply collapses—not physically, but within, as if the bulk of what's inside of her is made out of delicately heaped leaves that, out of nowhere, get blown away by a bit of wind, becoming scattered and displaced.

One week in February, after a few days straight of staying indoors because the weather was so cold and wet that none of us wanted to even open the front door, Chicago heats to unseasonable temperatures, and Lucy thinks it would be a good idea to get my mother out of the house.

"Just drive around with her a little. Roll the windows down so she can get some fresh air."

My mother dresses herself in black shorts, a black polo shirt, purple socks pulled up to her knees, and running sneakers. She still has bandages on both arms, which Lucy or I change every morning. A week earlier, the doctor assured us that she no longer needed them. Her skin, which was once raw and bubbled at the wrists, has healed enough that it should no longer be painful. It's not particularly attractive, though, since there are areas of her forearms where the natural texture of her skin has been erased, a patchwork of swaths that are flatter and shinier and more pink than the areas of skin surrounding them. So my mother insists she be wrapped up, one long ribbon of gauze pulled around and around until she is satisfied. I tried to substitute gloves once—long black silk gloves—but she refused them on the grounds that they did not look "official" enough.

That day, I steer my mother's eleven-year-old Toyota Corolla south along Sheridan Avenue to Lake Shore Drive. We pass buildings lined up along the side of the road like spectators at a parade. The icy blue body of Lake Michigan cracks under the sun. I put the windows down and my mother leans her elbow in the opening, resting her chin in her hand, as the crisp air whips in.

We make it all the way to Buckingham Fountain—we're stopped at a light—before either of us speaks.

"Did you find him?" she asks, so softly at first that I'm not sure I heard her.

"What?"

"Did you find him?"

"No."

She has her face turned from me, but I can see her reflection in the side mirror. She closes her eyes briefly.

"I haven't seen him in so long," she says when she opens them. "I wonder what he's doing now."

"Mom—" I say, then stop myself. I don't think there's any point in telling her he's gone.

She doesn't speak again until we're moving. "I tried to call him once, but a woman answered."

"And what happened?"

"I can't remember."

"Did you talk to him?"

"No. A woman answered."

"Did you say anything to her?"

"I think I hung up. I don't know. We were disconnected."

"You hung up or you were disconnected?"

She doesn't respond.

We pass the museum campus—the glass-faced aquarium, the sparkling dome of the planetarium. As we hurtle around a curve, the coins in the tray in the console slide. "You could have called back," I say.

"I don't know why I called in the first place. It was probably better that he didn't answer. I imagine he had gotten over everything by then. There was no need to open it all up again."

I shift my hands around the steering wheel. "I don't think so."

"You don't think so what?"

"I don't think he had gotten over it by then. I don't think he ever got over it."

"Oh, he must have eventually."

"I don't think so."

"Stop saying that! You're just trying to make me feel bad."

"No, I'm not. I mean, you should feel bad, but that's not

why I'm saying it. I just really don't think he got over it like you think he did." I nose around cars, switching lanes, suddenly anxious to go faster.

My mother takes a deep breath. "With all due respect, Mira. I don't think you have any basis for saying that. You don't know him like I do."

It feels like being punched, or what I imagine being punched—hard, square in the middle of my breastbone—would feel like. Slowly, I grind my teeth back and forth against each other and blink to keep my eyes from watering up so much that I can't see the road. I lean my foot a little harder against the accelerator.

Then, as if the discussion is over, my mother turns on the radio. Pointedly, I turn it off again. I swing around a black convertible with its top down into an open stretch of lane.

"You don't want to listen to the radio?" my mother asks.

"Didn't you think I wanted a father?" I ask. "I mean, there is no way, is there, *no way* that you couldn't have thought, wow, maybe Mira would actually like to know her father? Maybe, since he's not a bad guy like I let her believe he was, she might want to meet him one day or, I don't know, here's a thought, call him on the phone or, like, at least *know* that he's not a bad guy and that he cares about her and wanted to be part of her life. Is there seriously any way you didn't think that?" A back tire catches the edge of the shoulder and sends us skidding a bit. I feel shaky. My mother, in her own world, doesn't even flinch. She just looks out the window again.

"Because I honestly can't imagine a scenario where that wouldn't have occurred to you at least once."

"I thought that all the time."

"Oh my God! Then why didn't you do anything about it?"

Silence.

"Are you going to answer me?"

Silence.

"Because you could have changed everything. At any time. All you needed to do was tell him once that you still wanted him. He wouldn't have even needed to come here. It wouldn't have had to be a big production. But one phone call or one letter and you could have changed everything. I can't believe you don't know that. Or . . . never mind. I'm sure you did know it. You had to have. I can't believe you didn't do anything about it. I just think . . . it's so shitty! You have no idea the kinds of things I thought about him my whole life, and if it were up to you, you would've let me go on thinking them, and I can't even tell whether you feel bad about any of it. Mom?"

Silence.

"It's like you rolled this ball down a hill and you chose to ignore the fact that, if you wanted to, you could stand up and run after it and pick it up off the ground and save it. Instead, you set it in motion and let it keep going until it landed in this ridiculous, stupid ditch, and it's just so—" I stop. Then I shriek as loud as I can. The long, withering sound echoes within the confines of the car, filling it like a flood, and draining out again just as quickly.

"What do you want me to say, Mira?" my mother asks softly.

I can barely even feel myself driving. I'm just zooming through a blurry city, over potholes and through yellow lights, a skate park on the left, condos on the right, skyscrapers farther afield, streetlights hanging on bowed cables, the wash of gray pavement below and blue sky above. I'm just racing and thinking about it, what do I want her to say? That she's sorry? That she regrets it? That she would take it all back if she could? That if this stupid fucking disease eats me up, too, the way it's devouring her, she hopes it's the first thing I'll forget? What? What is it, exactly, that I want from her? Is there anything she can offer me now? Or is what I want from her the thing that she already chose not to give me, the thing that there is no way to go back and get now? My father. Isn't that what I want from her? Somehow, to learn that she could produce him out of thin air. But of course that's not going to happen. It's not going to happen. And I take a breath. And another. It's over now. It's over.

A long wailing sound slices through my thoughts. My mother bolts straight up in her seat.

"Mira, pull over."

"What? Why?"

"The police."

The officer writes me a ticket for speeding. He says if I hadn't been going quite so fast, he could have let me go with a warning on account of my spotless driving record, but twenty-five miles over the limit is excessive. He has no choice. I don't argue. Even after he pulls back onto Lake Shore Drive and motions for us to get off the shoulder and onto the road, I keep the engine off. I need a second to let my head clear. I'm amazed that I'm as composed as I am. My mother is staring out the window again, silent as a rock. Vehicles speed by on the road beside us, shaking our car in their wake. After another minute, my mother flips the vent on the dashboard open and closed a few times, then flattens her hand over it. "Damn it," she says. She rounds her shoulders and drops her cheek against her outstretched arm. Then she starts crying.

My suitcase stays, still packed and zippered shut, in the basement for more than a month. I shoved it in the crawl space when I got home with every intention not to look at it again for as long as I could stand it. I wouldn't need any of the clothes inside it for months anyway. But in late February, just after midterms, Asha calls me in a panic because she needs a copy of *Principles of Geology.*

"I have to write a paper comparing the impact of Lyell's views with either Darwin, Marx, or Freud for my earth science class, and every single copy of it is checked out of the library, and you know interlibrary loans take too long, and I don't have any money to go buy a copy because my parents have totally cut me off financially because of the hair thing."

"They did?"

"Can you believe that?"

"Because you cut your hair off, they cut you off?"

"Mira, please! It's really not funny."

I tell her I'll put my copy of the book in the mail for her. She says no, she's going to drive to Evanston to pick it up herself.

"The mail will take two days!" she wails. "You think I have the luxury of two days? I'm behind enough as it is. I haven't even read it yet, even though it's been on the syllabus since the beginning of time. I can't believe I let you talk me into taking this class. I was so happy just sailing through my chem major."

"I didn't talk you into it."

"And I really can't believe we have to write a seven-page paper now. We just finished midterms! Is there no mercy?"

"You can do what I do, and just write one page a day until it's done. Writing one page at a time is way more manageable than sitting down and writing seven pages all at once."

"You actually do that?"

"Why? It works."

"That's insane, Mira."

"No, it's not. It's totally reasonable."

"I honestly don't know, sometimes, who's a bigger nerd, you or Beth."

"Definitely Beth."

"I'll tell her you said so. You'll be around this afternoon?"

"I'll be around."

As soon as I descend into our basement, I smell the mothballs. Typically the basement smells like a combination of damp earth and the box of dryer sheets that sits atop the washing machine. The uneven concrete floor is ruffled where the smoothing tools came up off a drag. The walls and ceilings are striped with exposed wooden beams that have rusty nailheads popping out at various angles. But that scent. How can I describe it? Instantly it puts me in Panama again. Not as if I traveled back there again in my mind, but as if I stood still while the world around me transformed, blossoming into the place I was in months earlier. It's as if I'm standing in the middle of it again.

I yank my suitcase off the bumpy crawl-space ledge and let it land beside me with a thud. Lucy is upstairs with my mother, who is attempting yet another crossword puzzle. She still does them every day. "There's a house for each letter," she told me yesterday. "It must get expensive for whoever is building all of those houses," I said. "Oh, Mira, don't be stupid. They're not nice houses. Look, they're just little boxes. Two walls, a floor, and a roof, that's all."

I unzip the bag and dig hastily through my layered clothes for the book. I packed it at the bottom to cushion it, I remember. Under the mound of shirts and jeans, I feel it and pull it out. I'm about to close the bag and store it away again, when I glimpse a long, white envelope suspended in the mesh pocket lining the inside of the suitcase cover. On the front of the envelope is the letter M. The letter M, wide and artful. I stare at it for a minute as though it's a bomb I need to figure out how to disarm before handling it, and then quickly pluck it from the suitcase pocket. I know who it's from. It has to be. I don't want to read it.

But of course later that night, after Asha has come and gone and taken the book with her, after my mother is asleep, mumbling through her dreams, after Lucy is snoring on the couch with her feet popping out past the bottom of an afghan, after I'm alone in my room, sitting at my desk with my legs folded under me, I do.

> I know you're going to leave. That's okay. My life can go back to normal now. It was taking up a lot of my time showing you around every day. Nardo is always asking me, "Man, when are you going to drop that girl and come back to us?" So he'll be happy at least.
>
> I don't know what you want me to say to Hernán. I'll let him know that I took you to the woman and that you know the truth about your father. He'll be pissed at me, but whatever. He'll get over it.
>
> I guess you'll be in Chicago when you read this. I don't usually write letters to anyone so I don't really know what else to say. I knew you would leave. Even before you got your phone call. I knew that as you soon as you found out, you would want to leave. When you walked out of the apartment this morning, I knew it was probably the last time I would see you. I knew you wouldn't give me a chance to say good-bye. So I just started writing this. Whatever. It's

kind of a shitty effort. Sorry about that. I think you deserve better.

I hope you had a good trip back.

Danilo

It's written on Hotel Centro stationery. I slide the letter back into its envelope and put it in my desk drawer, next to a box of extra staples. For days, it stays there. For days, it's all I can do not to think about it. When Danilo wrote "at least," does that mean that Nardo will be happy, but that Danilo won't? And he said he doesn't usually write letters to anyone. Does it mean something that he wrote one to me? And the line I can't shake, the one I read over and over: he said I deserve better.

Three weeks after opening that letter, I get another.

Actually, I did write to my parents once. Hernán made me do it. He bought this fancy lined paper and gave me a pen and sat me down at the kitchen table and told me to write. I complained that I didn't have anything to say to them, so he dictated. I don't remember what I wrote exactly, but it was short. Just like, Hi, Mom and Pops. How's everything in Brazil? Maybe I could come visit you sometime. Or do you have any plans to come back to Panamá? You should give me a call. And then Hernán made me write down our phone number in case they didn't already have it. Can you believe that? I was smart enough to get it, you know. No one likes to believe that maybe I'm actually smart. But I understood that basically it was Hernán being like, Fucking come get your kid already! I'm tired of taking care of him. I mean, seriously, what's up? We folded that thing into some crazy shape to get it to fit into the only envelope Hernán had, and then we mailed it. I never heard back from them.

Anyway, you should call me sometime. Or you could write me back. You know the address. I know you're supposed to include the return address on the outside of the envelope, but I thought about it and I don't like the idea of that too much. It seems like bad luck or something. Like if I include it, then the letter could be returned. It's like tempting fate. And, you know, I do want it to get to you. So.

This might also be a good time to confess that I got your address from the hotel records. They still had a copy of your information in their file. I didn't know how else to get it. Don't rat me out, though.

Ciao.

Danilo

And then again a month after that.

It's going to sound like I'm making this up, but seriously there was a dude from Chicago in the hotel today. I asked him if he knew you, but he gave me a funny look and then held his arms out wide and said, "Chicago. Big." He didn't speak much Spanish. I saw him again tonight after dinner (I hung around the hotel today because Hernán said he needed the company). He was having a drink at the bar and talking on his cell phone. I think he's one of those real estate investors that are fucking everywhere in this city lately. Do you know that Donald Trump is building condominiums here? He's famous in your country, right? He's very famous here now.

I'm out of things to say and it's late. Hernán should be getting off soon so we can go home.

Danilo

And then a package another month after that.

Hernán wants me to tell you that he's sorry. He's gone to, like, thirty confessions about it already. He said, "Tell her that. Not less than thirty!" He wants to make sure you know that he was only trying to protect you. He says that hope is a very, very fragile thing and that when you steal it from someone, it can be like stealing their soul. He's convinced that taking away hope is much worse than giving someone the truth, and that those were the alternatives he was forced to choose between. You understand all that, right? He only did it because he cares about you. Fuck. I don't know. Are you ever going to write me back? Probably not, huh?

I ate a whole cake yesterday. I don't know why I just decided to tell you that, except that it seems a little funny. I rescued it from the trash. That bakery near our apartment was going to throw it out because the decorator fucked up and spelled the kid's name wrong whose birthday it was. I was just walking by when I saw one of the employees carrying it back to the huge metal garbage container out there. I asked what she was doing and she told me they were tossing it. Man, I could smell the frosting from where I was standing. I told her I would take it off her hands for her, and she didn't even hesitate. I was thinking I could stand there on the street and eat it, but then I got nervous that some of those street dudes would try to come over and talk themselves into a piece. Well, I don't know if I was nervous, but I just didn't want to deal with that. So I took the cake back to the apartment and put it on the table. I was just going to have one slice at first and save the rest for Hernán and me to share. But I don't know. I sat down, and the next thing I knew, I had eaten the whole thing. Shit was good, too. You might have liked it, even though the cake part was yellow, which I know isn't your favorite.

So, anyway. I guess that's all from this side of the world. I know you know a lot about the canal, like probably more than most of my paisanos do, but did you know that the dudes who used to work on it in the beginning when they were digging it all out used to say that they were cutting the world in half?

Hey, I know how you like maps, though. I know I said you couldn't find your life by looking at them, but I think I might have figured out a way. I just think there's more for you here. There's more *of* you here that you might want to find. Anyway, you should look at page 2.

Aren't you ever going to write me back? I probably shouldn't even send this one, even though I know I will.

Danilo

And oh yeah. More goodies! This girl I know makes these things and tries to sell them around the city but she's usually shit out of luck. No one's buying. I guess we aren't a very introspective people. But I had a little extra cash so I offered to take one off her hands. I asked for one that had a geology theme but my only choices were either this or a flower. You don't seem like a flower kind of girl. But I was thinking you could use it. You could write everything down. I know you're worried about forgetting everything, but this way maybe you won't. Even if it does happen to you one day, you would be able to read about your life like it was a book, you know. You wouldn't forget. So, anyway, use it if you want.

Page 2 is a map he drew. He sketched a globe and, popping off the surface like thought bubbles, inflated outlines of the United States and Panama. He drew a trail from Chicago to Panama City with an X at both ends. Standing next to the X in Chicago is a deft sketch of me: my Converse, my long bangs, my hair held back by what I assume are bobby pins, although that's more detail than he included. And standing next to the X in Panama City is a sketch of him: baggy pants, sneaker tongues up over the hems, messy hair. There are arrows along the trail, pointing from Chicago to Panama City. Across the top of the page, Danilo wrote in Spanish: THIS IS THE WAY TO FIND YOUR LIFE.

The "thing" he referred to is a blank journal. Hand-bound with burgundy twine. A cover made of sturdy green paper. A sticker of a frog on the front. Lined pages thin as newsprint. I fold the letter and the map and wedge them inside the cover. I squeeze my hands around it so hard that the edges of the cover dig shallow grooves into my palms.

I call him after that, before another letter has the chance to arrive and before I walk any further down the path that my mother already carved out.

The ring tones beat like a slow drum. Da. Da. Da. Da. Da. And then.

"*Aló?*"

"Danilo."

"Who is this?"

I can't speak.

"Miraflores? Is it you?"

"It's me."

Eleven

Vibration

I believe the earth has a memory. That everything that's ever happened throughout time has left its trace in fine, featherweight particles that fell and sank back into the earth like dust. The Sumerians tilled the soil. Mount Vesuvius blanketed Pompeii with ash. The Black Death slashed through Europe. Johannes Gutenberg invented movable type printing. Martin Luther nailed his Ninety-five Theses to a church door in Wittenberg, Germany. Copernicus conceived of a heliocentric solar system. Americans threw 342 chests of tea into Boston Harbor. The French rose up against the nobility. Napoleon and his troops—fewer and fewer of them the longer they went on—retreated across Russia. Charles Darwin wrote *On the Origin of Species.* Alfred Nobel mixed nitroglycerin with sand to make dynamite. The U.S. and British air forces firebombed Dresden at the end of World War II. Man walked on the moon. Two airplanes flew into the World

Trade Center in New York City. Mothers had babies. Somebody baked a pie. I scribbled all that ever meant something to me into a journal whose pages would one day disintegrate and fall away, just like everything else.

Humans forget everything eventually. Memories march out. They march away. But the universe keeps it all—in a rock, in the ocean floor, in the inner reaches of a mountain, in the fault lines in the crust—millions of years packed into the dirt. The universe holds on.

Over the next few months, my mother seems to plateau. She's taking various medications and vitamins, none of which improve anything, but they don't make anything worse, either, so we choose to see that in itself as an improvement.

Not long after the first time I talked to him, I called Dr. Herschel yet again and pulled myself out of school indefinitely. Even though it's the last thing my mother would want, there was really no option. I lost my scholarship funds, but Dr. Herschel very graciously told me that whenever I was ready to re-enroll, I should let him know and he would make sure it happened. I didn't tell him that it would likely be a while. By the time he and I spoke, my mother and I were quickly running out of money and I had already picked up an application from the Northwestern student center bookstore and from the Unicorn Cafe on Sherman Avenue. Juliette had given me the name of a manager she knew at Giordano's if I was interested in being a waitress. I haven't pursued any of those avenues yet. But soon. Very soon I'll have to.

Juliette and Beth and Asha check up on me often, sending me e-mails to keep me abreast of the news on campus, and calling me as they walk between classes to see how I am, to see how my mother is, to beg me to come back because being at school, they claim, isn't the same without me there. Which feels good in its way, and awful, too, because I know, and I've told them this, that I'm not going back for a while.

Beth drives to Evanston one day to have lunch with my mother and Lucy and me. When she arrives, my mother becomes agitated because she says that no one told her we were having company. I told her twice that Beth was coming, but I know by now that repetition has no bearing on anything. Information either sticks with her or doesn't, and these days mostly it doesn't. Lucy tells Beth and me to go on, sit in a restaurant together and enjoy the afternoon. She says she'll deal with my mother. She takes the car keys out of a bowl at the back of the hall closet, behind a bag of cotton balls, where she's been hiding them lately so my mother won't find them and take off to who knows where. "Thank you," I tell her.

At lunch, over a Caesar salad for her and a grilled cheese for me, Beth and I talk about nothing until she says that she was in Juliette's dorm room the other day, looking at the postcard I sent Juliette from Panama. "She had it taped on the wall by her bed," Beth says. "It had a picture of a church."

"Yeah, I sent her the Iglesia del Carmen."

"She said she was going to do an etching of it for her intaglio class. Whatever that means. But I was reading the back of it—she said I could—and you were saying how you didn't understand much about your mother's life before you were born."

"She never really talked about what it was like."

"I hope you don't mind, but I did a little bit of digging. I mean, I just went to Regenstein to see what I could find out about her hometown. I made some photocopies of a few things. I brought them with me."

"You didn't have to do that," I said.

"I wanted to do something."

That night, I sort through the sheaves of Xeroxed papers Beth had stuffed into the manila envelope she handed me. They don't illuminate much. They're all statistics, facts, figures—things I could find in almost any almanac. But she did include a profile of Highlands that appeared in *The New York Times* as part of a series about different communities around the state. The article is from 1960, a year after my mother was born. The third paragraph starts: "It would be impossible to visit this quiet town and fail to notice the military academy that is, in many ways, at its heart. The majority of the population here is in some way associated with it, even though there are those critical of what they see as its undue influence on the community at large. To be sure, Highlands' residents are on the whole conservative in their ideological leanings, and they strive to honor the best of the traditions that the Army has to offer. They look with suspicion upon those who are out of step with the unspoken 'marching orders' of the town." The piece goes on to talk about residents' "unapologetic conformity," before switching direction to write about the economy and the schools and the municipal parks.

All I have ever known about my mother's parents was that her father taught at West Point, the academy mentioned in the piece, and that her mother, no matter how she might have judged him privately, supported his every move without question. After reading the article, though, I understand the essence of who her parents must have been—people with very particular values, with very particular friends, with very particular expectations. I imagine my mother returning to them from Panama, her belly round as a globe, and I understand also how scared she must have felt. How much a disappointment. And I realize the strength it must have taken for her to leave. To leave everything. To only move forward from that moment on.

My mother quickly becomes the center of my existence. After a period of relative stability, she experiences a noticeable decline. It's agony watching her become unwhole, piece after piece flaking off and floating away.

I cook for her, even though she complains when I try to feed her anything but a BLT. I help her dress in the morning and undress at night, taking over with things like buttons and zippers, which have begun to confound her. She pleads to wear her pajamas sometimes day after day, and I give in because it's easier than fighting with her over it. Although much of the time she's still lucid, there are times when I sit at the kitchen table with her and have the same circuitous conversations we had yesterday, or the day before. I escort her to the bathroom and, unbeknownst to her, stand outside the door in case she needs me to remind her what to do inside, because I've read that one day that will happen. I mop the floor when, twice, she lets the sink overflow. I stand in the doorway of her room and watch her sleeping slack-mouthed in the middle of the day, to make sure that she hasn't yet forgotten how to do a thing like breathe.

And at night, I sit in my room and try my best to relax. Often that means bringing myself down off a cliff of frustration I have just scaled in trying to deal with her. Other times it means restlessly pushing aside the idea that I can't do this anymore, that I'm not cut out for it. I sit sunken in anger because I'm young! and I'm supposed to be in school! not doing this! I sit resenting my mother for making taking care of her my job. I sit scolding myself for having such a thought. And I cry a lot. In the dark, lying in my bed. I don't sob, but I weep, and the tears that come out are hot against my skin. It's enough to make up for all the times I didn't cry before, all that time I spent trying so hard to ignore what I was feeling. I've been trying so hard to keep the biggest goddamn news of my life from soaking in. I've been looking in every other direction to distract myself from what's happening with her.

I wipe my cheeks with the heel of my hand again and again. When I get tired of doing that, the tears just stream down the sides of my face, curling under my earlobes and dampening my pillowcase.

That summer, another family nearby wants to hire Lucy, and though she assures me she won't take the job if my mother and I need her, the other family is offering more than twice what I can afford to pay her now, even after insurance, so I tell her to go. She still comes by at least once a week to check in and make sure we're okay. When she does, she stays long enough to make lasagna or some other food that we can store in the freezer and live off for days.

Then something breaks. The delicate balance I think we have achieved is upended. I lose my footing. I lose my traction on the life I've gotten used to.

It starts when I wake up once in the middle of the night to the sound of my mother's coughing. I rush to her room and watch her, the way her tongue hollows against her lips as she sputters. I think, it's going to be over in a minute. She'll calm down and she'll be fine. But she goes on—that raw, wordless punch beating through the air.

"Mom," I whisper in the dark as I shake her arm. "Mom!"

She stops coughing, opens her eyes, and stares at me. She looks scared.

"Are you okay?"

She blinks wildly.

"Mom? Can you talk?"

She starts coughing again.

. . .

The doctor says she has bacterial pneumonia. At home, when she refused to speak even when she wasn't coughing, I loaded her in the car—in her pajamas and socks—as fast as I could and drove her to the hospital. Because I was scared and didn't know what else to do, I called Lucy and asked her to meet us there. She said she would.

The two of us sit huddled and anxious in the waiting room chairs with their blond wood and pilled navy seat cushions. It's October, and Lucy is wearing a crocheted red shawl, twisting the fringe tight around her fingers until her skin bulges and changes colors, and then letting it go again. I'm in my usual—sneakers, jeans, and a gray cardigan—and all I can do is pull my sleeves over the heels of my hands and release them to spring back up to my wrists, over and over. Everyone else in the waiting room is either dozing or flipping through a magazine.

When the doctor emerges, he calls my name. I gather my coat in my arms and stand. I wait for Lucy, but she doesn't budge.

"That's us," I tell her.

"No. It's you. You should go."

"It's okay. Come with me."

Lucy shakes her head. The doctor is waiting with the door open, his hand on the knob.

"You deserve to walk in there as much as I do," I say.

"Mira, go."

Later, I'll come to understand this exchange not as the selfless gesture I take it for at the time, but as Lucy's way of clipping my wings. I'll understand that she knew, as I must have known but didn't want to admit, that she won't be able to keep coming by forever, checking in on us, cooking occasional meals. Even if my mother hangs on for years, there's no guarantee that Lucy will be able to hang on with us. She already has another job. She could get yet another one on the other side of the city. Or she could be reassigned downstate. And if my mother does pass on, then what? Lucy might be generous enough to stick around as a friend for a while, but eventually I would have to figure out what to do for myself, with my own life. Later, I'll understand that she knew all of that. She was nudging me along.

The doctor closes the door to the tiny exam room behind me. My mother lies on the bed with her hands folded on her chest, a half-used tissue sprouting from one hand as if she's a magician and can, with a flourish, make a dove fly out. Her eyes are open, though unfocused.

The doctor invites me to sit. He gives me the diagnosis. He tells me what I already know: It's not Alzheimer's that takes people's lives, it's all the things that can happen to them because they have Alzheimer's. He says pneumonia is one of those things. My mother stares at nothing. She stares at a porous ceiling tile that looks like every other porous ceiling tile. The doctor says, "I've already told her all this." He goes on. When anyone else has pneumonia, the chances for recovery are generally favorable. But in the coming months, as the

Alzheimer's progresses, my mother could forget how to sit upright or how to walk, the sorts of activities that keep her lungs pumping. She could forget how to swallow, and inhale whatever it is she is trying to drink into her lungs instead, flooding them. Her body could forget to do the sorts of things that in anyone else would stave off infection. He doesn't mean to scare me, he says. He believes in being realistic. He's seen it before, when caretakers aren't prepared, when they aren't vigilant.

It sounds far-fetched. She can be treated. She can take whatever medicine she needs to take. I'll be there to administer it. There's still not that much that she forgets outright. It escapes her sometimes how to use certain appliances, like when she put the bread in the toaster and didn't push it down and stood there watching it, waiting for it to be ready, until she yelled to me in frustration that the toaster was broken and held up two floppy pieces of bread, waving them around like flags. She forgets to rinse the shampoo out of her hair on occasion, and I have to lean her head over the sink to sluice the suds out. She doesn't get dressed sometimes; and once or twice she's mistaken the ringing phone for a fire alarm; and she gives answers to questions I haven't asked; and she puts things away in places they don't belong, like her clean clothes under her bed, or her nail file in the silverware drawer. But those are the outstanding examples. She's still mostly fine. Maybe if she got pneumonia again in five years it would be different, but now she'll be fine.

"She isn't that far into her Alzheimer's," I tell the doctor. He says, "I know." Then he says, "She isn't yet."

Danilo comes to visit in November. We've been exchanging letters about once a month by then and calling on occasion besides. Living with my mother reminds me every day of how easily things can slip away. It reminds me that while there are some things worth fighting to hold on to, there are others that it's better just to let go of. There are things, like anger, that you can live without. I let go of being angry with Danilo and Hernán for lying to me like they did. It just wasn't worth it to hold on. In our most recent correspondence, I sent Danilo the postcard of Panamá La Vieja that I bought that day on Via España and invited him to visit me in Chicago. The next thing I knew, he was calling me to tell me that he'd bought a plane ticket.

When he arrives, it's snowing. A fine, diaphanous sort of snow. I wait in the heated car, stopped in the pull-through area outside Baggage Claim. Police cars are bleating their funny-sounding horns at vehicles that stay in one place for too long, and people wrapped in scarves and knit hats scurry with their luggage rolling along behind them to huddle under the heat lamps while they wait for their rides. My mother is sleeping beside me, buckled into the passenger seat. I keep my hands warm between my thighs, watching through the window, willing Danilo to appear before a police officer has the chance to ticket me for not moving along. Then I see him. That same brown hair and buttery skin, the same cargo pants and T-shirt, although now he's wearing an unzipped track jacket as well. He's carrying a blue duffel bag and looking around, looking unsure. I step out of the car and call his name. He smiles and jogs toward me, across the crosswalk zooming with shuttle buses and taxis. He hugs me, pressing his fingertips into my shoulder blades and shimmying me from side to side like the agitator on a washing machine. He pulls back. I smile. He slides his hands under my coat and under my sweater, his icy skin clutching my waist, and says, "It's fucking cold here, Miraflores! Feel my hands." I twist away at the shock, laughing and feeling my heart surge again at the possibility of him.

"Hi," I say.

For the next four days, Danilo helps me with my mother, even though it takes the two of them some time to warm up to each other. The first time he steps foot in our house, he doesn't mention the piles leaning against the living room wall. "She's putting everything in order," I explain anyway. "Lucy said that she needs to feel like she still has control over things." Danilo raises his eyebrows as if it all sounds a little crazy to him. He harbors a muffled fury toward her for all that she did and for the way she irresponsibly and irrevocably altered other people's lives—mine and my father's—in order to keep herself comfortable. He's told me that, in not so many words, and I've told him that I appreciate his anger on my behalf, but that if I've let it go, he should, too. I remind him of that and, maybe because he can see how much it means to me, or maybe because upon seeing my mother, he realizes that anger toward a helpless target is futile, after less than a day with her, he does.

For her part, my mother eyes Danilo curiously and suspiciously all of that first afternoon, hunching over her crosswords and meals as though she believes he's going to snatch them away from her at any moment. But the next morning, as Danilo labors over a pan of eggs for us, she marches up to him in the kitchen and says, "Are you a friend of Gatún's?" It must be something about his Spanish or his accent or his Panamanian features that reminds her of my father. It sends a shiver skittering along my bones to hear her say my father's name out loud. It takes Danilo less than a second to figure her out. With the spatula in his hand, he says in English, "He is a good man, no? He tell me about you. He tell me to come here take care of you girls." He smiles big.

For the remainder of his visit, he makes eggs for us in the mornings and picks up fast food in the evenings. At my mother's request, because she read somewhere that it helps slow the progression of her disease, he generously sprinkles turmeric on everything he makes for her.

Beth and Juliette and Asha drive across the city one day to meet him, and although they stay for no longer than an hour because they don't want to get in the way of what is already a chaotic day (they all are now), Juliette whispers her approval as she hugs me when they leave. "It's not like that," I try to tell her. "We're just good friends." Danilo and I have established that unequivocally by now. Juliette holds up her finger, though, and with a playfully beseeching look, says, "Please, Mira. Just let me believe." I agree to it, because I know that people need to believe in things sometimes even, and often especially, when they aren't true.

Whenever there's time, Danilo pulls me outside for stolen minutes to play in the snow, a phenomenon that he can't get over. He holds his upturned palms toward the sky, trying to catch some of it, and when the flakes melt into his skin and his hair and his pants, he declares that he thought it would be colder. He spins around in circles, kicking up snow in his wake, catching it on his tongue, until his cheeks are bright pink and wet. He runs and slides against the slick grass on his belly with his arms outstretched like Superman. I show him how to make a snowball, and he pelts me with them, laughing like a madman when they break apart upon impact. He attempts to save handfuls of snow by shoving them into a brown paper lunch bag he finds in one of our kitchen drawers and storing the bag in the freezer. He says he wants to take it back with him when he leaves, and though of course he has to know it won't work, there's still something sad about watching him, the morning I'm scheduled to drive him to the airport, open the freezer to find a brown paper bag that has frozen into something brittle, without anything inside.

But we spend most of our time together, the good and significant time, in the hushed house while my mother is sleeping. We sit at the kitchen table and talk while Danilo attempts to teach me rummy and while the wind outside scrapes the bare tree branches against the house, or else we lie in my room in the dark and have conversations until one of us falls asleep, something the other realizes only after asking a question and getting no response. Danilo sleeps on the floor next to my bed, buried under two flat sheets, two cotton blankets, and a comforter I borrowed from George Grabowski for just this occasion. When I went to George's house, I told him some of what had been going on with my mother. He said matter-of-factly, "It's an awful disease. I've seen it firsthand. It steals people. But your mother . . . Catherine . . . well, no matter what it takes of her, she'll still be more than most people ever are." He smiled. "Don't tell her I said that."

Danilo doesn't complain that he's still cold, but when he asks if I have a pair of sweatpants he can borrow and when I see him in my crimson women's volleyball sweats that I bought on clearance at the University of Chicago bookstore, I grab the afghan from the couch and throw that on top of him as well.

Our conversations are like they've always been, dipping and rising, jumping from meaningless to meaningful. We don't once talk about my father or the future and whether he and I will manage to stay in touch. In a way, promising we will forever or even for years seems unlikely, as far apart as we are—he in Panama, me in Chicago. But in another way, I want to believe that distance doesn't matter. If he lived in Michigan, would it be much different? Or if he lived in

Japan? There is only Here or Not Here. And people make Not Here work all the time. It's only geography, after all. An illusion. You can live in the same house or in the same neighborhood as other people and, if you draw the right lines around yourself and build the right walls, be as far removed as if you were a continent away. That's how my mother lives. I want to be different.

I apologize to Danilo for not being able to take him around Chicago the way he took me around Panama, and for his entire trip instead to be about my mother. He says, "Doesn't matter. The only thing I wanted to see in Chicago anyway was you." He tells me that Hernán ordered a new Shakira video and that he watches it with his headphones on in the morning before he leaves for work. I ask him to tell Hernán that I'm sorry for not having said good-bye. And I tell him that I've been thinking about what he wrote in his letter, about how the men building the canal thought they were cutting the world in half.

"For me, it was my mother's disease," I say. "There was my world before it and my world after it, but the Alzheimer's runs right down the middle."

I think about it a lot, actually. Of course, the world already has its halves—the hemispheres. Hemispheres of the earth. Hemispheres of the brain. Except that my mother's brain—her mind, her life—fractured, is fracturing still, into a thousand pieces. But I don't know how to say all of that in Spanish. It doesn't matter. As usual, Danilo understands me.

"I know," he says, and nothing more.

My mother and I drive him back to the airport the day he leaves. From the backseat, Danilo holds his hands on my shoulders the whole time, until I have to pull over just past Pita Inn on Dempster because I'm crying so much that I can't see. I don't even ask if he has a license. I just let him switch seats with me and drive while my mother compulsively tunes the radio and I navigate, telling him when to turn and when to merge onto 294. A hundred times I consider giving him directions that will send us looping back to my house.

When we pull up to the curb outside the international terminal at O'Hare, my mother says, "I've always thought your country is very lovely." Danilo says, in English, "It is. You would like to see it again, anytime you are welcome."

My mother smiles and says in Spanish, "Thank you for the offer."

Standing next to the car as it runs, the exhaust puffing into the brisk early-winter air, Danilo hugs me for what feels like a full five minutes before letting me go. "You'll write to me this time?" he asks.

"Yes," I tell him.

"And you'll come to Panamá sometime soon?"

"Yes."

"You know where I am. And you have your map. You know how to find me."

And that might be the end, or the end might come later, when one day I make it back to Panama, or one day I don't and continue my life in a different direction, or one day my mother passes away, or one day the tangles and plaques in my own mind start sprouting like weeds and I can't remember what came before and I can't predict what will come next. I don't know. It's impossible to say where things begin and where they end. Memory doesn't have seams to hem it in. It just goes on and on in both directions. And so, there was this story, but before that

and before that,

and before that,

and before that,

and before that,

and before that,

and before that,

and before that,

and before that,

and before that,

and before that,

and before that,

and before that,

and before that,

and before that,

a woman named Catherine is born. She crawls on the hardwood floor and sucks her thumb. She brings a cheese sandwich to school for lunch every day. She sits in the backseat of a wood-paneled station wagon while her parents sit in the front, not speaking to each other or to her. She gets in trouble for spilling grape juice on the front of her school uniform. She dreams of horses. She sews her own prom dress. She shaves her legs with soap and a razor. She meets a boy named Brant Strickland. She says yes when he proposes. She moves to Panama. She meets another man. She understands what it means to fall in love. She lets other people decide her life. She misunderstands what it means to be a good girl. In a way, she breaks her own heart. She has a daughter. She is alone. She grows gruff and stubborn as steel. She is short with cashiers. She works as a pizza delivery driver, a waitress at a chain restaurant, a receptionist, a receptionist again, a receptionist once more. She dreams of a life as an actress, a life less practical, full of whimsy. In a different way, a life of escape. She has brown eyes embedded with flashing flecks of gold. She has freckles that march across her slender shoulders and over the bridge of her nose. She talks in her sleep and sings in the shower. She takes pride in dressing up and doesn't understand the philosophy behind dressing as though you don't care to impress. She cooks dinners at home. She grows scared of the stove. She forgets to turn it off. She forgets a lot of things. She doesn't feel them slip away, but when she goes to look for them later, they're gone. She is stern with the rules. She reorganizes everything. She has her soft moments, those times when she is tender and bruised, but mostly she is a plank of wood, braced and erect, weathering anything and everything. She puffs her chest out to the world and walks through it—all the way to the end of it—without taking a breath.

Acknowledgments

With deep, deep gratitude to Megan Lynch, Kate Lee, Diana Spechler, my parents, and as always, Ryan Kowalczyk. Additional thanks to Tracy Mobley for generously sharing her knowledge and herself.